STILL HIS FIRST LOVE

Trip lifted her chin and pushed her hair from her face. "I feel like I'm losing my mind every time I'm around you, and yet . . . I can't get enough."

Emery was too shocked to respond, and then his hands were on her hips, his eyes dipping down to hers, and suddenly there were no words. Only action.

His lips crushed into hers, stealing away her worry and doubt, erasing each fear with his warm touch. She leaned into the kiss, gripping his shirt, securing him to her, and parted her mouth, inviting him in. Trip released a soft groan, and the kiss intensified, heat spreading from her chest out, coating her in it like a blanket, sparking each nerve from her head to her toes. All these weeks, all the tension, built up to this moment, this kiss, and Trip wasn't the only one who couldn't get enough. . . .

RACING HEARTS

A Hamilton Stables Novel

Melissa West

LYRICAL SHINE
Kensington Publishing Corp.
www.kensingtonbooks.com

LYRICAL SHINE BOOKS are published by

Kensington Publishing Corp.
119 West 40th Street
New York, NY 10018

All Kensington titles, imprints, and distributed lines are available at special quantity discounts for bulk purchases for sales promotion, premiums, fund-raising, educational, or institutional use.

Special book excerpts or customized printings can also be created to fit specific needs. For details, write or phone the office of the Kensington Sales Manager: Kensington Publishing Corp., 119 West 40th Street, New York, NY 10018. Attn. Sales Department. Phone: 1-800-221-2647.

Lyrical Press logo Reg. U.S. Pat. & TM Off.

First Electronic Edition: October 2015
eISBN-13: 978-1-61650-825-8
eISBN-10: 1-61650-825-6

First Print Edition: October 2015
ISBN-13: 978-1-61650-826-5
ISBN-10: 1-61650-826-4

Printed in the United States of America

*To the women of the world who dare to step into
male roles and succeed—Thank you.*

ACKNOWLEDGMENTS:

As always, thank you to God for giving me the strength and courage to put my words out there and the blessings of people willing to read them.

I am forever thankful to my agent, Nicole Resciniti, for her continued support and genius in this industry. Thank you to my editor, John Scognamiglio, for being a true joy to work with and thank you to Rebecca Cremonese and the rest of the editorial team at Kensington and Lyrical.

Thank you to Todd Pletcher and Christine Hosier for answering questions about racing, breeding, and numerous other questions that were very likely idiotic. Also, thank you for not directly saying said questions were idiotic.

Thank you to Siobhan Clayton and Jennifer Jabaley for reading early drafts of this book.

Many thanks over to Rachel Harris and Cindi Madsen for your continued friendship and wisdom in all things writing. I feel so blessed to call you friends.

Finally, thank you to my wonderful husband, Jason, my two beautiful daughters, and the rest of my very supportive family. I could not write a word, let alone a novel, without you. I love you all dearly.

This Kentucky Derby, whatever it is—a race, an emotion, a turbulence, an explosion—is one of the most beautiful and violent and satisfying things I have ever experienced.

—John Steinbeck

PROLOGUE

*A*nd they're off in the Kentucky Oaks! It's a slow start for Blasting Sun. And there goes Gambler's Way right off to take the lead. It's Gambler's Way to the front! Firecrest and Xray Vision on pace, and Matching Tree settles into fourth. Then there's Chromelite, Park Place, Merryland. In behind True Star is Marching Soldier to the outside, and Victorian Blue is third last with Shouting Call in the backfield.

They went twenty-three and three in the opening stretch. Now, Firecrest is just off the leader, with Matching Tree three lengths off the lead. Xray Vision rides the rail six lengths off the lead and it's a long way back to Marching Soldier. They're forty-seven and four at the half mile.

Round the turn and now goes Firecrest to the front, but Gambler's Way is on her neck! And no! Gambler's Way hits Firecrest, and there goes rider Emery Carlisle to the dirt, Chromelite and Xray Vision spilling over as well. And now jockey Brian Crane manages to stay on his mount, Gambler's Way the unofficial winner as emergency crews make their way to Emery Carlisle . . . who has yet to get up.

CHAPTER ONE

Jockeying for position

The air was cold outside, the kind of air that made it easier to breathe, easier to exist. Emery drew a breath and wrapped the afghan she'd grabbed on her way out tighter around her. Her granny had made it, like so many other things inside her parents' guesthouse, and not for the first time, she wondered if everything she touched was first touched by someone else. It was a peculiar way of thinking, but these days all Emery had were her thoughts.

She closed her eyes, and like a vicious nightmare that refused to let go, she was back there, on her way to her second Kentucky Oaks win. Thrill and adrenaline ran like blood through her veins. And then the spike of fear as she felt the hit, felt Firecrest buckle, and the ground rushed toward her. Pain burst through her leg, her side, her head, and then all she could hear was the wail of the ambulance and the muffled sobs of her parents beside her.

Shaking off the memory, she pushed through the gate by her house, steadying it with her cane as she slipped inside. Then she began her trek down the long path to the main house on the farm— her parents' house. She could drive, but she liked to walk down the concrete road, cradled by the quiet woods, the birds not yet up, the day still half-asleep. Drawing a breath, she took in the pine and dew scent in the air. It reminded her of the comfort of home and better days, before she'd lost everything and couldn't find her way back to the light.

Thoughts worked through her mind as she continued, ways to convince Daddy to trust her again, trust the sport he'd loved all his life. Each morning she came to him—and each morning he turned her away. She'd just decided that she wasn't against begging when she saw a woman walking aimlessly down the road, wearing nothing but a thin nightgown and a look of rage. Several of the pins in the woman's hair had fallen out, so half of her gray hair fell around her shoulders, the rest still wrapped in a bun. The woman looked like she'd either been caught in a storm in the middle of the night or abducted by aliens who'd promptly decided she wasn't worth the trouble and tossed her back.

"Good morning, Mama."

Mama's steely blue eyes turned on Emery, a combination of fear, anger, and exhaustion within them. "I've been up for four hours. My body's drenched in sweat like I'm burning in hell. It is *not* a good morning. I swear to God, if this doesn't end soon I'm moving to Alaska!"

Emery thought her daddy and the rest of the staff might appreciate Mama moving to Alaska. Or anywhere, really, so long as she left the farm and stopped screaming all the time.

"Can't Doc Paterson give you something? Hormones?" *Crazy pills?* She thought of her mama when she was little, all sweet words and soft hands as she braided Emery's hair. Now . . .

Grace Carlisle focused on her only daughter, tears welling in her eyes. "You must think I'm a moron. A silly, miserable, idiotic woman. That's exactly what your father thinks."

"No, Mama—"

"Why else would you ask if Doc could give me something, when you know I've asked. A thousand times, I've asked. *It's menopause,* he says every time. Tells me to wait it out like I am a mare in foal! He doesn't know, 'cause he's a man. Damn self-centered gender thinks we women are nothing but trouble, but I'll show him trouble!"

"Oh . . . I'm sure you will." Emery pointed to the house. "Is Daddy inside or at the barn?"

"He's reading the paper." Then her mama tilted her head, her voice softening, the change so sudden Emery contemplated the abduction thing again. "But you know he's not going to budge on this, darling. You are his baby."

Yes, well, she wasn't a baby. She was a twenty-five-year-old woman, and it was time she got a little voice about her when it came to her daddy. "We'll see." She continued on up the stairs of the large manor house, through the front double doors, and down the long hall to the kitchen, the smell of bacon and eggs hitting her nose. The same breakfast Daddy ate every morning, despite his cholesterol.

"Good morning, Daddy, I—"

Beckett Carlisle lifted a hand, then tapped the coffee cup in front of him, the paper up, blocking his face. "I'd like at least one cup in before we start this argument."

Sighing, Emery sat across from him and crossed her arms, bouncing her boot against the tile floor. He lowered the paper and peered over his reading glasses, his salt-and-pepper hair and face full of age letting her know he'd lost his patience twenty-five years ago and never found it again. "Fine, go. But it's barely five a.m.—don't you sleep? When I was your age—"

"When you were my age, you were an assistant trainer to Bob Bailor, and you woke at the crack of dawn, determined to beat him to the barn every morning. If anything, I learned my sleep habits from you."

He looked away. "Yes, well, I wasn't healing from a major injury."

At that, Emery leaned in, forcing him to look back at her. "Neither am I, Daddy. When are you going to see that? I've been healthy for nearly six months now. I'm ready."

"Ready to risk your life again? Ready to put yourself in the ground and break your mama's heart?" He shook his head, pushing away from the table and storming over to the coffeepot, only to stand there, staring out the window above the kitchen sink like he wasn't sure why he'd gone there in the first place. "You didn't see what we saw, Em. The bruises and blood. The fear in every doctor and nurse's eyes. I never want to see you like that again." He faced her, the stubborn man he'd always been before her. "The answer is no. Today, tomorrow, next week. The answer is no. Besides, I'm retired."

"But, Daddy—"

"I said no." He worked his palm into his chest, a grimace spreading across his face, and guilt punched at Emery's stomach. There'd been a time when he was the one pushing her, helping her through her fear and challenging her to be more than simply a fine rider. He'd urged her to be the best. Now, that desire to be the best was firmly planted, and one fall couldn't erase it. She didn't want to put him through this misery, but she couldn't give up, either.

She'd started to say more when Beckett turned away, and she

knew the conversation was done. "All right," she said, balancing on her cane as she headed out the back door to the stables, wishing she could drop the cane. Maybe then he wouldn't see her as crippled. But she knew the moment she gave it up, the moment she admitted she was well enough to walk on her own, she'd have to face her fears and get back on a mount. Begging her daddy to hire her again, to find her a mount, wasn't the same thing as actually getting back on. She told herself she would do it as soon as she had a horse to ride, but the truth was . . . she was scared. Not of falling off; no, that happened. She was scared she wouldn't be as good as she was before, and then what?

Thoughts of everything she'd given up coursed through her, a different life, so many possibilities, yet only one ever felt right. She'd dropped out of college junior year to focus on her jockey career, and from that moment, she'd all but put the idea of love out of her head. She'd dated, but what she wanted was someone who would see her through the tough times, and she see him through his tough times. The problem was there was only one person she wanted around her during her toughest times . . . and he'd left.

Two years had passed with nothing but healing and physical therapy and far too many antidepressants to count. Then six months ago, her doctor gave her a thumb's-up to ride, but despite the ache in her chest to get back on a mount, she couldn't bring herself to do it.

Emery thought of how all the staff came over to the training ring to watch. Only for her hands to shake and her eyes to water, and before long, she backed away from True Star like he was a monster, ready to drag her to her death. But while every moment of that horror stayed with her, it was nothing compared to the look in her daddy's eyes. The look that told her she might ride again, but he would never put her back in a race.

As a world-renowned trainer, Beckett Carlisle had trained some of the best Thoroughbreds out there, so when Emery decided to become a jockey, it went to reason she would work for him. She never hired an agent—she didn't need one. Daddy set her up with a mentor, taught her how to think like a trainer but ride like a jockey, and before long, she won race after race after race. And while falling was always a risk, she never once considered her daddy would blame himself. That the guilt would eat at him every day of her recovery.

So, she didn't push it, let him deal with his grief, while she dealt with her injuries. But the time had come and she was ready. She had to be. She knew in her heart if she didn't get on a mount now, she never would. The truth was, she needed someone to push her— needed a new trainer. But of course, a good trainer would look at her, a broken jockey with a cane, and laugh.

The thought made her want to rush into the stables and throw a saddle on True Star and show everyone that she was still the best female rider in history, but she knew that wasn't possible. Not yet. She needed to feel connected to her horse, body and mind, like it was a part of her very soul, and she knew from the moment Mr. Sampson, their lead trainer now that her father had retired, brought True Star to her that he wasn't her match. He was someone's match, perhaps, but not hers.

It was a different way of thinking for a jockey. Most simply accepted whatever contract they were offered, riding any colt or filly the trainer assigned them. They were paid, plus a percentage of the purse, and then they were done. No dedication to the trainer or the owner or the horse. But Emery's passion wouldn't allow her to be so carefree, and her agreement with Daddy, while painful at times, gave her one great advantage over other jockeys—she would know her horse, through and through. She would select him. She would assist in his training, and when they crossed the finish line, Emery would know that she'd genuinely earned it.

Of course, to be that rider again, Emery needed to actually *ride*. And the problem was that True Star wasn't Mr. Sampson's first attempt. Or second. Or tenth. The poor man had brought Emery more Thoroughbreds than she could count, all boasted to be champions in the making, but Emery couldn't bring herself to ride. Part of it was that she hadn't felt that spark she craved, but she also knew Mr. Sampson wouldn't force her. It was easy to back away. She needed a trainer who didn't accept *no*, who pushed and demanded and didn't accept anything less than a win.

And only one trainer fit that description.

A memory hit of a young man, tall and strong, with a scruffy face and callused hands and a smile so warm it stopped you in your tracks. He'd worked with her daddy for over a year, learning all he could, watching Beckett like he was a god. And truthfully . . . he was. Four-time Eclipse Award winner, Hall of Famer, no one trained racehorses the way Daddy trained them. Until the young man became all man, and putting those years of learning to good use, he'd trained more champion racehorses in the last four years than any other trainer in the world. He was the next Beckett Carlisle, and exactly what she needed.

Goosebumps rose across her skin at the thought of him, of the special moments they'd shared . . . of her promise to never forget him when he left. She told herself that if nothing else, they would always be friends, but things were different now. He was a superstar and she was a nothing, broken and sad, with no mounts and no prospects . . . and he had refused to meet with her.

She balanced on her cane and knocked lightly on the weathered door of the trainers' quarters, letting Mrs. Sampson—and, by default, Mr. Sampson—know that she would be in the stables. Of course, they already knew. She'd knocked on their door every morning for the last three months. She'd become obsessed with watching the horses go through their morning workouts, eager to feel that spark she craved, but it never reached her like it should—like it used to. Since her accident, only one horse had made her sit up and pay attention—a colt, beautiful and strong, born ready to run. But he was sold at the sales.

Maybe she should give up racing altogether, and instead become a trainer. Her daddy had taught her everything he knew. She felt sure she could become a lead trainer in no time, especially with Mr. Sampson at her side.

The thought gave her hope, until she realized that would also mean losing everything she loved about racing—the adrenaline rush, the danger, the complete faith in the animal below her. Deep down she would be submitting to her fear, allowing it to take control. She couldn't do that, and besides, she was a born racer. One of only three female jockeys to have any hope of winning the Kentucky Derby. Of course, all of that was before the accident. Now . . . she wasn't sure she could finish a race, let alone win one.

Emery stopped just inside the stables and stared down the long path, a few horses already peeking out of their stalls to see who was coming. The smell of hay and horses mixed with the scent of rain in the air, and she drew a deep breath, letting it wash over her. She loved the stables in every way, especially from this vantage point. Her daddy'd had his architect design the plans so when you peered inside it was the perfect picture of strength and elegance. Tall red oak beams stretched high, crisscrossing on their way, so even the ceiling was beautiful.

"Trying to beat the sun again, I see," a voice called from behind her, and she peered around with a smile at the familiar wrinkled face of Mr. Sampson, his two boys on his heels to cycle soiled hay for fresh. Mr. Sampson took it upon himself to be her second father, overbearing and all, but in a quieter way than her daddy, making it impossible not to love him.

Emery shrugged. "I like to watch them in the morning," she said, though that wasn't the full story. She came out every morning hoping she would feel that pull in her gut, that twitch and prick in her spine that rippled through her until she got on a horse. For three long months, she'd come out to the stables, and for three long months her body had done nothing more than breathe. It made her feel sick and ashamed. She was a jockey! Where was her spirit?

Mr. Sampson studied her, like he saw straight through her lie. "You know, Ms. Carlisle, Lemon Grass would be a fine option for a morning ride."

Lemon Grass, an old mare with as much gait as a turtle. Emery was offended for a moment, and then her offense was quickly replaced by sadness. How had she allowed herself to fall from True Star to Lemon Grass? Still, Mr. Sampson had a point. Riding Lemon Grass would be easy, like an injured runner walking instead of taking to the track. A small step.

She thought of the upcoming Sandbar Maiden, a tiny race compared to the Triple Crown, but the place where she should begin. A solid win would throw her name back into the circle for the next Kentucky Derby. She needed to train every single day to have a chance. Instead, she had yet to even sit on a horse. The thought made her angry with herself, and with every bit of the spunk she once wore like a cape, she said, "Saddle her up. I have a call to make."

Emery rotated on her heels and walked out of the stable, jerking her phone from her pocket as she strode far enough away that Mr. Sampson couldn't hear her voice. She ducked behind a nearby tree and dialed the number she had called every day for the last week. And every day she'd been told he wasn't available, wasn't in town, a different excuse each time. Which was exactly what they were—excuses. But her farm in Crestler's Key was just a town over from Triple Run, and if he refused to talk to her on the phone, she would come to his house and pound on his door. Dignity be damned.

Enough was enough.

* * *

Trip's cell vibrated from the pocket of his worn Levi's. It was five in the morning, and already it felt like he'd forgotten something. Every day ran that way—a to-do list so long he had no choice but to check off the most important things and leave the rest for the next day. Only to start the process all over again. He told himself he'd slow down eventually, but so far *eventually* hadn't come.

His cell vibrated again, and he peered down at the number, recognizing the main office and cringing. He pictured his father at his grand cherry desk, tapping a pen against its surface, an annoyed look on his face. He'd been on Trip for the last week to meet with Gerald Lancaster, a wealthy businessman who had a hand in everything from real estate to oil and now had his sights set on Thoroughbreds. He wanted Trip as his trainer, but Trip didn't trust the man, his motives, or that conniving grin that said his words were no match for his thoughts. Besides, Trip had already built a solid relationship with owners he trusted. Why add one who could end up being nothing more than a thorn in his side? This was the great difference between Trip and his father; Carter Hamilton always sought more, when Trip was content to keep things steady. Enjoy his successes instead of always seeking the next gain.

Carter used to be that way, too, until he lost his wife, Trip's mother, to a ruptured brain aneurysm, and his father's heart refused to bounce back. They never saw it coming, and Trip often wondered if knowing would have helped his father—being able to properly say good-bye— or if that only would have made things worse for him.

Trip eyed the number again, readying himself for an argument, and reluctantly clicked the call. "Hamilton."

"Trip?"

"Yes . . ." Trip hesitated. Definitely not his father. Peyton, the office admin, must not be in just yet, so the call had forwarded to his cell. Suddenly, he wished he'd ignored it. He didn't like the slip in the female's voice, the brief break, like she was mustering her courage— or preparing to go off on him.

He tried to remember if he'd angered any women lately. Hell, who was he kidding? Angering women was his second best skill. He thought of Lexi Price's long legs and come-here smile and promise that she, like him, was too focused on business for a relationship. That attitude held for a whopping two weeks before her manicured claws set in, and once again, he had to have the conversation that'd branded the Hamilton brothers as womanizers. Though the title held no truth, it interfered with business, so their father had ordered them to stay away from any and all women involved in racing.

Of course, Trip had always been selective in the rules he chose to follow, hence the Lexi issue. He trudged on with the conversation carefully. "Who's asking?"

There was a pause on the other end, then, "It's Emery."

He sucked in a breath, the name hitting him like a punch to the gut. Memories poured in, flashes of endless blue eyes and coy smiles and afternoons laying in the fields behind Carlisle Farms, the clouds making shapes above them, his heart speeding away in his chest for reasons he couldn't understand. But that was all stuff of his youth, before his mother died and he watched his kind father break in two, unable to return to the man he'd once been, his kindness replaced with coldness. Then his brother Nick lost his fiancée to cancer, and Trip vowed to never be that man—lost to his feelings and grief, his career stunted by love. Nah-ah, not him.

Which was the very reason he'd avoided Emery's calls all week. Now what the hell was he supposed to do?

Trip focused back on the phone, drawing an annoyed breath, prepared to let her have it for calling him personally. There was a protocol, for God's sake—he talked to agents, not jockeys. But then he caught the desperation in her voice as she started to speak again, barely there below the confidence, and instead of barking off an angry reply, he found himself asking, "How are you?"

"I would be better if you agreed to meet with me," she said, her silky voice dropping just a touch. He had always liked the sound of her voice, the way it was both strong and feminine. It had been to blame for one or two of his greatest transgressions. He couldn't believe he hadn't recognized it immediately. A woman's voice had always been his undoing, but this was different, complicated, the last thing he wanted to add to his already jam-packed schedule.

"Look—"

"I know what you're going to say, but please . . . one meeting. If you like what I have to say, I'll ride for free. Whatever you ask. And just so you know, I'm not against stooping to blackmail."

"Blackmail? That's a new one, even for you." Trip couldn't help but smile. Years had gone by, but she was still the same Emery, all heart for the race, all love for the horses. She didn't need the money and really didn't care about the fame—Emery raced to prove to herself that she could. Her guile, coupled with that voice of hers, made him reconsider her offer . . . if only for a second.

"I still have the photos."

He stopped walking. "You don't."

"Oh, I do. You lost the bet fair and square. It's not my fault you were forced to sit on a mount. *Naked.* It must have been a cold, cold day, because—"

"Hey, now," he said, unable to keep from laughing. "I think we'd have a greater problem on our hands if I'd shown my real size, if you know what I mean."

Emery released a small laugh, the sweet sound hitting him straight in the chest. Damn, it felt good talking to her. Too good.

"Come on, Trip. It's a meeting. Just hear me out."

He sighed and started back for his training ring. "Your father would kill me."

"Wouldn't be the first time you've taken that risk."

Trip grinned. Sure enough, he'd taken lots of risks back then, but he was older now. Wiser, he liked to think. He opened his mouth to reply with as much when he heard a squeal from the training ring. Clark, his assistant trainer, had a new colt out that'd just come in from auction, a purchase by Sarah Anderson, a longtime friend of the Hamilton family. He listened, curious if they'd worked through their problem, when he heard a shout from Clark.

"Son of a bitch . . ." Trip whispered.

"Sorry?"

"Not you, obviously. We just got a new colt, and by the sounds of it, he's working my assistant trainer into the ground."

"From the sales?"

"Yeah, Sarah Anderson bought him. Actually . . . come to think of it, she bought him from your farm."

Emery sucked in a breath. "Did you say a colt?"

"Yes. Why?"

"I'm coming over."

Trip nearly dropped the phone as he skidded to a halt. "You can't come here."

"I can, and I will. We need to talk about this, and I need to see that colt. If he's the horse I'm thinking, I can help you."

Trip released a breath and peeked back over at Clark, who looked like he might piss his pants any second. "There are plenty of trainers."

"I don't want to work for just any trainer. I want you."

His breath caught at her words, at the intimacy of them. At the way her voice had dipped back down, as it had in the beginning of the call, like she couldn't hide her plea. He started to tell her—again— that he couldn't, this was too complicated, when a sharp scream cut through the early morning silence.

Trip spun around to find the colt reared up, Clark on his back, and then Trip ran, the words, "Be here Thursday. Seven a.m.," rushing out of his mouth before he could convince himself otherwise. He shoved his phone back into his pocket and leaped over the fence. His pace slowed as he reached the horse and steadied him, his mind still on Emery's silky voice as she said *I want you.*

CHAPTER TWO

Hitting his (her) stride

Emery made her way into Brighton's Sandwich and Pastries for lunch the next day, the smell of fresh bread hitting her nose and soothing her soul, despite her body still being keyed up from the call with Trip. Was it her imagination or had he laughed at her throughout the conversation? The thought made her both scowl and smile.

Her entire life she'd felt like a young girl among adults. Her parents still called her baby and patted her head like she was a ten year old, instead of the twenty-five-year-old woman she'd become. Her accident, while tragic in its own right, did nothing more than detract from her age in her parents' eyes—in the eyes of everyone on the farm. But Trip was different. He didn't laugh at her because he thought she was a kid. He laughed because he understood her, knew how she ticked, and it amused him.

Whether that was a good thing, she couldn't be sure. She'd told herself as soon as they ended the call that this was for her career. That if he hired her on, their relationship would remain professional, nothing more. Her heart wouldn't get involved. The problem was, her heart had never once been safe around Trip Hamilton.

Emery glanced around the sandwich shop in search of her lunch date, ignoring the curious stares from everyone within reaching distance. Brighton's was every bit as small town as the rest of Crestler's Key, Kentucky. Small glass tables covered in floral tablecloths. Wrought-iron chairs. Pictures on the wall of every famous person who'd ever stepped foot in the town, including her. And a mess of town folk ready to gossip at the first word worthy enough to spread.

She frowned, which didn't go unnoticed as she slipped into a chair across from her best friend.

"Good God, Em, what'd old Mrs. Wilbanks do to you?" Kate asked, her freckled face lit with humor. She had her red hair pulled back in a bun, a blue paisley wrap around her head, making her blue eyes even more pronounced.

"Why do they have to stare all the time? It isn't like my face changed from yesterday." Emery pulled her cloth napkin into her lap and sat tall. God forbid she forgot her manners and ate without it.

Kate's face softened. "They're just worried about you, hun. You're the only one in this town worth worrying about, so they make it their mission to keep up the job. It'll pass as soon as you're racing again."

Emery cleared her throat and lifted her menu to hide her face, which Kate promptly pulled down so she could look at her friend. "Em . . . why do you look like you stole someone's mail on the way over?"

Crap. She'd thought she could hide her secret a little better.

"I don't. It's . . . I don't."

Kate pinned her with that kindergarten teacher stare of hers, waiting. She'd mastered the look at just six years old, when she'd demanded that Emery tell her what Curtis Trink had said about Kate's request to marry him—again. Needless to say, Kate's desire to be loved never went away, nor her ability to suck the truth out of someone by scrutiny alone.

"All right, fine," Emery huffed and leaned in. "But if you breathe a word of this, I will make it my mission to tell Matthew Bridges just how deep that crush of yours runs."

Kate flinched, before smoothing out her expression and crossing her arms, faking ease. "Well, that would be a waste of time, see. I don't have a crush on Matt anymore. That was *last* year, and . . ." She trailed off at Emery's cocked brow, and her shoulders slumped. "Okay, okay, but I'm nearly over him. For real this time."

Emery sat quietly while her friend tried to explain away her feelings. It was one of a hundred conversations they'd had about Matt, and Kate had yet to act on her feelings, too shy to take the first step.

Seeing her best friend wasn't buying it, Kate dropped her head. "Fine, I promise. Now, spill it. I'm dying here."

Emery glanced around, lowering her voice. "I made an appointment with Trip Hamilton for Thursday."

"You *what*?" Kate said too loudly, causing several heads to turn.

"Lord Almighty, keep your voice down," Emery said, smiling to the few who had turned to look at them. "I think they heard you in China."

Kate's eyes were still wide, but she dropped her voice to a whisper. "Okay, I'm listening. Quietly. But I have a lot to say on this. A lot. So speak quickly so we can get to the part where I tell you what a horrible idea this is."

Sighing, Emery set down her menu on the table and leaned back in. "Look, I know exactly what you're thinking, but it'll be fine. It's just a meeting, anyway. He could say no."

"No to what exactly?"

Emery chewed on her left thumbnail. "Well, I kind of asked him to hire me."

"You what!"

"Jesus, be quiet. I think you just blew up Mr. Black's hearing aid."

Kate drew a long breath and clasped her hands together in front of her, her mouth opening and closing twice before she spoke. "Um, do I need to remind you that this isn't just any trainer? This is Trip. The boy who broke your heart. Doesn't that matter to you?"

"Of course it matters." Emery's gaze fell to the table, before she revealed just how much. It mattered more than she would ever admit to anyone, even herself. "But he didn't even know my real feelings, Kate. He didn't leave me. We weren't anything serious. He got a job—it happens—and I was only seventeen. What was he supposed to do?"

Kate tossed up her hands, drawing more looks, and Emery thought she might kill her friend before they made it out of this conversation. "Sorry. It's just . . . you were absolutely something. Maybe not with a title and promise rings or your names carved into an old oak. But you were something. It mattered. It would have been nice if he'd called you once or twice in the last eight years. Instead, he just left, went on about his life. Doesn't that bother you?"

What bothered her was that she wouldn't have left him. If he'd asked, she would have gone anywhere with him, done anything, but she couldn't admit those feelings. Besides, she didn't want to be that kind of woman. "What would you say I did these last eight years? I have a shelf full of trophies and a body full of scars to prove I lived, too. We were young, but we're adults now, and feelings aside, he's the best. Owners want to work with him, he's smart and talented and—"

"Too hot for his own good." Kate shook her head. "You're sure about this?"

Emery stared out the shop's window, watching as an old Ford pickup truck went by.

"I'm sure I need to get back on a mount, and he's the best trainer to get me there. For now, that's all I need to know. Anyway, the appointment is Thursday morning."

Brighton's teen daughter, Mary Elizabeth, stepped up then to take their order, her braces-lined teeth showing for all to see. "Doing okay, Ms. Carlisle? Ms. Littleton?" she asked, her smile widening. "What can I get y'all today?"

They placed their order, and then, as soon as Mary Elizabeth was out of earshot, Kate leaned back in. "Okay, initial reaction is over and now I'm to *wow*. This is just so wow. How did you even get him to take your call? I thought you said he wouldn't talk to you about it."

Emery grinned. "I have no idea. The call went directly to his cell, like fate or something. I couldn't believe it."

Kate shook her head, smiling. "You are the luckiest person I know," she said, and then, realizing the deeper meaning of her words and just how very *unlucky* Emery had been, she started to apologize as Emery waved her off. "What time do you have to be there?"

"Seven."

Mary Elizabeth brought their chicken salad sandwiches, and Kate took a bite from hers before saying, "I guess I have plans Thursday morning?"

Emery smiled that pretty-please-with-sugar-on-top smile she knew worked best on Kate. She'd spent the last ten minutes trying to figure out how she would ask Kate to ride with her for moral support. Leave it to her friend to see through her ploys before she'd even conjured them. "I would owe you forever."

"Will there at least be some hot guys there? Cowboy hats who say things like, 'Hello, darlin'?"

"Um, well, I think he has two brothers, both younger, though I can't remember their names. Maybe one of them?" Emery wondered how she would feel if Kate actually *did* date one of Trip's brothers. Kate was adorable, and she knew all three brothers to be very handsome, but Kate dating a Hamilton brother would only remind her of the fact that she couldn't.

Kate picked up a bagel chip and popped it into her mouth, seeming satisfied. "Fine. But you're buying lunch."

Emery nodded as she sunk back into her chair. "Absolutely. And what about Matt? Are you really over him?"

"Matthew Bridges?"

Their gazes snapped up to find Mary Elizabeth standing over them, floral tea pitcher in hand as she shook her head in disappointment. "You're too good for him. He's a *mailman*, Ms. Littleton. You should date someone from the fire department. Firemen are hot. Mailmen are so not. Maybe Chris Dickens?"

"No chance," Kate said. "His name contains the word di—"

"Kate!" Emery kicked her under the table and Kate cried out, causing Mary Elizabeth to drop her pitcher and sweet tea to run everywhere. Several people nearby came over to help clean up the mess. Including half the fire department. Kate cringed as she slowly lifted her eyes to each of them, then stopped when she locked on Chris Dickens, the expression on his face revealing he'd heard every word of their conversation.

He flashed Kate a shiny grin and edged close. "Yes, it does, which should tell you I know just what to do with that word. And I'm willing to show you Friday night if you're willing?"

Kate's face went scarlet. "Um, thanks. I'll, uh . . . think about it."

Emery burst out laughing, still giggling as they left Brighton's. They walked down the sidewalk, enjoying the afternoon sun, everything about the moment easy and light, until Kate stopped and turned to Emery, biting her lip in that way she did when she wasn't sure how to say something.

"What?"

"Well, there's just one thing."

Emery's eyebrows threaded together. "About Chris Dick-ens?" She laughed again. "He said he's open for a date if you're willing."

Kate smacked her arm. "Not about Chris, though . . ." She thought for a moment, then shook her head. "Nah, too beefy."

"Then what?"

Her friend's eyes softened. "What are you going to do if Trip asks you to ride?"

Fear washed over Emery, settling into the base of her spine, all the easiness from before replaced by worry. She straightened before her weak backbone dropped her to the sidewalk. She couldn't even sit on Lemon Grass and had spent all of yesterday thinking about what she would say if Trip asked her to ride, playing out scenarios in her mind, coming up with excuse after excuse. But at the end of the day, Trip was a trainer, and he had owners counting on him to put the best jockeys on their mounts. If he trusted her enough to hire her, she couldn't let him down.

She started back down the sidewalk. "Then I'll ride."

Trip had spent the better part of the last twenty-four hours cursing everyone in his path, but mostly himself. He replayed his conversation with Emery again and again, wondering how she'd broken through his careful facade so easily. Hadn't he told her no? Hadn't he been stern in his delivery?

But this was Emery.

He thought of the first time he'd realized he couldn't stay away from her. They were friends, nothing more, and he'd ordered himself to be good out of respect for her father. And then one night everything changed. She had come home from a date with some loser on the football team, and the guy had kissed her, but clearly he had no clue what the hell he was doing. She laughed about the kiss as she described it in detail to Trip, their legs hanging over the second story of the barn, staring out over the farm, the night warm above. He'd looked into those amazing eyes of hers and told her she deserved to be kissed by someone who knew what he was doing. A breath passed between them, and she whispered, "Someone . . . like you?" And then his lips were on hers, and he'd spent all night answering her question, losing himself more and more with each kiss.

Trip shook himself from the memory, angry that he'd let the one person who dropped him to his knees back into his life. He blamed Clark for losing control with the new colt. *His thoughts were on other things*, Trip told himself. But the truth was, he couldn't find the will to deny her, not when he heard the break in her voice. Emery Carlisle had always been Trip's greatest weakness. Even her name stopped him in his tracks. Now, he'd all but handed her his man card by allowing her to come to Hamilton Stables after he'd already said no. Twice! What was he thinking?

And there was the problem—he wasn't. Trip never thought clearly when it came to Emery. He remembered the first time she'd raced, the thrill in her eyes when she'd returned to the farm. She hadn't won, not even close, but she was so excited no one cared. They'd celebrated her loss like she'd won the Triple Crown, and as he'd watched her laugh and dance with excitement, he knew she'd become a part of him. His thoughts, his dreams. He saw her in them. To him, she was everything.

But then he had that dreaded talk with Mr. Sampson, followed by his mother's death. Trip returned home to his father's tears and that was the end of it. He left, and she never called, so their lives continued on in parallel yet separate directions. A part of the same world, but never sharing the same life. And the truth was he missed her. When the quiet overcame the noise and rain beat against the roof and nothing occupied his mind but the sound of his heart, he thought of her. Until he ordered the thought away, closing up his heart once again.

Now, he invited this misery to his barn. What kind of suicidal shit was that? He pushed away his dark thoughts and continued on to his father's office for their weekly meeting.

Trip nodded to his father's administrative assistant, Peyton. "Doing okay today?" Trip asked.

She winked. "I am now."

He smiled, but somehow he couldn't bring himself to flirt with her like he should—like he would have just days before. All the things he'd once found appealing in her paled in comparison to his memory of Emery. Trip had spent eight years trying to forget her, and now he would see her again. He wondered if she looked the same, if she still wore her hair back—if her skin still smelled like wildflowers.

Freaking hell, pull yourself together, man!

He dropped his head and pushed through the conference room doors, his father and brother Nick already seated around the long rectangular table. Nick was the middle Hamilton brother and always early, just like their father, which virtually made him the favorite.

It all began two years before, right after Nick's fiancée, Brit, died. For three months, he barely got out of bed, unable to function, unable to work, unable to be the Nick they had always known. But then, one day, he showed up at the office, and it was like something had switched on in his head. He dove into work and never came up for air again. Sure, he found female comfort, but he was very private about it and very selective and never committed to anything beyond work. Though Trip dedicated himself to his work, too, he liked to think he still experienced life. Then again, he could be kidding himself.

"Right on time, as always," Nick said, grinning up at Trip. He had that floppy kind of blond hair and wore thin-rimmed glasses, set against a golden tan and a Crest commercial smile. He was polished, where Trip was rough.

"What can I say? Creature of habit." But the truth was Trip valued his own time far too much to ever be early for anything, but he also respected the time of others too much to be late. He was notoriously on time, to the second, whereas his youngest brother—

The door burst open from behind him and he turned slowly, his smile widening as Alex Hamilton, the youngest of the three, came strutting in, everything about him, from his mussed hair to his open-at-the-top collar shirt, screamed carefree. Or, to their father, reckless. Alex went through careers like others went through socks—pre-vet student, professional bull rider, Starbuck's barista. You name it, he'd done it. And while Trip certainly wasn't the line-walking son of Nick, he had a strong business sense and an innate ability with the horses. In short, he earned his place in that meeting. Alex? It was questionable.

Alex pulled out a chair beside him and plopped down, leaning back in the chair for good measure.

"Late night?" Trip asked, unable to stop himself.

Alex smirked, his green eyes sparkling. "Always."

The brothers all leaned in, eager to hear a good story, as Carter Hamilton cleared his throat and all three men straightened in their chairs, trying not to laugh. It was amazing how easily they became boys again when they were all together. There had been a time when they saw one another every day, but life and work kept them all busy.

Carter opened up a folder in front of him. "All right, let's begin with Industries. Nick?"

Nick began his spiel about Hamilton Industries, the various land, oil, and investment companies in which they still held a significant share. Nick, at the age of twenty-six, was the VP of operations, and while his job held many responsibilities, to Carter Hamilton, the core one was to ensure that none of the other "suits" screwed up the business his father and grandfather had built. Thankfully, sales for that quarter were good, with a strong GPM, which all meant Nick could sleep peacefully for now.

When Nick was done with his part of the meeting, Carter turned to Trip. "Now, stables?"

Though no one expressly said that Trip ran things on the farm, everyone knew he and he alone handled that side of the business. From maintenance to financials, he had a hand in it all, which was exactly how he liked it. Trip gave a rundown of the basics—status on a barn renovation, new arrivals, entries—then added at the end, "I may have a jockey for Sarah Anderson's colt."

"Oh?" Carter asked. "She'll be pleased to hear it. Who are you going with?"

Trip hesitated. He had considered keeping the meeting with Emery a secret, but he knew his father had an ear out for everything and would learn about it on his own. Then he would question Trip on why he'd kept the information to himself. He didn't need the added trouble, so he drew a long breath and said, "Emery Carlisle."

The other men began to speak all at once. Talk of risk and falls and doubt—all the reasons this was crazy. And they were right, yet Trip couldn't convince himself to listen. If he hadn't listened to his own doubts, he sure wouldn't listen to theirs.

Trip sat back in his chair and crossed his arms over his chest, waiting for the shock to die down. "Do I need to be here for this discussion or can you continue it without me? I have a broodmare foaling any minute."

His father leaned in closer, his hands threaded together on the table, his stare fixed on Trip. "Is this some kind of joke? Sarah expects a champion, and a champion needs an experienced rider. Forget that Emery's female; she hasn't been on a mount in over two years."

"True enough," Trip said. "But Sarah bought that colt from her family's farm. Emery knows him, and right now, I'm nowhere near where I should be in his training. She could help. I'm meeting with her on Thursday. I'll make the call then."

Nick stared at Trip, forcing him to look over. He was the only one who knew about Trip's feelings for Emery. The way he'd almost accepted Beckett's offer for a permanent position, just so he could be near her—Mr. Sampson and his threats be damned. So Nick knew this situation wasn't simple. No, it ran layers deep, each layer more coated and difficult to process than the last.

"It's fine," Trip said before Nick could start his psychobabble. What did he expect Trip to say? The truth? Hell no. He couldn't admit the truth. That he'd spoken to Emery and simply couldn't refuse her. They wouldn't understand. Their father and Nick were both devout businessmen, and Alex's spirit was too wild to be swayed by a woman. Everyone in that room had been to the races, but not one of them felt it deep in his bones—not like Trip. And not like Emery. He knew plenty of riders, but he rarely talked to one he felt gave two shits about the horse beyond what it could do for them. Emery was different. She'd always *been* different, which was part of the problem. He'd resisted her once. How in the hell would he do it again?

Trip realized they were waiting on him to continue. "Look, she's been in the money in every race she's ever run. Her performance is unmatched."

Alex scratched his chin. "Yeah, well, talk around Crestler's Key is she can't even get on a horse. Have you seen her ride?"

Trip glared at his brother. "What are you doing in Crestler's Key?"

"Hey, women are women," Alex said, holding up his hands. "And there are only so many in Triple Run. Man's gotta eat. But this isn't about me, bro, so stop changing the subject. Have you seen her ride?" He watched Trip, his eyes narrowing. "You haven't, have you?"

"Alex . . ." Nick warned, blowing out a breath at the same time Trip's fists came down on the table.

"I don't owe anyone in this room an explanation. I'm the lead trainer for Hamilton Stables. Every trophy on that damn wall—" He jabbed a finger at the impressive display across from him— "is because of me. I don't see any of you down there checking feed tubs at four thirty in the fucking morning. So until you're ready to get your palms dirty, you don't get to ask me questions. Got it?"

Trip eyed them one by one, daring them to argue. But all they did was stare back, and then, finally, Carter spoke up. "Okay, then," he said, his voice as calm as ever. "Emery Carlisle will ride Sarah's colt . . . what's his name?"

"Craving Wind."

Carter nodded, letting the name settle in his mind. "Craving Wind. It's good."

"It is," Trip agreed.

"And what about the broodmares? Are you still determined to split Hamilton Stables into breeding and training?"

Trip heard the hesitation in his father's voice. The same hesitation he'd heard when Trip had decided to open Hamilton Stables, but Trip had long had an interest in breeding. Not like with training, but he wanted to have his hand in all sides of horse racing. Besides, he liked the idea of being a one-stop shop for owners—buy from Hamilton Stables and train at Hamilton Stables. Trip had their trust and felt this would be an easy expansion. But of course, nothing was ever easy. What he needed was someone to manage the breeding side of the business and allow him to handle training. He would oversee both, but if he had someone he could trust . . .

"Still my goal," Trip answered finally. "But we're working through some kinks. I need someone to manage it, so I can focus on training, but I've yet to find the right fit."

Alex turned to Trip, his expression unreadable. "What exactly are you looking for?"

Trip shrugged. "Someone who understands the business, the science. Can analyze and predict the best matches, see champions even before they're born."

Carter started to move on to the next topic on the agenda when Alex interrupted. "What about me?"

"What about you?" all three men answered.

Alex sat taller. "Look, I know y'all think I'm unwilling to do the whole hardworking Hamilton thing, but you're wrong. I'm done with that life and ready to take my place in these meetings." He turned to Trip, his expression serious. "I was halfway through vet school. I can do this. I know the science, but more importantly, I know you. I know what you expect and I'll deliver."

All eyes fell on Trip, but he already had the stress of hiring Emery on his back. He didn't want to add his brother to the list, and though he knew Alex to be the most intelligent of the three of them, he'd quit every time something got tough. And Trip knew it would destroy their relationship if he put all his trust in his brother only for him to pull an Alex and bolt.

"I'll think about it," Trip said. Tomorrow. He had enough to think about for today.

They wrapped things up with a reminder from Carter to return the following week, same time, even though they'd met every Wednesday for years. And then the brothers were all outside, Nick needing to catch a flight out west, Alex planning to go to some bar later, where a local band would be playing.

"Want to get together tomorrow night for drinks?" Nick asked, before slipping into his Mercedes. Trip knew exactly why he'd asked to meet and wanted no part of it. But he knew his brother too well to hope Nick would let this go.

"Do I have a choice?"

Nick laughed. "Nope."

Trip started to turn for his truck when Alex called, "Yeah, then maybe you can tell us how Emery Carlisle really convinced you to work with her."

He cocked his head and tapped a finger against his lips. "You know, I think I've made my decision on the breeding manager position."

Alex's eyes widened. "Oh, yeah?"

"It's a no."

He started for his truck as Alex shouted after him, "Dude, it was a joke. I won't mention the name Emery Carlisle again. Just give me the job."

Trip smirked. "Yeah . . . I don't think so."

"Come on!"

Trip's phone vibrated with a text from back at the barn. The mare had foaled, but Trip had to get to the races. Hesitating, he turned back to his brother. "You serious about this?"

"Dead."

He blew out a breath and glanced over at Nick, who gave a single nod. "All right. Bright Candy just foaled, and someone needs to get over there to make sure everything's fine. I need to get to the races. Can you go?"

"Seriously?"

Trip shut his truck door and hung out the window, a smile breaking across his face. "Tell them I sent you. And try not to hook up with any of my staff before I get back."

Alex laughed. "Yes, sir."

CHAPTER THREE

Put him through his paces

"I still don't understand why I had to pick you up way out here," Kate said, eyeing the trees that surrounded Emery in the darkness. The fairway cut through the woods like a curving stream. Daddy had the small nine-hole course put in two years earlier in an attempt to teach Mama how to play golf without an audience. To this day, she still had never stepped foot on the course.

"I had no choice. Mr. Sampson is in the barn at the crack of dawn every morning. I couldn't take the chance that he would see me leave so early."

It was five a.m., the sun had yet to wake up, and the sounds of outside still resembled something out of a horror film. Which was Kate's real problem. Despite being an adult, she still harbored terrifying illusions of getting attacked by a serial killer in the woods. It all went back to their horror-movie marathon in the third grade. They'd rented every one of the *Friday the 13th*s, and by the third movie, Kate had resigned herself to never going in the woods again—or to a hockey game.

Kate eyed the darkened depths around them again. "You realize that you're twenty-five, right?"

"Do you? I mean, seriously, are you going to pee yourself out here? Should I go get you a change of clothes?"

Kate rolled her eyes. "First, stop changing the subject. And two, gross! I have never peed my pants in my—" At Emery's expression, she stopped and pointed her finger at her friend. "You promised to never bring that up! It was seventh grade and I laughed too hard. It happens!"

Emery grinned. "Sure it does." She placed her bag in the trunk of Kate's Prius, hoping against hope that she found the courage to put on the riding boots she'd tucked inside. This was it, her one and only chance to convince Trip, to regain her family's respect. Hell, to regain the entire racing world's respect. Everything rested on this appointment.

"I'm sorry," she said, slipping into the passenger seat. "I promise not to bring it up again starting now."

"You just remember that I know your secrets too, little Emery Carlisle."

Emery smiled. "That you do." She felt bad asking Kate to drive, but she knew carsickness would find her friend if she rode instead of drove, and besides, she owed Emery for that cross-country stint in college, which had resulted in an empty gas tank and a three-mile hike in the desert out west to the nearest gas station. Needless to say, this was cake compared to that disaster.

Kate pulled off the side road, back onto the main highway that led to Triple Run. "I thought your meeting was at seven."

"It is."

Kate's gaze shifted to Emery and then back to the road. "Um, am I missing something here? It's five."

"I figured we could hang out until then. Patty's Place should be open by the time we get there. We can have fresh scones and coffee."

"Patty's? Are you insane?" She held up her right hand. "No, don't answer that. I know you're insane. Why else would you eat breakfast with your aunt's nemesis and then meet with your first love?"

Emery jerked up like she'd been shocked. "What? I didn't love him."

"Ha! You loved him down to your toes, girl. Every bit as much as Annie-Jean *hates* Patty. She'll crucify you if she finds out we ate there."

Emery stared out her window, not willing to touch the love topic and hating how much it hurt to hear Kate say it. Never once had Emery said she loved Trip out loud, never once had she even allowed herself to think it. Feeling it, though? Well, feelings were their own animal, and hers refused to be tamed.

"Then we'll just have to make sure she doesn't find out."

"Yeah, is that like making sure your daddy doesn't find out about this meeting? Why don't you just tell him, Em?"

"You know it's complicated."

And she did. Kate knew exactly how hard it was for Emery to stand up to her daddy, especially after the accident. She remembered her parents' faces when they came into her hospital room after her second surgery. She had two broken ribs, a broken leg, and a face full of bruises. She was a destroyed woman, and she was their only child. Her mother had had countless miscarriages before Emery, so they viewed her as a blessing from God—a blessing they held clutched to their chests.

Emery didn't even allow them to speak before she looked them in the eyes and simply said, "Please." The room grew quiet then, but they knew exactly what she was asking—please don't make her stop racing.

She had no idea then how deeply her fear would set in, how the animal that had once held a piece of her soul would cause her hands to shake so badly she couldn't even grab the reins. Coming to Trip was a risk, in more ways than one. She just hoped it'd be worth it.

"All right, well, if Annie finds out, I wasn't with you. She scares me when she's mad."

Emery laughed. "She scares everyone."

They fell into a comfortable silence, switching from station to station, Emery's nerves twisting around and around, doubt replacing Kate as her new best friend.

"Hey, Em?"

"Hmm?"

Kate cut her eyes over. "What was it like to talk to him again?"

Emery thought of his voice, the perfect combination of smooth and rough—all man, all confidence—and the hint of a smile lingering at the end of each word. Her heart beat in her chest, warmth spreading all around. "It was like a sunrise. All dark and then it just peeks up, and suddenly you're nodding and smiling, because it was always there, hidden behind the night."

Kate looked at her again. "Um . . . what was that?"

A laugh burst from Emery's lips, and she tossed the ChapStick she'd been playing with at her friend. "Hell, I don't know!"

"God, you're in so much trouble."

Emery sighed. "Don't I know it."

They drove through downtown Triple Run, all the streets cobble-stone, the stop signs wooden and painted bright red and white. There were few cars on the road and the stores that lined the street were just beginning to open up. Emery eyed each of the stores, curious which ones Trip frequented the most—the hardware store, perhaps, or the diner, or maybe he was fond of Patty's Place. Emery couldn't blame him. Despite her aunt's hatred, Patty was an amazing baker.

"Are you sure, like sure-sure about this?" Kate asked as she parked in an open space in front of Patty's Place. The lights were on inside, a few of the tables already full, and then there stood Patty behind the counter, laughing and waving her hands around as she spoke, like she couldn't keep them still if she tried.

Emery didn't know exactly what had happened between her aunt and Patty, but she knew they'd been best friends all their lives, both women never married, and then suddenly Patty had moved to Triple Run and Annie-Jean never spoke kindly of her again. Though a part of her wanted to trust that her aunt had reasons for her hatred of Patty, another part of her knew Annie could be unreasonable. This whole fight could be over something trivial—like a recipe.

Regardless, the diner down the street still sat dark inside, which meant Patty's was the only place they could go for a good cup of cof-fee, and Emery needed five if she hoped to survive this morning.

"Let's go."

She shut the car door and opened the door to the bakery, the smell of cinnamon and brown sugar hitting her nose. Patty's gaze locked on Emery as soon as the door closed behind them. For a moment, Emery worried she might ask them to leave, but instead, she just looked sad.

The rest of the diners all peered over at Emery and Kate, seeming to recognize out-of-towners, and truthfully, if they knew Emery and Kate were from Crestler's Key, their quizzical stares would turn downright mean. There had always been some animosity between the two towns, going back so long it was hard to remember where the issue had originated.

All Emery knew was that an article in the *New York Times* had called Crestler's Key "Kentucky's horse country." Well, a week later,

Triple Run changed their "Welcome to Triple Run" sign to read "Welcome to Triple Run, Kentucky's horse country." And that was that. Crestler's Key's mayor at the time had ordered Triple Run's mayor to change the sign, but it was done, and then the *Times* article was forgotten and everyone in the racing world had started referring to Triple Run as horse country, driving that knife deeper into Crestler's Key's back.

All that was to say, Patty didn't open her bakery in Triple Run by coincidence. It was an intentional slap in the face to Annie-Jean.

Emery motioned to a table by the window—making it also superclose to the door in case they had to dash out—and within a minute, Patty stood beside them, her hands on her hips, a tight smile on her overly made-up face.

"Good mornin', ladies. What brings you to town?"

A hush fell over the small bakery, all eyes on Emery. Crap! She hadn't thought through her reasons for being in town, what she would say. She couldn't mention Trip or Hamilton Stables. Though she doubted anyone here would step foot in Crestler's Key to tell her daddy about her visit, she couldn't chance it.

"Oh, just passing through."

Patty's eyes narrowed, her white bob shaking, like even her hair didn't believe Emery. "Driving through to where, honey? Atlanta's the other way."

"Oh, well . . ." She glanced hopefully at Kate, but her stare was locked on a guy by the counter, oblivious to the disaster happening at their table. "It was . . . You see . . ."

Just then, the guy walked over to their table, a grin on his face. "Well, hello there, Patty. You look lovely this morning."

Patty laughed and swiped a hand through the air. "Oh, you are such a flirt. But I'll take it." She laughed again, and Emery turned in her chair, eyeing the door. Could she run without drawing attention?

The guy laughed, and Kate laughed harder, causing all eyes to turn to her. *What are you doing?* Emery mouthed, for her friend to just shrug and waggle her eyebrows, then nod toward the guy. Subtlety was so not Kate's strong suit.

"Care to introduce me to your friends, Ms. Patty?" he asked.

For a second Emery thought Patty might say no, but then she plastered on that sugar smile of hers and motioned between them. "Alex Hamilton, this is Kate Littleton and Emery Carlisle."

Alex Hamilton? Hamilton? No, no, no!

Alex's gaze landed on Emery. "Right. I thought I recognized you. You're here for—"

Emery jumped up and grabbed his arm, dragging him to the counter. "Yes! Thanks for the offer. I'll take whatever you bought. Come show me."

Alex tried to resist, but when Emery dug her nails into his forearm he screamed. "Damn, woman, what the hell did I do to you?" he asked as they reached the counter. "I didn't think we'd been together before." He cocked his head, studying her. "Have we?"

Emery glared at him. "*No*. What is wrong with you?"

"Me? You just assaulted me in the name of blueberry scones!"

Trying to calm herself down, Emery closed her eyes, but when she reopened them she found everyone in the bakery watching them. Gah! Why couldn't she live in some massive city where people minded their own business?

"Look, no one knows I'm here today to talk with Trip. You can't say anything."

Alex's brows lifted. "Oh . . . kay. And why is that again? Don't you think people are going to notice if you start riding for Trip?"

"I don't know. Yes? Maybe? But that isn't happening today, see. We're just talking. I've got time to . . ."

He grinned, and she thought maybe she didn't like Trip's brother all too much. "Come up with a lie?" He took in her expression and burst out laughing. "Damn, I'm right, aren't I? First Trip went all crazy in the meeting about you, and then you're keeping the whole thing a secret? What's really going on between you and my brother?"

Emery had stopped listening at *Trip went all crazy in the meeting about you.* "What do you mean, he went crazy?"

"Ah, just all his decision. He'll do whatever the hell he wants. All that shit." Alex dipped down so he stood eye to eye with Emery. "But that doesn't explain why you're all worked up right now. Is there something going on?"

"No!" Emery glanced around and lowered her voice. "I mean, no. We're just—we're nothing. It's just a meeting."

Alex laughed again. "Yeah, you said that."

Emery opened her mouth to tell Alex where he could shove that laugh when Patty came up, and Emery pleaded to Alex with her eyes to keep his mouth shut—or else she wasn't against shoving those delicious blueberry scones down his throat.

"Everything okay over here?"

Alex smiled down at Emery, then flipped his crooked grin over to Patty. "Yes, Ms. Patty. Emery was just asking for directions to Lexington. She and her friend are going up there to that new antique shop. You heard about it, right?"

Antiquing? What? Emery was twenty-five. Twenty-five year olds didn't go antiquing. Patty would never buy that. Stupid Hamilton brother.

But then Patty said, "Oh," and her expression turned thoughtful. "No, I don't think I have. I'll have to check it out, too."

Emery released a breath as Patty left them, and Alex leaned down, that annoying smirk still on his face. "I'll tell Trip you're on your way." Then he glanced down at his forearms, to the tiny crescent moon–shaped indentations turning red. "And warn him to wear gloves."

Trip awoke with a start, the remnants of a dream still clouding his mind. A certain woman. A table. A voice so full of intensity and want that it took his breath away. He groaned as he pushed out of bed, all evidence of just how *involved* the dream had been still showing in his boxers. Damn, how had Emery impacted him so fully after just one call? He blamed his current self-imposed drought. Racing season was upon them, and the last thing he needed was a clingy woman distracting him. He'd made a deal with himself—stay focused on his goal of having one of his horses win, place, or show in every major stakes, and he could celebrate with as many women as he liked.

The problem was, Trip wasn't the many-women kind of guy. He hated the idea of commitment, but he also didn't like the complications of dating around. He preferred to mix with one woman at a time, keep it fun and simple, then move on. At least, that had been his mantra throughout his twenties, but now that he was approaching thirty fast, he'd begun to wonder what he was doing with his life. Didn't he want a wife to hold in his arms after a long day? Didn't he want the quintessential two-point-five kids?

The truth was, he wanted what his parents had, but he'd met enough women to know that women his age had different interests— interests that began with dollar signs. He had only met one woman who possessed the core values he craved—a solid moral compass, unwavering passion, and a drive for more than what his money could buy. And that woman would be at his farm in an hour.

He thought of the last time he'd seen Emery. It had been two years ago in Saratoga, and she'd pretty much become the face of horse racing. An article had just been released in the *New York Post*—"Beauty & the beast, an inside look at racing's newest champion"—and suddenly everyone was talking about Emery and whether she would take the Kentucky Derby. Back then, Trip had done little more than mock her as a marketing ploy, angry that she'd let them present her as a pretty face instead of the athlete she deserved. But one passing moment between them in the backside told him she didn't care what he thought, didn't care about him. He was in her past.

If only he could tuck her away so easily. Instead, she filled his dreams with her long black hair, porcelain skin, and those damn blue eyes.

He turned on the shower at the thought and ran the water as cold as he could handle it in hopes of calming himself down. She would arrive soon, and he wanted to be on his game. He still wasn't sure that he would actually hire her. After all, he had a reputation to consider, and Alex was right. There was talk that she hadn't even gotten back on a horse. He figured the rumors were just that—rumors. But what if they were true? What was he getting himself in to?

Trip pushed out of his house and shut the door, only to turn around and spy his brother sitting in his golf cart, tapping the wheel to a song only he could hear.

"Howdy, brother," Alex said, continuing his beat. "Thought I'd give you a ride over so we could talk about a few things."

With hesitation, Trip slipped into the cart and immediately felt like an idiot. He hated being the passenger, hated handing over the controls to someone else. Alex managed to get all the way to the end of the driveway before Trip waved his hands. "Enough. Stop."

The cart slammed to a halt and Alex peered around. "What? Did I hit something?"

"No; get out."

"What?"

Trip walked around to the driver's side of the cart. "Get out. I'm driving."

"You're serious."

"Don't I look serious? My cart, my rules. Get out."

Alex shook his head and slid over, motioning dramatically toward the driver's seat. "She's all yours. And something tells me she's not the only *she*."

Trip stopped in midmotion to getting into the cart. "What did you say?"

It was six thirty in the morning, and already Trip felt like he was running late. He'd yet to have coffee, hadn't taken the time to shave, and knew Clark would already have the morning workouts going. In short, he was in no mood to deal with his brother's shit. He started down the driveway again, ignoring his brother's stare.

"I said—"

The cart jerked to a stop again, lurching both men forward. "I heard what you said. I want to know what you meant."

Alex made a show of gripping the seat, like he held on for his life. "Should I get out now, before I find myself in a death-by-golf-cart crash?"

"You can say whatever it is you're here to say before I get aggravated and tell Nick about that time you got too drunk and hit on Brit."

Alex recoiled. "She dyed her hair. I didn't know it was her!"

Trip shrugged. "Somehow I don't think Nick will care."

"Yeah, well, I've got dirt on you, too, now, so we'll see who's threatening who."

"Dirt on me how?"

Alex rested back in his seat, relaxing with his newfound power. "I ran into someone this morning at Ms. Patty's. Care to guess who?" At Trip's glare, he continued. "That's right—Emery Carlisle. And not only did she manhandle me into secrecy about her reasons for being in town but she acted every bit as crazy as you did in the meeting yesterday. Seems a little odd, don't you think?"

"Don't know what you mean. And don't care."

Trip parked the cart beside the barn and started to walk away as Alex matched his step, refusing to let it go. "You know exactly what I mean, and I gotta tell you, this is a bad idea. Frankly, I'm a little disappointed in you."

"Me?" Trip spun on his brother, growing frustrated and annoyed that he had to explain himself. Again.

Alex grinned, enjoying the fact that his always-responsible big brother was being anything *but* responsible. But then he caught something in Trip's expression, something like fear, and the smile slipped away. "Shit." He took a step toward Trip, making sure no one was around. "I was just messing with you. I didn't think you really had feelings for her. You don't, right?"

Trip stared down the road, watching as the wind moved through the trees, causing them to stir. He didn't want to answer his brother, didn't want to have this damn conversation at all. Because if he opened his mouth, there were only two possible outcomes—he admitted the truth or he lied to his brother, and he made it a point to be honest with his family.

"Trip."

Finally, he glanced over, unable to delay any longer. "Look, she'll be here soon, and they need you up at the foaling barn."

Alex opened his mouth, but one look from Trip had him closing it again. "All right, but just remember, this isn't just your career you're messing with. It's all of us."

"Like I could forget," Trip murmured as he continued around to the training ring, eager to lose himself in work before Emery arrived.

Clark had Craving Wind out, getting him ready for Emery to see him, and already the horse looked like it wanted to rear and kick Clark out of the way.

"Trouble?" Trip asked as he neared.

Clark laughed. "Yeah, though by the sound of that conversation you just had, you're in it worse than me."

"That obvious, huh?" He didn't look over at his assistant trainer and friend. He didn't have to. Clark's thoughts oozed off him, slapping Trip in the face and yelling for him to pull himself together.

"I've known you a long time," Clark said, "but I've never seen you make a snap decision. Never once seen you act with your heart instead of your head. So what's this really about?"

The colt walked around, seeming thankful for the men's distraction. He'd eaten all his morning feed and had grown well in the weeks Trip had stabled him here, but he couldn't help wondering if the horse would do better at the track.

"Ah, hell."

Trip shook himself from his thoughts and peered over at Clark. "What?"

"Just tell me now. Is there something going on between you and Emery Carlisle? 'Cause if there is, I'd like to know now so I can start looking for a job before your father axes us all."

Trip wasn't sure what annoyed him more—Clark's assumption that he'd get involved with an employee and risk all their jobs or his belief that Carter Hamilton had the final say in anything on the farm. Industries? Sure. But the farm was Trip's, through and through, and damn if he'd allow his father to tell him what to do.

"There's nothing going on. Damn, why can't any of y'all believe that I'd hire a female jockey? She's not just good. She's the best female jockey in history. That kind of thing needs to be on my payroll."

Clark stared at him. "So, that's it then? Just a business decision?"

"It's the only kind I know."

"All right. Just make sure you keep everything on your terms."

"What do you mean?"

Clark started toward the colt, clearly hoping to state his peace and leave before he pissed Trip off. "Well, she's a woman, and a looker at that. She's coming here to ask you for a job, not the other way around. She doesn't get to make the demands, you do. Just remember that. Set the terms and keep to them."

Trip let the advice work through his mind. *Set the terms.* He could do that. Hell, he hadn't seen her in years. The spark between them could long be gone, and then it would be all too easy to treat her like every other jockey. Whose virginity he'd taken. But still. Irrelevant detail.

"Set the terms?"

"Set the terms," Clark called back, already over to the colt. Trip wanted to step in and micromanage the situation, but Clark didn't need Trip doing that. He was a fine trainer. This colt was just a little more complex, like the woman scheduled to arrive any moment now.

"How's he doing?" Trip asked in an effort to change the subject.

Clark swiped his forehead with his shirtsleeve. "Stubborn as a mule."

Trip nodded, taking in the horse. He was a rich chestnut, his mane shiny, his conformation nearly perfect. The horse trotted away from Clark, shaking his head as though to say, "*Not this one again.*" He watched the episode for another solid minute before walking over.

Clark backed away from the horse, giving his boss room, and instantly the colt turned, hyperaware of the new presence in his domain. Taking slow steps, Trip approached him, closer and closer, their eyes locked, until finally he stopped several yards away and lifted his arms out. He nodded for Clark to step out of the gate, then he focused back on the colt. "It's just you and me, boy." He took another step and the horse squealed, stepping back. Trip focused on his breathing, keeping it steady, and began to lower his arms. The horse reacted immediately, taking another step back. He didn't trust Trip, but he wasn't afraid of him either. That was a good thing.

There were barely any sounds on the farm just yet, everything quiet, the morning just beginning. Trip loved this point in the day, how a world of possibilities lay before him. No two days were the same on the farm, which was the very thing that made him fall in love with it all those years ago. He liked to spend time with every horse, and he had never once turned away a horse because he couldn't train it. There was always a way.

He focused back on the animal before him, stubborn and feisty, so much like Emery, but his conformation and pedigree all but guaranteed a champion. He just needed time. Trip took one long look at him and then stepped back, showing that he would respect that time. For now.

He reached for the gate, and before he'd even turned around, he felt the change in the air. The intense gaze on his back. The increase in his heart rate.

Taking longer than necessary to close the gate, he dipped his head and drew a long breath. *Set the terms*, he reminded himself. And then he faced them, and it was like time had stopped and he was back there, getting introduced to her for the first time and knowing he'd just met someone who would forever impact his life. All bright smiles and caring eyes and unyielding passion. Without thinking, he started slowly toward her, unable to pull his eyes away, unable to slow his pulse.

At first glance, her features appeared harsh—black hair, ivory skin—but then you took in those huge blue eyes and suddenly all you could think was *damn, she's beautiful.*

And she was. So damn beautiful.

Eight years had passed, yet somehow it felt like nothing more than a moment, a breath, a blink, and then she stood there in front of him again. He ached to go to her, to pull her against him and trace a hand down her face and tell her he was a fucking moron for leaving. Because damn.

But then he reached her and tipped his Stetson down and saw a wicked flicker in her eyes, and though time hadn't aged her a bit, something had changed. She was older, more experienced—in more ways than one, if that look meant a thing.

Memories hit all at once—the first time he saw her, the first time he reached for her hand, the first time he pressed his lips to hers, unable to stay away. She was seventeen, almost eighteen, and he was twenty, the age on his mind yet not. They were so similar the small gap didn't matter—outside of the fear of Beckett having him arrested. He smiled at the memory of them nearly getting caught, their hearts racing.

He took a second to take her in, ignoring the warning bells sounding off in his brain. He knew her face, had a thousand memories of it, had seen her in the *Post* article and in countless mentions of racing, and none of it, not the photos, not his memory, had done her justice.

Trip cleared his throat and stepped up to them, tipping his Stetson down with a polite smile. "Emery."

CHAPTER FOUR

Riding for a fall

Emery tried, and failed, to keep her mouth from falling slack. She'd Googled Trip's name the night before, unable to stop herself, and while she knew age had served him well, every expectation she had paled in comparison to the person before her. He wore faded jeans and a fitted flannel shirt that showed off his broad chest and thick biceps. Rugged cowboy boots stuck out from his jeans and an equally beaten-up cowboy hat graced his head, but even with it on, she could see his chocolate brown hair curling out at the ends. A memory hit of her hands in that hair, and she had to look away to keep from blushing. Trip was manly to the extreme. His expression, hooded and sexy. But none of that compared to watching him with the colt.

She and Kate had parked behind the stables and walked over. Kate had just begun to speak when Emery motioned for her to wait, her eyes on the training ring and the man inside it, his every move controlled—graceful. She'd never seen anything like it. They eased up to the fencing and watched, and the longer she watched, the more two things became apparent to her—the man was undoubtedly Trip . . . and the colt was hers.

"Wow, he's gotten big. He's beautiful, isn't he?" Emery said, nodding to the horse. The truth was, she found it easier to look at the horse than the man before her. Somehow, she never expected to feel so intimidated by Trip. Sure, they had a past, but that she could handle. What she couldn't handle was the surge of emotions waging war inside her head and heart at the way he said her name—Emery. Like her name meant something to him, even now. Looking into his eyes was like looking into the depths of a well, dark and forever and yet, somehow, peaceful. They were mesmerizing.

And the last thing she needed distracting her in that moment. He should have aged crappy, gotten flabby and worn. Instead, he looked even better than she remembered.

Damn him!

Trip turned around, a smirk on his face, like he knew just what she was thinking and got a little more than joy from her frustration. He'd always been able to read her thoughts. "He is," he said, then focusing back on Emery, added, "a little spirited, but a beauty all the same."

Their eyes held, the moment drawing long, and then Emery cleared her throat and adjusted her footing, forcing Trip's gaze to drop—and land squarely on her cane. His brow furrowed, like he couldn't quite make sense of it, and she felt her cheeks burn. She knew this would happen. Kate had suggested she leave it in the car, but the thing had become her security blanket. Without it, she wasn't sure she could stand tall against a man like Trip.

This time he cleared his throat, his eyes darting quickly to Kate. "And you are . . . ?"

Kate grinned, reaching out to shake his hand. "We've actually met once before, but it was a long time ago. Kate Littleton, teacher." Trip's gaze shot to Emery, and Kate laughed. "No, no. Not her teacher. Even I'm not patient enough for that."

"Oh, really? So what do you teach?"

"Kindergarteners."

Trip burst out laughing. "I see. So, it would require more patience to teach Emery than it does five year olds?" He laughed again, and Emery found herself gritting her teeth together to keep from blurting out just what she thought of Trip and his too-sexy laugh.

"Can I see him?" Emery asked, her tone full of aggravation despite her best efforts to hide it. Why did she have to wear her emotions on her sleeve, for all to see?

"Who, this one?" Trip replied, still chuckling a little, until he caught the determination in her face. He knew, even before she had to say a word. He crossed his arms and stood taller. "He's a little wild right now." His gaze fell to her cane and then quickly back up, like he'd made a mistake. "Is that a good idea?"

Emery stared back, unable to hide her hurt. After the time they'd shared, she never once thought he'd focus on her injury. That he'd be like everyone else. She held him higher than the class of people who saw her injury first, Emery second, and the disappointment was unsettling. "I'm not a cripple."

Kate adjusted beside Emery. "Hey, Em, let's—"

"Then what's with the cane?" Trip shot back.

The hurt spiked, transferring into anger. "What did you say?"

"You don't need it. So why are you using it?"

Emery's hands balled into fists, despite her best effort to keep her emotions in check. "You don't know a thing about me."

"Don't I?"

Everything about the moment felt overly raw, from their too-close stance to the intensity in their eyes. They tested each other, seeing who would falter first, and Emery had no intention of allowing it to be her.

She took a step forward, refusing to allow her cane to keep her from standing up to him. "You barely knew me then, how in the hell could you possibly know me now?"

The air sparked with tension, even the colt behind them backing away, as though he, too, wanted away from Emery's glare. She knew her words were a lie, but she couldn't admit the truth—that he'd known her better than she knew herself. Which made it hurt all the more when he left. Maybe she was the reason he'd left. She'd wondered that very thing too many times to count, but it didn't matter now. Now she needed to act tough. It was easier to throw attitude at him than allow herself to feel all the things her heart wanted to feel.

"Tell yourself whatever you want," Trip said. "But I know you, and I know this—" he motioned to the cane—"is beneath you. If you plan to work for me, then you do it without that cane."

Emery pointed at Trip, and Kate, sensing her friend's feistiness coming to life, darted forward, pulling Emery back. "Em, let's look around first. Then maybe you can—"

"I want to see the colt. Now," she said to Trip, refusing to back down. "You know as well as I do that it's a smart decision to hire me. I'm the best female rider in—"

"Fine, have it your way. Clark?" he called, glancing over at the man. "Saddle up Prankster Pit. Let's let Ms. High and Mighty show us what she's got."

Emery's hand dropped to her side, all the blood draining from her face, her lungs refusing to take a breath. "What . . . what are you doing?"

"You're a rider. So ride. Prove it to me."

He was challenging her now, and she hated him all the more for it. "I don't have to show you anything."

Trip laughed. Laughed! "You really are something else. This is my farm, not your daddy's, and you'll follow my rules or you can go. Simple as that." He crossed his arms and, unable to stop herself, Emery stepped up in front of him, refusing to accept this mean, arrogant man in front of her. He might know her, but she knew him, too. And this wasn't Trip.

"I can't do that," she said, her voice low as she lifted her head to look him in the eye. "But I will. If you know me like you think you do, then you *know* I will. For now, I'd like to see him." She motioned to the horse behind them. "Please."

Trip exhaled, his gaze locked on hers, his heart beating noticeably in his chest, and she thought maybe she'd pushed him too far, maybe he wanted her to leave, when he released another breath and with effort said, "Fine . . . after you."

The gate seemed an eternity away with the cane in tow. Emery considered tossing it, but then, how would she stand? How would she brace herself when she reached up to stroke the colt's mane? Rushing would only make things worse, so she took her time, sliding the cane in the dirt, then taking a step, until she reached it, ignoring the stares from both Trip and Kate. She could handle almost anything but pity, and it rolled off both of them in nauseating waves.

Trip unhooked the gate and held it open for her to step inside. Immediately, she felt the presence of the horse across from her, heard his breath rush out in uneven bursts. She remembered the white diamond shape between his eyes, the way he'd gotten up immediately after he'd been born, like he couldn't remain still—like he was ready to run.

"What'd Sarah name him?"

Trip stopped just behind her. "Craving Wind."

A smile spread across Emery's face as she pictured the name at the races. "It's perfect."

The sound of Trip taking another step toward her hit her ears, his body undeniably close. If she leaned back, she would touch him. "It is?"

Emery turned but remained where she stood. Her five-two height left her a full head and a half below him, so she tilted her head up, squinting in the morning sun. "I saw him being born, and it was like he couldn't *wait* to take off. Like his spirit yearned for the track."

Sounds of the farm's staff at work echoed all around them—commands from other assistant trainers managing the morning workouts, the quiet chatter from those busy in the stables. She knew she should step away from Trip before someone saw whatever this was passing between them, yet she couldn't force her body to move.

Trip's tongue swept over his bottom lip and her eyes immediately drew down, wondering if they felt as full as she remembered. Wondering how they would feel now. She shuddered and turned back to the horse, who walked around like he wasn't sure about anything at all. Emery could relate.

She took another few steps toward him, watching for his reaction, waiting until he calmed, then took another few steps, and then she stood right beside him, listening to his breathing.

Emery closed her eyes and gingerly reached out her hand . . .

Trip's insides coiled up like a rattler, every fiber in him screaming for him to step between the colt and Emery. He didn't know this horse, couldn't predict his responses. He'd almost kicked in Clark's face, for Christ's sake, and now, here was Emery, five foot nothing, tiny and meek, her body's weight resting on that black cane of hers. He still couldn't make sense of her using it when she very clearly didn't need it. But need was a very subjective thing.

Time slowed down as he watched her extend her hand to the horse, her palm out flat, reassuring. He held his breath, telling himself to stay put, despite everything in him screaming that he should intercept. But then her hand was flush against the colt, holding there, not moving, just rising and falling with the horse's breaths. It was the most beautiful thing he'd ever seen, and for the first time in his life, he questioned his own ability. No one had touched that horse without him flinching. Until now. It was like Craving Wind remembered Emery, cared for her. This was different than the standard rider-horse relationship. Trip just couldn't decide if different was a good thing or a very dangerous one.

He gave Emery another five minutes alone with the horse, watching as her mouth moved in hushed whispers, appreciating how quickly they'd reconnected—their bond undeniable. Damn, how did he allow himself to get in this situation? Emery was injured. Even if he hired her, he couldn't put her with this colt, who by all accounts was expected to become a champion. He needed an experienced rider to get him there, and Emery hadn't been in a race in years. Clearly, Trip was losing his mind. He shook his head and released a breath, forcing the trainer in him to return.

"I have other horses to show you," Trip said as he approached her.

"I don't want another horse."

"Well, I refuse to let you ride this one."

She dropped her hand from Craving Wind, and the look on her face nearly broke his will. Like she was losing her best friend, like she was losing herself. "I told you, you don't have to pay me. Just let me ride." She lowered her eyes, and he knew she was trying to rein in her emotions. "I can do this." Her watery gaze returned to his.

He swallowed hard, wishing he'd never invited her here in the first place, but at the same time, he didn't want her to leave. The feelings that had settled over him since she arrived couldn't be ignored. He enjoyed being around her, enjoyed listening to her voice and watching her with Craving Wind. Still . . . "I can get you back on a mount. Just not *this* mount."

Emery spun to face him. "Why?"

There were a thousand answers to that question, all of them more important than the last, but maybe the truest answer of all was that he didn't trust her. A part of him wanted to, but that part was also the one urging him to forget that eight years had passed and pull her into his arms. He couldn't depend on that side of himself right now, which only left the sensible side, and anyone with good sense would laugh at the idea of putting Emery on Craving Wind. He would prove to be a champion. Trip could feel that in his bones. And champions needed dependable, experienced riders. Not riders with canes and two years' worth of pent-up fear, who refused to ride for him today.

"Are you going to continue analyzing every aspect of this situation or are you going to answer me? It's a simple question."

He almost laughed at how well she could read him. Maybe he hadn't changed that much after all. Though she was wrong about one thing—this was anything but simple.

"I have other horses," Trip repeated.

"*This* is my horse."

Trip shook his head. "See, this is part of the problem. He isn't your horse. He's Sarah Anderson's horse, and she expects him to win a title this year. That isn't going to happen with an inexperienced rider. So, like I said, I have other horses."

Both Clark and Kate adjusted their stance, sensing the tension rising.

Emery walked away from the colt, toward the edge of the fencing, gripping the side and staring over the pastures. "You don't get to call me inexperienced. Not you. You've never seen me ride."

"I've seen you—"

She whirled around. "You've watched a race. That isn't the same thing and you know it. You have never been part of my winner's circle. You don't know how I ride or what I'm capable of. Besides, my résumé speaks for itself."

"Two years ago it might have."

"*Might?*"

Clark cleared his throat and mouthed the words *your terms* and Trip nodded. "On second thought, you're right. The answer is simple. My farm, my rules."

She started to say more, and Trip readied himself for the argument that was sure to follow, but then her gaze went back to Craving Wind and her shoulders drooped. "Okay. Okay, I get it. And I know this is crazy to you. Trust me, I've heard it all before. But I can't ride just any horse. I . . . I can't." She drew a rattled breath, and with one more stroke of Craving Wind's mane, she walked out of the gate. "Thanks for your time. I'll just . . . go."

Trip ground his teeth together and placed his hands on his hips, anger pulsating through him in waves. Anger at the horse. Anger at Emery. But mostly, anger at himself. He thought of the expression on Emery's face when she said *okay,* like it was the most difficult word she'd ever uttered, and he knew he couldn't allow her to just leave.

He pushed through the gate and took off in a light run, rounding the corner of the stables just as the women reached their car.

He bit his lip, searching for some way out of this—some way to keep her there on his terms, but Emery had never operated on anyone's terms but her own. Frustrated, he opened his mouth and blurted the first thing that came to mind, "I'll let you ride him on one condition."

Emery turned, her face lit up. "Anything."

"You show me that you can."

"I—"

"I know you say you're ready to ride, and I believe you. Or I *want* to believe you. But this is a multimillion-dollar horse, owned by a close friend of my family. I need to trust that the jockey I put on his back is the best jockey there is for the job. And I don't know that of you. Not yet. Prove to me you're that rider and the mount's yours."

They stared at each other, Emery's face unreadable, and then she smiled triumphantly and said, "Thank you for the offer. I'll let you know." And then they were in their car, the taillights disappearing down the drive.

Trip shook his head. *What the hell just happened?* Then he realized—she'd manipulated him. Completely and totally manipulated him.

Clark walked up beside him, a smile playing on his lips.

"Shut up."

His friend laughed. "Not saying a word."

CHAPTER FIVE

Odds-on favorite

Emery rode in silence the entire drive back to Crestler's Key, unable to wrap her mind around what Trip had asked of her—demanded of her. She still couldn't decide what she thought of the Trip Hamilton of today. He had a way about him, a sincerity that was hard to ignore. But then, there was that arrogance . . .

"Em, we've sat in the car for twenty minutes now. Are we going to talk about this out loud or are you going to continue chewing away your nails?"

Emery's gaze dropped to her thumb, and sure enough, the nail had been whittled away to the wick. Her mama would have a few choice words about that, a habit she'd had since she was a kid that tended to reappear when she was under stress. Stress like going against her daddy for her dream, or worse, for a man that made her heart beat out of control. She'd genuinely thought her feelings were gone, healed, or at the very least under her control. Now she knew that was laughable.

"I just . . . I have to tell him no, right? That I changed my mind. I mean, I ride for Carlisle Farms. I can't just turn my back on that."

"But the thing is . . . you aren't riding for Carlisle Farms. Your daddy refuses to let you ride."

Of course her friend was right, so what should she do? Emery went to work on her other thumb, the decision too great.

It was no secret that her riding for her daddy was frowned upon. Jockeys were hired by trainers to ride on their horses. They never owned the horse themselves. Jockeys were contract employees, paid hands. But the rules stated *the jockey* couldn't own the horse. It said nothing about family. So, Daddy trained the horse and Emery worked for him. Their setup received too many sharp looks to count, especially given how much he paid her. It was a little too close to the rule, but Daddy never gave a damn what anyone else thought of him. He'd been bending rules his entire life. He knew Emery wanted to be a jockey, and being his only daughter, he wasn't about to let her ride for someone else.

So Emery chose her mounts, and then Beckett paid her to ride them. Only, riding for her daddy had its drawbacks—she played too safe. Sure, riding was a risk. Racing was a risk. But she never pushed herself, never took a chance on a mount, because anytime she suggested taking a chance, Daddy would turn her down. Emery loved her parents, loved Carlisle Farms, and loved every single person who worked there. They were a family, blood or water, but she didn't really live her life, didn't state her opinions. She did what she was told to do, ignoring her gut at times, because she was twenty-five and Daddy was the expert. For years she'd told herself it didn't matter, but now things were different. She couldn't get on a horse, could barely stand beside one back home, and he refused to put her back on a mount. Deep down, Emery knew she needed the change. She needed to accept Trip's offer and prove to him she was the best rider for Craving Wind.

But by accepting his offer, she would break her family's hearts.

Emery realized Kate was watching her work all this out and glanced over. "What?"

"You're going to do it, aren't you?"

She bit into her pinky nail, giving her thumbs a break. "I don't have to decide today."

"No, I guess not," Kate said. "But you do have to decide, Em. And the decision shouldn't involve anybody but you." Emery's eyes lifted back to Kate's, and she opened her mouth to respond as Kate cut her off. "I know what you're going to say, and you're right. They're your family. That matters. It's thick and real and it matters. But this is your life, Emery. Your career. Your future. And Trip's handing you the opportunity of a lifetime. The best jockeys in the world would kill for this opportunity."

"You think I should take it?" Emery stared at her friend, a part of her wishing she could make the decision for her. Why couldn't life be that easy?

"I think you will never get on another horse if you stay at home. But I think . . . if you go with Trip, if you take that leap, you could be something amazing, Emery Jane Carlisle. This is your chance."

Tears welled in Emery's eyes, and she brushed the heel of her hand over her cheeks. "Well, I don't have to decide today."

Silence fell between them again, and then Kate said, "So, has enough time passed for me to ask the real question on my mind?"

Emery rested her head back against the seat, hesitating. She knew her friend would eventually question her about Trip. She just didn't know how she would answer. Seeing him again had brought all those old emotions to the surface.

"Go ahead. I was waiting for it."

"Oh, come on now," Kate said. "Don't be like that. You would be the same exact way if it were me."

Emery smiled at the thought. "Yeah, probably."

"Does that mean I can continue without getting crucified?"

"Go already."

Kate squealed loudly. "Good! Tell me everything you know about him."

"Him? Trip? He's—"

"Not Trip. The brother."

"What?" Emery's eyes went wide and she turned toward her friend. "No. No, no, no. You can't get involved with Alex Hamilton."

"Why not? I'm not a jockey. My daddy isn't their competitor. The way I see it, I'm just an innocent bystander to this whole disaster."

"Hey! It's not a disaster."

Kate laughed. "Oh, it's capital D disaster."

"But you said—"

"Oh, I still think you should do it. Sometimes we know the crash is coming, but we've still gotta go through with the ride. Learning, and all that crap. That's why I went out with Chris Dickens."

Emery hit the radio dial, leaving the car in sudden silence. "Wait, what? When did you go out with Chris Dickens?"

"Last night."

"Last night? And you're just now telling me this."

Shrugging, Kate reached for her bottle of water and took a long pull before dropping it back in the cup holder. "You had a lot going on, and besides, it wasn't a big deal."

Somehow it bothered Emery more than it should that her friend hadn't told her. She didn't want to be this complex, chaotic mess who became detached from the rest of the world. She crossed her arms and peered over, studying Kate's face. "Well, how did it go?"

She shrugged again. "Fine, I guess. We kissed. It was . . . interesting." Her shoulders shook a bit, and then she was laughing. "God, who am I kidding? It was horrible."

"Horrible?"

"He did the whole lizard thing. You know, the—" She stuck her tongue out rapidly, and Emery burst out laughing.

"Oh, no."

"Oh, yes."

"So what are you going to do?"

They turned onto the main stretch toward Carlisle Farms, and Kate smiled over at her, but it didn't reach her eyes the way it should. "I don't know. It's something, right?"

Emery slowly shook her head. "No. It isn't enough to be just okay. It needs to rock your world. The whole sparks-flying thing, or it isn't worth it."

Kate parked outside the guesthouse and peered over at Emery. "I don't know if that's real. I've never felt sparks. Have you?"

A flash hit her of the moon high above, a slight chill in the air, of Trip laying her back onto a blanket, his lips pressed to hers. Emery wasn't sure if it was possible to feel love at seventeen, but she'd felt something amazing that night, something so intense that it scared her. *Still scared her.*

"Yeah . . . I think I have."

She waved good-bye to Kate, but instead of going inside, drowning in her thoughts, she jumped in her Jeep, desperate to be around someone else who'd disappointed the Carlisle family. Funny how as humans, whenever we were bad, we wanted to be around someone who was just a little bit worse. Make the whole thing a little easier to digest. And no one did *bad* like Annie-Jean Carlisle.

Emery drove as close to the one mile an hour mark as she could down the old gravel road, which was less gravel and more dirt and holes and other things capable of ruining a perfectly good car. Finally, she pulled up to the detached garage and stepped out of her Jeep, eyeing the peeling paint and cracked window in the second story. Well, at least she was consistent.

Up the front steps, Emery didn't bother knocking on the door—

Annie-Jean wouldn't hear her anyway—and went on through the screen door, following the chorus of a woman belting out to Diana Ross and the Supremes. Emery rounded the corner into the kitchen and stopped, her eyes going wider with each new observation. It looked like someone had bombed the place. Flour decorated every inch of countertop. Other places were covered in dough (Clearly, the flour had morphed into something at some point.) And then, in other places, there were dozens of cookies, cooling on racks.

"You overbooked again, didn't you?" Emery asked her aunt with a sigh. "How many and when?"

Annie-Jean pushed her glasses up high on the bridge of her slightly crooked nose and ran a hand through her black hair, sprinkling it with flour. "One hundred. Nine a.m."

"Tomorrow?" Emery squeaked. "One hundred cookies due by tomorrow morning?"

Annie-Jean laughed. "Don't be ridiculous. One hundred *dozen*. Now, are you going to keep staring at me with exasperation—I swear, you were carved from the same tree as your daddy—or are you going to help? I assume you came here to pour your soul. Might as well bake while you do it."

With another sigh, Emery grabbed a spare apron from one of the hooks by the doorway and draped it over her neck, unsure if it would do her any good, but Annie-Jean had her rules, and aprons and hair ties were two of them. Emery pulled her hair back into a ponytail and motioned to her head and the apron. "Okay to enter, Chef?"

Annie-Jean flashed the smile that had broken hearts all over town in her day—still to this day, really. "Enter, and hurry. I'm only at three dozen."

They spent ten minutes scraping the first three dozen from their pans, the work providing the silence Emery needed to think. Until finally, Annie shut the oven door and twisted around. "All right, spill it, before that sour look of yours seeps into my cookies. What happened? Did Beckett say no again?"

"Actually, no."

"He said yes?"

"Well, no. Not exactly."

Annie set down the wooden spoon in her hand. "Look, honey, I've never been a fan of carousels. So can we quit this cycle and you just get on with it?"

Emery closed a package and pushed it across the counter to meet the other two. "Trip Hamilton's agreed to hire me on at Hamilton Stables."

"Agreed?"

"Well, see . . . I sort of . . . blackmailed him into it." She closed her eyes tightly and dropped her head onto the counter, refusing to face her aunt's judgment. But Annie-Jean was never one to dish it out by look alone.

"I guess it's good I have a spare bedroom."

Emery peeked up. "Is it that bad?"

"Yes . . . if he finds out. He'll be devastated. But the thing is, honey, it isn't his life. It's yours. What does your gut tell you to do?"

She rested against the counter and stared out the large bay window of Annie's breakfast nook. "He's working one of our colts, Annie. It feels like destiny or something. I couldn't even get near another horse without shaking, but with this colt—Craving Wind, they're calling him—I'm me again. I can stand. I don't want to lose that, not when I'm this close."

"Then I think you have your answer," Annie said, mixing in cranberries to her batter. "But I don't think you have to tell Beckett. Yet. See how it goes first. Why break his heart when it might not work out anyway?"

"So, you're saying keep it a secret? Lie to him?"

Annie fixed her gaze on Emery. "I'm saying a little lie for the greater good can't be all devil. Wait and see." She slid another tray into the oven. "Still . . . I'll prep my guest room just in case."

CHAPTER SIX

Back the wrong horse

Trip sat down on his brother's couch, his eyes glued to the game on the widescreen in front of him. It felt good to lose himself in the familiar, and hopefully with another beer or two in him, he could get his mind off Emery Carlisle and how easily she'd slipped back into his life.

He thought of her cane again and said a little thanks to God his father hadn't seen her with it. That cane would have ended Emery's career with Hamilton Stables faster than she could blink those long lashes of hers. But for Trip, the cane wasn't so much the issue as her reasons for using it. She was afraid, he could see it in her eyes, and that fear could prove a liability if he actually put her in a race.

"Dude, take this before I drink it myself."

Trip's gaze swept from the TV only long enough to take the beer from Alex's hands, and then he sat back down beside Nick, Alex on the other side.

"I'm not leaving again. Every time I leave, there's a turnover."

"Or maybe," Nick said with a grin, "you coming back is the problem."

Alex punched his arm. "Screw you, man. This is my house."

Nick started to argue that the house was in fact Trip's, which wasn't a lie exactly, when Trip's hand shot up. "Shut it, both of you."

All of their eyes fell on the screen, and then they all jumped up, screaming and high-fiving, glad their team was up for the first time all game. Trip had just reached for another slice of pizza when Alex said, "So are we going to talk about Emery now or later?"

"We aren't going to talk about her at all."

"Don't be ridiculous," Alex said. "There's something there. A past or something. Did you know her before?"

Trip eyed Nick, curious if his middle brother would call him out, but Nick said nothing. Hesitating, he considered lying to Alex, sure Nick wouldn't disagree, but honestly, it didn't matter if Alex knew. It was years ago. So why did he feel the need to protect his past, to protect her?

Alex's gaze went to Nick, then back to Trip. He pointed between them. "He knows but I can't? How fair is that?"

"He knows because he was there."

"Where?"

Trip set down his beer, the alcohol in his veins making it all that much harder to ignore his feelings. "When I came home from Carlisle Farms. Nick was here."

Realization crossed Alex's face. "I remember that. You worked at Carlisle Farms under Beckett for a year. But Emery had to have been . . ." He trailed off.

"She was seventeen."

"Jesus."

Trip nodded once, because there was nothing to say. She'd been seventeen years old, and yet that couldn't keep him away from her. He told himself she was nearly eighteen and he had just turned twenty—the age difference wasn't significant. But then he thought of Mr. Sampson's face, and a wave of guilt washed over him. Beckett had always had tremendous respect for Trip, but what would he think if knew the truth?

"Well, it doesn't matter now," Nick said. "It was in the past. Right?" Both brothers' eyes fell on Trip, but he couldn't bring himself to return their look.

"Right . . . the past."

Trip parked his truck by the main training center and stepped out, enjoying the peaceful morning air. The sun had yet to peek up, the farm still asleep.

"You're here a half hour early," a voice called from behind him.

Well, almost everyone was asleep.

Trip turned to see Mama V behind him, a travel mug full of coffee in her hand. Every morning Mrs. Vivian Marshal made breakfast for the staff in the stable house, and then made it her job to find Trip as soon as he arrived to force coffee and breakfast into his hands. Something about losing his mother all those years ago, and her asking Mama V to make sure her boys ate. Trip felt his mother likely meant to watch out for the Hamilton brothers, but Mama V took the job seriously.

He reached out and took the coffee mug with a gracious smile. "Thank you. I didn't think anybody was up."

She smiled back. "I'm always up. And I made blueberry muffins." She held out a perfectly Saran-wrapped muffin. "You look uneasy this morning. Should I have made tea? Your mother used to make you tea when you were little and something was bothering you."

Trip grinned. "I was eight then. And she would force the stuff in me whether I wanted it or not."

"Even so . . ." She studied him, and Trip looked away.

The problem was, he didn't know why he was so uneasy. He'd hired plenty of jockeys over the years. Though Hamilton Stables preferred to work with the same lot, there was always an up-and-coming star, and that star would end up here. Every time. So why did this have to be different?

Because this was Emery, and everything about her was different. From her attitude to that unyielding fire to that face of hers that refused to be ignored. He could still remember the slightly floral scent of her hair, the intensity in her eyes as she watched Craving Wind. The sick feeling in his gut when she drove away.

God, pull yourself together.

He should call her now and take back his offer. Nothing good could come of her being here, beside him day after day.

"Trip?"

His gaze focused in on Mama V. "Sorry, what did you say? I was . . ."

"Distracted?" She offered a small smile and patted his shoulder. "Take the muffin and go on in." She nodded to the stables. "You'll feel right as rain."

Trip hesitated, but then she shot him that grandmotherly look of hers, and he laughed. "All right, old lady, fine." He reached for the muffin and strode toward the stables, already feeling more at home.

The shedrow at Hamilton Stables held twenty or more Thoroughbreds, depending upon the year and Trip's eye for a champion. He tried to commit to training only the horses that had the combination of pedigree and conformation to win, but there were always exceptions. A gut feeling. A moment. Just like with Emery.

He tried to tell himself that she'd proven her ability as a rider. Hell, she was well on her way to winning the Kentucky Oaks for the second year in a row until the accident. And he'd been there—watching in horror as her small body hit the dirt, only to stay there, unmoving. It took everything in him not to race down there, but he wasn't her family, wasn't even a friend anymore. Six years had passed at that point. What would he say to Beckett? So instead, he'd watched, unable to sit down until he'd heard she made it to the hospital, heard she'd gotten through her surgeries. Looking back, he should have gone anyway. Ignored the uncomfortable feeling in his gut and just gone. Oh, the number of times he'd dialed the hospital, then later her cell phone—programmed in every new phone he ever bought or carried, like he was afraid if he lost her number he would lose her forever—only to hang up before the call could go through.

The sound of someone already in the stables made him look up, and he nodded to Clark. "Here early, aren't you?"

Clark grinned. "Now we both know you don't consider this early."

It was a hint after five in the morning, and Clark was right. It wasn't early. It was closing in on late, but he wanted to hear Clark's response. Trip walked over to the first stall and reached out his hand to stroke the neck of a filly, a closer through and through, but she hadn't quite figured out the right time to kick it into gear to actually win.

"So what's the delay?"

"My morning exercise boy is running late. Car accident."

Trip nodded. "So who's riding?"

Clark fidgeted. "Marcus."

Trip's hand went still on the filly. Marcus. Even the name made Trip's spine tighten. Marcus was an experienced jockey, his performance unmatched, but with the sort of arrogance that grated on Trip's nerves. His father had contracted him to ride for them this year on Hot Lightning, the best colt at Hamilton Stables, already favored in the Derby, but Trip had yet to trust the man. Had yet to even have a conversation with him that didn't end with Trip walking away angry. He'd almost fired him twice but had forced his temper into check. After all, Trip was the head trainer here. Marcus would obey or he wouldn't ride. End of story.

"Sorry, boss, no choice."

Before Trip could respond, he heard the telltale heavy sound of Marcus's boots and turned.

"Early morning for you, isn't it, Mr. Hamilton?"

Trip arrived at the stables at five thirty every morning, like clockwork. Which Marcus knew as well as everyone else on the farm. He didn't respond, instead walking over, his six-two height towering over the small jockey, who stood at five-three, one hundred twenty pounds at best. Marcus grinned, enjoying Trip's response. "I hear you hired Emery Carlisle."

Trip straightened, peering over his shoulder at Clark, who merely lifted his hands as though to say *I didn't do it.* "I've extended her an offer, yes. I fail to see how this involves you."

"Doesn't it? I'm your top rider."

"You are a contract employee, and you are replaceable. Never forget that fact."

"So you've been saying, yet I'm still here. Something tells me I'm not as replaceable as you would have me believe. Besides, we both know I'm the favorite for the Derby."

Trip laughed. "Lightning is the favorite. People don't bet on jockeys. They bet on horses. I can put someone else on that mount, someone who'd appreciate it, and no one would be the wiser or care." Trip grinned to push away his annoyance. Patience. He reminded himself that part of the business side of training was dealing with less than ideal people. Marcus was number one on that list. He cared about his share of the purse and nothing more. Not the horse. Not this farm. Only the money. Little did he know that someone with heart, real heart, would beat him every time. Heart beat monetary drive. Trip had seen it happen more times than he could count.

"Someone like Emery?"

Trip's back tightened, and he had to draw a breath to keep from lashing out at the man. "You worry about earning your paycheck and let me worry about new hires. How does that sound, slick?" Trip patted him on the head condescendingly, then shot Clark another look. "I want him working for the next hour. If I see him leaning against a fence, it's both of your jobs. Understand?"

Clark nodded, and Trip strutted out of the stables, needing air. Marcus mentioning Emery's name had rattled him. But why? Hadn't he offered her a job? Wasn't she just another jockey on his payroll?

Only he knew it wasn't the case. He'd made an emotional decision with Emery, and in this business, emotions could lead to heartbreak. He needed to get his head on straight, focus on the job at hand—prepping these horses for the races.

Clark ordered several of his stable boys to help start the morning workouts, and Trip tried to lose himself in the morning training—galloping, gate schooling, short speed works, eventually getting up to 5/8th of a mile. But despite his best efforts, he spent the rest of the morning thinking about Emery Carlisle, and whether she would meet his challenge. A large part of him wanted her to do it, wanted to see her rally back. But another part of him knew he was playing with fire, and something told him the second time around he was bound to get burned.

CHAPTER SEVEN

Under the wire

"Last batch, baby, don't die on me now," Annie-Jean said to her double oven, her hand gently rubbing the side like she was talking to a dog. Or a man.

Emery laughed. "You know, the oven's not going to keep you warm in the middle of the night."

Annie-Jean spun around, her eyes filled with mischievousness. "I disagree. This thing gets me hotter than any lover I've ever had. You should give it a go. See for yourself."

Emery laughed again. "Thanks, but I prefer my lovers in human form."

Annie-Jean smirked. "Is that right? I'm pretty sure you hung your heart on a horse as soon as you could walk and never looked back." She went on packaging another perfect box of oatmeal and cranberry cookies.

"That's not the same thing. I'm about more than just horses."

Annie-Jean's eyebrows went up.

"What?"

"Name the last man you dated who wasn't affiliated in some way with farms or horses or racing."

Emery's mouth opened and snapped back shut. Huh. Had she really restricted herself to the racing industry and nothing more? "I . . . well, what about you? You speak of having one great love, but he disappointed you. What did he do?"

Annie set down the package in her hand and turned around, her expression distant. "I was sixteen when I first met him. He'd just moved to town, and the moment he walked into the cafeteria, I knew there was something there. Some strange spark, though I'd yet to even speak to him." She smiled a little.

"So what did you do?" Emery leaned in, eager to hear another of Annie's stories.

Annie pushed up onto her counter and crossed her legs. "I did nothing for about a week, and then, finally, I couldn't take it any longer. He came into the cafeteria, same as every day. Got his lunch and went outside to eat in the sun, and I stormed out after him. I told him he was to ask my name that very second or else." She laughed.

"You didn't!"

"I did."

"What did he say?"

She smiled up at the ceiling, her eyes so full of happiness that Emery wondered why she didn't speak of the boy more often. "He shot me a grin and told me he already knew my name. Then he patted the space beside him, and I swear, I would never have gotten up again unless forced. We talked about music and poetry and his dreams of law school. And then he asked me on a date. It took an evening of fine dining and then parking out at Old Key Point for him to kiss me, but good Lord, what a kiss."

"But Annie, I don't understand. What happened? Why didn't you stay with him?"

Her face turned sad, and then she wiped it away and pushed off the countertop, busying herself with a pack of semisweet chocolate. "He went to Notre Dame and I stayed here. We were together for a whole year before we both realized it wouldn't work out. That was the hardest decision I've ever made."

"You ended it?" Emery couldn't imagine ever walking away from someone she loved, rational decision or not.

"I think I walked away before he could. My ego couldn't take the blow of him leaving me. So I left him."

Emery closed her eyes. "God, Annie, I'm so sorry."

She brushed off the sentiment. "It was years ago."

"I don't think a thousand years is enough to get over our first loves."

"You might be right. But then, what is love? Longing for someone who doesn't want you back? That's not love. Love is an everyday commitment to each other—a determination to make it work through the thick stuff, because there's no one else you'd rather fight with. Find someone who makes your heart race when you're arguing and you know you've found the love of your life."

Emery laughed. "You know, you're the only person on the planet who'd tie love to arguing."

"I speak the truth, child. Whether you choose to listen is another story."

"So whatever happened to your great love?"

Annie sighed, then went back to her work. "He found a greater love."

The words hit Emery square in the chest, refusing to let go. Had Trip found a greater love? Was she even on his list of loves? They'd never said the word, never truly spoken about the future or where their relationship would go. They'd already known it couldn't continue, and somehow that knowing made it easy to tuck away those three little words. Saying them out loud would make it all that much harder to watch him go. At least that was what she'd told herself. But then she watched him leave, never once saying the words, and for months she wished she had. She ran over moments in the fields, secret dates, and hidden kisses—a thousand opportunities to tell him just how much he meant to her. But she was seventeen. What did she know of love?

"Oh, no."

Emery's gaze snapped over to Annie. "What? Did you burn something?"

Annie's eyebrows scrunched up. "Are you insane? I'm a baker. I don't burn things. I'm oh-noing you and that pathetic look on your face. You felt it, didn't you? Eight years have passed, but not a minute for your heart. Which is why you shouldn't go work for him. Your heart's too in it."

"Wait, you said earlier that I should. And I'm not talking about dating him. I—"

"Right, you talked about Hamilton's reputation and the colt. For about thirty seconds. Then you spent the last two hours telling me about his dark hair and brown eyes and the way he wore his Stetson. You just need to make sure your reasons for seeking Trip out are strictly professional and have nothing to do with wishful thinking."

Emery felt her face burning. "He's the best in the business. If I ride Craving Wind for him, I could win. I feel it."

Annie-Jean cocked her head. "Well, feelings are a fickle pickle. You're better off trusting that pretty head of yours. And I'm betting it's telling you to run, faster than that Thoroughbred you're so desperate to ride."

Silence overcame them as Emery went about boxing more cookies, the smells of cinnamon and nutmeg in the air from the latest batch cooking. By the time they were done, she was going to have a bellyache from the smells—and her thoughts.

She knew her place was with her family, but she couldn't help feeling like she'd made mistakes in her career. Been too careful, and yet she'd ended up broken, two years of nothing but her thoughts. Emery didn't want to make the same mistakes. She had one goal in her life—to win the Derby. And the only way she stood a chance of doing it was to accept Trip's challenge. She'd sensed the connection as soon as she saw the colt again, as soon as she slid her hand across the horse's mane. For the first time, her hand didn't shake, her heart didn't pound, her eyes didn't go wide with fear. She was home.

"You're going to do it, aren't you?"

Emery glanced up at her aunt, the only person she trusted beside Kate. Annie-Jean pulled another tray of cookies from the oven, all as perfect as the last. "How did you know baking was what you wanted to do? How did you know this would make you happy?"

Annie-Jean laughed. "I didn't. I saw an opportunity, and I jumped."

The sentiment hit Emery square, and she leaned back against the counter, deep in thought. Could she jump?

"Life is never easy. Decisions are never easy, but I'd always rather move forward than stand still. I can correct my mess-ups, but I can't bring back a lost moment. I can't ask for the rainbow to reappear, the wish to return. It's all a gamble. You have to choose whether you want to watch the race . . . or run it. I'm not sure working for Trip is a smart idea, but I can't argue with the spark in your eyes." She studied Emery. "It's been a long time since I've seen that spark in you. I'd hate to see it disappear again. No matter what, the choice is yours. Remember that."

Emery's heart swelled, the decision working its way through her. She pushed off the counter and walked around to the cooling rack, transferring the dozen to their white and pink boxes, the logo *AJ's Creations* across the top in a fun, swirly font. Annie-Jean was the only Carlisle to step away from the farm, and it had labeled her an outsider at every family function. But she couldn't argue with the smile on her face, the happy aura that trailed her, a glow instead of the dark cloud her father carried with him. Emery wanted that aura. She craved it.

"You've decided."

Emery's eyes lifted. "Yes."

"You're going to do it?"

She licked her lips, stalling. "I have to, Annie."

Her aunt nodded slowly. "Well, do me a favor, then. Don't tell your daddy. Not yet."

"Annie—"

She swished her hand through the air in the Southern gesture that said *hush, you.* "Now, I know what you're going to say. You can't lie to family. God'll strike you the moment the words slip from your lips. But this is different. He needs to see you better. He needs that more than anything, and he won't really see it if he's stubbornly got his eyes closed."

"This is going to break him no matter what. I don't think delaying will make it any better."

"Time can do a lot of things. Maybe if he sees you racing again, he won't care who you're racing for."

Emery shot her favorite relative a look.

"All right. He'll rage. But my gut says to wait."

"Are you sure?"

"I'm positive."

She said good-bye to Annie-Jean a few minutes later, needing time to think. Could she do this? Leave her family for a competitor? Lie to them about what she was doing? A part of her knew it was a bad idea, all of it, but if she was going to take this leap, she'd prefer to tackle one hurdle at a time. Hurdle one: Get back on a horse.

Time to return to Hamilton Stables.

Trip slipped into the batting cage, his brothers in each of the spots beside him. The air was warm but light—the sun hidden behind a patch of gatelike clouds, refusing to let it free.

The brothers used to all play ball in high school, long before adulthood took them under. Now they made it a weekly ritual—hit the cages, take out their frustration, and then grab a few beers at Rudy's after. It was the only time they saw each other anymore, beyond their father's weekly meetings, and let's be real, those weren't moments of visitation. Those were moments of survival.

"So, has Carlisle accepted the job?" Alex asked as they set up. "Or are you still refusing to talk about her and we have to hound Clark?"

Clark might be Trip's favorite person on the planet, certainly his favorite assistant trainer, but even he didn't know Trip's true feelings for Emery. Trip wasn't sure he himself could explain them.

"Haven't heard from her," Trip said, swinging as the first ball sailed toward him. They'd chosen to have the pitching machine throw real baseballs instead of the rubber balls, convinced they were still agile enough to handle them, but something told Trip he'd be paying for that decision the next morning.

"Are you hoping to hear from her?" Nick asked, huffing his way through a strike. "You worked at Carlisle Farms, fell for their golden girl, then left. Now you're hiring her at our barn? This sounds suicidal, man."

"She's hot," Alex said. "I wouldn't mind her hanging around the barn." A loud smack filled the air as his bat made contact with his first ball, followed quickly by another smack, and another.

"Damn, what do you live down here or something?" Trip asked, annoyed at his youngest brother's youth. And his insinuation. And at his praise of Emery. She *was* hot, but that didn't mean he wanted his brothers saying it—or noticing it, for that matter. If she accepted the job, she'd be around a lot more. The last thing he needed was Alex screwing things up for him.

He paused at the thought, unsure where it'd come from. Screwing things up for him? He chalked it up to his thrill at the idea of helping her get back on a mount, nothing more, but he couldn't shake off the nagging feeling that there was more there. A hell of a lot more.

Alex smirked, rolled his shoulders back, got into his best batting stance, and hit again, this time with more force, causing the ball to ricochet off the back netting. "What can I say? God-given talent."

"Talent my ass," Nick said with a laugh. "I bet he comes every day. What the hell else does he have to do?"

"What is that supposed to mean?"

The air became tight as the two brothers squared off, Trip between them in his cage as the only thing tempering their mood. This was a constant argument between them. Nick knew only drive and success. He slept six hours a day, rose before the sun, and set out to the office, determination his only friend. He'd been more relaxed in his Brit days, her easiness bringing out the best in him. But losing her had nearly destroyed him, and instead of bouncing back and finding another love, he had countless flings and otherwise devoted himself to his work.

Alex was different. He lived and breathed for spontaneity, had spent a year in Australia just because, and had only recently settled into the Hamilton family business, something he'd yet to discuss with Nick.

Trip eyed Alex, pressing him to tell Nick that he'd taken over the mare and foaling barns. In truth, Trip was waiting for his brother to bolt—some insane opportunity in some remote location in Africa or some shit—but instead he'd shown impressive devotion to each project. If training and racing were Trip's business, then breeding was Alex's.

When Alex turned back to the pitching machine, refusing to meet Trip's gaze, he knew the secret would continue.

"Easy for you to judge, Nicky boy. You're the golden boy. Can-do-no-wrong son. Besides, I *am* working."

Nick opened his mouth, likely to fire off some sarcastic retort, but Trip shot him a look, his eyes narrowed, and his brother went back to focusing on the incoming pitch. "So, about Emery."

"What about her?" Trip knew his agitation showed more than he wanted, but he couldn't help it. He *was* aggravated. At himself. At his offer. At the whole damn thing. How had he let this happen? And what's worse, he was almost equally aggravated that she hadn't responded yet. He wanted to know where they stood, her plans. And okay, he wanted to see her face light up with excitement and know he put it there. Something about seeing her fall to her worst and having a part in bringing her back again would be special. Beckett sure as hell wasn't helping her get back on a mount. The few times he'd been interviewed about Emery, he all but said he'd never let her race again. No wonder she'd turned to Trip, and though he knew this situation was as screwed up as they came, he couldn't turn his back on her, too. She needed support.

"Is she going to live at the farm?"

Trip shrugged. This conversation was getting worse by the second. "No. I don't know. Maybe. Probably not, though. None of our other jockeys live on-site."

"So she's going to commute in from Crestler's Key? Is it true she hasn't ridden since the accident? Have you seen her on a mount?"

"I don't know."

"How can you not know? What exactly *do* you know?"

Both brothers had stopped to stare at Trip, their voices so similar he wasn't sure who'd actually asked the questions. He opened his mouth and shut it again, wishing they'd hit Rudy's first. He needed a few hundred shots to survive this shit. But under their weighted stare, all he could do was tell the truth.

He turned to spit out that he didn't know a damn thing when the pitching machine threw again, the ball zooming toward Trip at 60 mph before he could step out of its path, then the crack and pain as it hit his side, and he went down on his knees, but not before the machine fired again. He had only a second to spin away, landing with a groan face-first in the green turf, his brothers' laughter the only thing he could hear.

"I think I'm done here," Trip managed. The sentiment true in more ways than one.

CHAPTER EIGHT

Right from the horse's mouth

"Catch that dog before it runs loose!"

Emery cracked open the front door to her parents' house the next day as a giant ball of white fur flew through the opening, knocking her back in its effort to get outside. Or escape.

Her mama stood over her a moment later, her hands forever on her hips, her sharp blue eyes creased with worry. Emery wondered if the line between her mama's eyebrows had been marked by her and her alone. "Heavens, child. Didn't you hear me call?"

There were no words that wouldn't result in another sharp look, so Emery simply said what she always said to her mother. "Yes, I guess I did. Sorry, Mama. But Princess Diana couldn't have gone far."

Grace Carlisle spun on her heels and walked down the long wrap around front porch, her delicate hand over her brow as she peered into the woods that cradled the house, sure she could see through the leaves. Or, at the very least, could spot a flash of white.

"What are you doing here so late?" Mama asked, her gaze still trained on the woods and the diva dog who would keep her in knots all day and night, only to reappear on their front steps the next morning. As innocent as ever.

Truthfully, it'd taken her that long to muster up the courage to go there. Talking about lying was a whole different thing from actually telling the lie. She still wasn't sure she could go through with it.

"I was with Annie-Jean." This explanation tended to explain everything, but instead of accepting it, Mama turned, her keen eyes zeroing in.

"Nothing else?"

Emery's chest tightened under her mother's stare, and she had to remind herself that she was not some sixteen-year-old girl. She was twenty-five. She could do whatever she liked, when she liked, and she sure as heaven didn't have to answer to her mother.

Mama's head tilted down, as though she knew just what Emery was thinking and had words on such thoughts, but she held them in. For now. "Your father's in his office if you're looking for him. And dinner's in an hour if you're hungry."

Dinner? Emery checked her watch. She knew it was late, but she hadn't realized she'd spent all day again at Annie-Jean's, doing little else other than sulking. Life had turned hard overnight, and something told her it wasn't going to be getting easier any time soon. She needed to make a decision, and though a part of her knew she'd already made it, this was more complicated than agreeing to work with Trip. He wanted her to ride, wanted her to prove she was still the rider she'd once been. Emery wondered if that meant he didn't trust her, but she couldn't really take offense at the idea. After all, she wasn't sure she trusted herself.

She walked into the house and stopped in the study, her fingertips gliding over a hundred different spines as she thought through the truth of her situation. The way Emery saw it, she had two options. Force herself to remain loyal to her family, support her father's pride ... and never ride again. Or she accepted Trip's challenge, dropped out of the plane, and prayed the parachute opened. Despite racing for all of her adult life, she'd never considered herself a risk taker. She did what her father told her to do. It was only now that she realized she'd never really grown up, never spent a day of her life as an adult. And she hungered for it. She wanted to fail and rise again. She wanted to do things all on her own and know without any doubt that she got there by her bare hands and her passion and little else.

With that thought fresh on her mind, she stepped into Beckett Carlisle's office, the hint of cigar smoke fresh in the air. Clearly, he was in a mood. Otherwise, he'd never risk smoking in the house, when he knew Mama would hit the roof and never look back if she caught him.

Scottish plaid curtains accented the French doors of the large room, bookshelves on two walls, awards and degrees in expensive frames on the others.

Daddy used to say his office helped him think, brought all the chaos back to neutral. After all, it was the only room in the house designed by him, decorated by him, and used by him and him alone. This fact had driven Mama crazy, until she realized she needed her free time, too.

"Daddy?" Emery said. She realized her spine was hunched and cowering, and she tightened it, if only for show. Beckett lifted his eyes, peering over the tops of his glasses from where he sat at his desk. The sound of his desk clock ticking caught Emery's attention, and she had to fight the urge to look over at it. She'd just stepped inside his office, but already it felt as though she'd been there for an eternity.

"Emery." He said her name with the slightest bit of softness, a tone rarely used by any of the Carlisle men, and certainly not her daddy. It picked at her resolve.

She'd made the decision to go in there and profess that she'd be contracting with Hamilton Stables for the next year. One year. And then she'd return home to her family and do whatever he asked. For however long he asked. Just give her a year without guilt, without that look in his eye that said she'd disappointed him . . . again.

And that's when the lie took shape in her mind, Annie-Jean's words so fresh—"Don't tell him." Maybe she could keep it to herself, see how things went with Trip. See if her gut was right, live a little while in her own shoes and her own opinions. She bit her lip, desperately searching her mind for some way out of this without crushing her family or lying, but there was nothing, so she opened her mouth, and before fear silenced her tongue, she said, "I've spoken with Hamilton Stables, and I'm going to do a little work there."

At this, Daddy set down the pen in his hand, removed his glasses, and sat up. "You spoke with whom?"

"Trip Hamilton."

"All right, you have my attention. What exactly will you be doing there that you can't do here?"

"Um, see, I . . . he has that white-diamond colt from Tiger's Curse. The one Sarah Anderson bought? They're having some problems with him, so I agreed to help out." The air in her lungs became weighted, difficult to push out, difficult to breathe in new. She wondered if all lies were this heavy.

"Help how?"

Lord, did he have to make this so difficult? "I . . . exercise rider?" Her eyes widened, as the words settled over her. "Yes! Exercise rider." She cleared her throat. "The colt's proving difficult with training, so I agreed to help with his morning workouts. Give him someone he's used to, you know?"

"No. Absolutely not. Besides, that's one of our colts. There's no chance he's difficult. A good trainer would know how to work him into shape. This is, it's—" He stood up, reaching for his phone, and started away from his desk.

"Daddy, who are you calling?"

"Carter Hamilton. How dare he orchestrate such a mess."

"No, please. Don't call Mr. Hamilton. You don't understand. This is my doing, not theirs."

He set down his phone slowly, his eyebrows threading together. "Yours?"

Emery cleared her throat, calling up the last bit of her courage, wondering if she would always feel like a child before her father. "I visited the stables a few days ago, saw the colt, and I remembered him. I offered to help."

Beckett stared at his daughter for a long moment, taking in the excitement on her face. The hope. "An exercise rider?"

Emery swallowed again, but her throat refused to function right, the lie too large to go down easily. "Yes."

"Okay."

Her eyes flew up. "Okay?" Emery felt her heart lift, hope floating.

He crossed the room and placed his hands around her arms. "I want you to be happy again. I want you riding again—just not racing. If this will make you happy, then go ahead. But promise me you'll be careful."

"I will, Daddy."

He kissed her cheek, then went back to work, and Emery left, feeling both better and worse. She'd lied to her father, betrayed him. Now she just had to make the lie worth it.

Time to ride.

Trip flipped a bottle cap into the air and caught it easily in his hand, his gaze trained on the game on the widescreen in front of him, though he wasn't even sure who was playing. He couldn't get Emery out of his mind, his curiosity too intense. Would she accept his offer? Did he want her to?

He flipped the cap again, and Nick swiped it from the air. "Beer for your thoughts?"

Nick slid a fresh bottle toward him, his eyebrow cocked. "You've barely said a word since we got here."

Trip shrugged, unsure of where to begin. Or even if he wanted to. "I'm just taking a gamble, and for the first time in my life, I'm not sure I'll win."

Alex's face broke into a grin. "Now, see, that's the difference between you and me, bro. Those are my favorite kind. What's the fun if you already know the outcome? Kind of takes away the excitement when you win."

Trip liked this sentiment, even if he wasn't sure he could adopt it. He was a planner. It was part of what made him so successful. He made it his life to win, never allowing himself to grow attached to anyone in the business. Even the horses. He treated them with the respect they deserved, but he had never loved any of his horses. That love would blind him to a true winner, and he couldn't let that happen. His reputation depended on his name being beside the winner of the race. But this was different. It was cement thick with emotion, sure to harden any second and lock him into something he couldn't get out of.

A pair of women on the opposite side of the bar flashed them a grin, and Alex's attention shifted. "Be right back."

Trip nodded, wishing he could be distracted so easily, as Nick took Alex's seat.

"This doesn't have to get complicated."

"Oh, it's already complicated." Trip took a long pull of his beer,

Nick did the same, then, without looking at Trip, asked, "So what actually happened eight years ago? Between you and Emery."

The evening crowd had set in, chatter all around them, the sounds of glasses hitting wood from shots being taken, balls clinking at the pool table to the far left. People made happy look so damn easy, but it wasn't easy. Or it hadn't been easy for Trip in a long time.

He thought of his last days at the Carlisle Farm, and the final moment between him and Emery. Her lips on his, her long black hair all around him, his heart out of control in his chest. And then Mr. Sampson walked in on them, the look on his face very clear. It took less than twenty-four hours for him to come to Trip and order him to leave, else he would tell Beckett everything and ruin Trip's career before it'd officially started.

So Trip left, telling himself he would come back for Emery when she turned eighteen and could make her own damn decisions. But then his mother died, and suddenly he wasn't so sure. Days turned into months, then years, and before long, too much time had passed. Their lives went separate ways, and his heart turned harder and harder with each year.

He'd never told anyone what really happened, including Emery. She thought he'd taken another job because his time with them was over, but he didn't want it to end with her. Now she was back, all woman, able to make her own decisions, and he couldn't deny a part of him wanted to pick up where they'd left off.

"Trip?"

"What? Oh. What happened? What always happens—we went our separate ways. Can I ask you something?" Trip said, his gaze on Alex over at the end of the bar, talking it up to two women who'd just come in.

Nick adjusted on his stool. "Shoot."

He hesitated, unsure how to ask what he wanted to know without suggesting things he didn't want to suggest. Curiosity won out. "Do you think you'll ever find another one?"

"Another one what?"

"Partner. Wife. Do you think Brit was your one and only chance, or do you think you'll love again?"

Nick went rigid beside him, and he felt like a jerk for bringing it up. Nick rarely ever talked about his fiancée, the pain clearly too much, but Trip had long since thought he needed to talk about it more. And he was just the selfish asshole to force it.

"Some days I think I shouldn't want anyone else. I should live my life and just be glad I had the time I had with her. But then . . ." He shook his head. "I think if it were me, if I were the one who was gone, I'd want her to find someone. I wouldn't want her alone for the rest of her life out of some misplaced loyalty to me."

"So why haven't you dated anyone seriously?"

Rudy brought over a fresh round of beers, giving them a moment to breathe from the intensity of the conversation. "I haven't met any-one worth the guilt. What about you?"

Trip took a long pull of his beer and set it back down. "I think a part of me hoped the next person I dated seriously would be her."

"But you know it can't be."

"I know."

"Then why are you doing this?"

Something happened in the game and the bar erupted in applause, giving Trip time to think. "Ask yourself what you would do. If it were Brit and she needed your help. What would you do?"

Nick took a sip of his beer and then slid it away from him. "I'd do whatever she needed me to do."

"Exactly."

Alex came over then with three women, likely touring horse coun-try. Hell, they could've toured Hamilton Stables for all Trip knew. They ran tours in the afternoons, and he spent his afternoons at the races. "Gentlemen, meet Mandy, Carly, and Amy. They're sisters." Alex's eyes sparkled and Nick groaned. Nick liked to keep his flings private, and Rudy's was anything but private.

"Hey there," the blonde said. Mandy maybe? Trip hadn't paid at-tention. "Are you Trip? I've seen you on TV."

Trip glared at his brother before finishing his beer and standing. "Nah, that's a much better-looking guy." Then he turned to Nick. "Listen, I'm out. Early morning tomorrow."

His brothers started to argue but then just nodded. They knew when Trip needed his space. Outside, the air was less heavy, a chilly evening with stars dotting the black night. He climbed into his truck and started back toward the farm, just as his phone vibrated against the cup holder. He peered down at the number, not recognizing the area code. He wasn't in the mood for business talk, but he didn't want to miss something important either. With trepidation, he hit Accept.

"Hamilton."

"Trip?"

His chest tightened at the voice, the depth and the warmth. The hint of girl behind the woman. "Did you change your number?"

This seemed to trip her up, and he cursed himself for being so ob-vious. "Uh, yeah, I did. Right after the accident. The press had gotten hold of the number and wouldn't leave me alone, so I switched it. How did you know?"

He leaned back in his seat, searching his mind for an answer, but all he found was the truth. "I didn't recognize the number."

"You remembered the old one?"

Damn it all to hell. "I had it in my phone."

"You have the same phone you had eight years ago?"

Christ Almighty, give him a gun now so he could put himself out of this misery. "No . . . I transferred it over."

"Over how many phones?"

He scrubbed his face with his free hand. "Not many. Just six . . . or so."

She went silent, and he worried he'd freaked her out. Hell, he was freaking himself out. "You added my number to six different phones? But we haven't spoken in eight years."

"I know."

"So, why . . . ?"

He wasn't sure if she was talking to herself now or him. "You know why."

Silence settled between them, and he wondered where she was and what she was doing. If she still twirled her hair around her finger when she was deep in thought. If she still slept in mix-matched pajamas. If her lips still tasted like vanilla and honeysuckle . . .

He needed to bring this back on point and fast. "So, what's the verdict, Ms. Carlisle?"

She laughed, and the sound drew his eyes closed, eager to bask in it. He could listen to her all day and never grow tired. "I think seeing someone naked earns a first-name basis. Don't you? Besides, you're my boss now."

Boss. Trip both loved and hated the sound of that. "Does that mean you accept?"

"On just one condition."

Trip couldn't help but grin. She was the only jockey who'd dare ask Trip for something. Most took the job with a handshake and a smile, scared to utter a word lest Trip change his mind. "I'm listening."

"You keep this between us. No publicity. No one knows. For now."

"My family already knows, Emery. I can't keep this from them or the staff." He heard her fidget on the other end, curious why she'd want this a secret. "Is this about Beckett? What did you tell him?"

"That I was just an exercise rider for Craving Wind. Nothing more. My riding for Carlisle Farms is important to Daddy. This will devastate him. I need to keep it as private as possible . . . for now."

"But I thought he wouldn't put you back on a mount?"

"He won't."

"Then why—"

"I know this doesn't make sense, but I know Daddy, and it's for the best. I'll tell him once we know this is going to work out."

Trip considered what she was saying. He understood. He'd try to protect his family, too, but he wasn't sure this was a good idea. Stories tended to come out, whether you wanted them to or not. "All right, then. I'll tell them you're an exercise rider. You can ride early morning, before most of the staff get here. Sound good?"

She released a breath. "Thank you."

He opened his mouth to say more, or maybe just to continue the conversation. "Emery . . ."

"Yeah?"

He released a long breath, then put his truck in drive. "See you tomorrow."

"See you tomorrow, *Mr.* Hamilton."

CHAPTER NINE

Off and running

Fog had set in the next morning, giving the farm an eerie, foreboding vibe. A hint of some disaster to come, perhaps? Or—*Stop being so dramatic.*

Emery shook out her hands and drew a long breath, but as she stepped out of her Jeep and walked toward the stables, she couldn't help feeling she'd made a life decision by coming here. This wasn't small. It was big, big, big. Somehow that realization both gave her pause and filled her with excitement.

She stopped just outside the stables, and with one glance down the long row, her heart picked up and a smile stretched across her face. Wow. Carlisle Farms was beautiful, and her father made it a point to ensure the stables were equally gorgeous, but they were nothing like Hamilton Stables. Nothing so grand. She lost count of how many Thoroughbreds she could see—bay, roan, brown, chestnut, even the occasional pure black. They were beautiful, their coats shiny, their strength and size evident even from here. She knew Trip trained the best, but she had no idea he stabled so many.

"Having a change of heart? Now's the time to tell me."

Emery turned, eyes locking with Trip's. Her skin flushed under his penetrative stare, that crooked grin of his far too sexy for this early in the morning. "Hey there, cowboy."

He tilted his head down in a hello and tucked his hands into his jeans' pockets. Emery had to order herself to swallow and breathe, swallow and breathe as her gaze swept down him. Trip wore jeans the way others wore gloves, all fitted to perfection, with just enough wear to show that when he was at the barn, in his element, he intended to work. He had on a red and tan flannel shirt, loose over the jeans and rolled to his elbows. The same cowboy boots she'd seen on him before stuck out from the bottom of his jeans. She bet he never wore another pair. In place of the Stetson, he sported an Atlanta Braves baseball cap that looked like he'd had it since he was a boy. The rim was torn in spots, the *A* no longer red but burgundy from dirt and wear. Dark chocolate strands curled out from the edge, tickling his neck, and Emery had to fight the urge to reach out—to see if his hair felt as soft as she remembered.

She cleared her throat. Twice.

Forget getting on the damn mount, this man was going to be the death of her. How anyone worked around him, with that soul stare and those broad shoulders and—

Dear God, enough with the descriptions!

She blinked hard to fix her thoughts ot else she was really going to embarrass herself. Trainers weren't supposed to look like Trip. They were old and whiskered and had more wrinkles than good sense. She knew firsthand; she'd been around her fair share. But Trip had never conformed to the typical trainer stereotype, which might be why he'd so quickly become the best.

He bit his lip, a smile twitching at the corners of his mouth, and she got the distinct impression he knew just what she was thinking. "He's not in here," he said, pointing down the row of stalls. "I had Clark take him to the training ring out back. Would you like to see him?"

Emery's heart screamed yes while her head screamed no. She wanted to see the colt like she wanted to breathe, but she knew Trip would ask her to ride; then he'd see that she was still a chicken and retract his offer. He'd never said when she had to fulfill his challenge, and Emery hoped she could delay it a little longer.

She needed to get over her nervousness. So what if she was thrown from her horse? It wasn't the first time it had happened in her life and wouldn't be the last. But the throwing wasn't the scary part, nor the trampling, though the memory of the pain would remain with her for the rest of her life. It was—

"Emery . . . ?"

She glanced up and straight into those chocolate eyes. Damn, melted M&M's had nothing on this man. "Yes?"

He took a step toward her, the move so simple yet full of purpose—no one had ever read Emery the way Trip could read her. The thought warmed her more than it should. "No one's forcing you to do this, to be here," he said. "You know that, right? Not your family and certainly not me. Especially if you're not ready." His gaze dropped to her cane, and she held her breath, waiting for the pity to come, but it never appeared. Instead, he returned to her eyes, his head slightly cocked. "The show's yours, lady girl. You gotta decide if you're ready to perform. Nobody else can take the mount for you."

Emery licked her lips and leaned into the cane, then put all her weight on her left leg, testing it. There was no pain, but then, she hadn't felt any pain in months. The cane was a crutch—both literally and figuratively. A crutch she needed to ditch if she hoped to return to her old self. The moment had come.

It reminded her of when she rode for the first time. She'd been around horses her entire life, but she'd secretly always been afraid of them. Every time the horse cantered, she felt her heart hit the dirt, cowering away. She'd stayed up all night the day before her first galloping lesson, sure she would die of fear the moment she sat on her horse. But then something magical happened. She reached the training ring and pushed through the gate and made a decision to leave the fear behind. It was one of the best days of her life.

Here and now, she knew this moment was a repeat of that lesson. She had a choice—put down the cane (and her fear) or resign herself to never riding again. Emery couldn't do that.

She drew a long breath, thankful that Trip hadn't said any more. She needed silence right now, needed to feel her way through the moment. Slowly, Emery leaned her cane against a nearby empty stall and balanced her weight on both feet, careful not to cringe or hint at her fear.

Trip waited, watching—forever patient—and she could feel all those old feelings floating up, tempting her to succumb to them. She didn't blame him for leaving—she was only seventeen—but that didn't keep her from wishing every day for a year that he'd come back to her.

"Ready?" he asked.

"Ready."

They walked around the stables to the training ring out back, Clark already inside with Craving Wind. Emery's pulse sped up with each step, beating from her head to her toes, nervousness and excitement fighting it out for control of her emotions. She forced herself not to limp as she walked, not to lean on her good leg, to forget that she'd ever had a bad leg. This was her time.

Trip held open the gate, and her breath caught as his palm gently rested on the small of her back. "After you."

She glanced up, and then to the horse, relieved to see an exercise rider on his back. Calling all her strength to the surface, she started over, but suddenly each step felt weighted, more difficult than the last. The air outside turned hot, her hands clammy as she recounted article after article about her accident. Speculation if she'd ride again. Crude comments that suggested she'd never be the same even if she did.

"I . . ."

"Emery?"

"This . . . I . . ." She shook her head, unwilling to say the words *I'm not ready* aloud. Because she was ready. She'd already been through this, said the words, made them real. She couldn't take them back now. What was she doing?

And then Trip waved his hand in the air. "Bring him around." The exercise rider rode over, a look of sheer fear on his face. Emery couldn't help but smile.

"Is that look because of the horse or Mr. Hamilton here?" she asked.

"No, ma'am, I'm fine," the boy replied, though his hands shook.

She laughed at how surely his face disagreed with his words. A sense of ease washed over her. "I'd say you're anything but fine. What's the problem?" Without thinking, she walked over, Trip close behind, and stroked Craving Wind's mane. "Are you scary? You don't look so scary." Emery leaned in and whispered close, "I'm betting it's Mr. Hamilton. Whatcha think?" She peered around at Trip and cocked her head, her eyes narrowing in scrutiny. "Looks pretty damn frightening to me."

Clark broke into fits, and Trip shot him a look that made Emery laugh still harder. The sun had burned away the fog, and now the birds crowed, telling the farm to wake up. Workers busied about, feeding horses, saddling them up for their morning workouts, cleaning and brushing. The whole place had a sense of community about it, different than other farms she'd been around—different from her own. Like every person worked hard because he wanted to, not because he was paid.

"Haven't you ever heard of teasing?" Emery asked Trip with a smile. "All work and no play for Mr. Superstar Trainer?" She knocked his stomach lightly with her fist, too comfortable and too in her element. But the moment her hand made contact with his rock-solid abs, she felt herself flush. God, why had she done that? She couldn't seem to be around Trip without staring or flirting—like no time had passed and nothing had changed between them. She needed to get herself under control.

Trip cleared his throat and ducked his head, but she caught the edges of his lips curving into a small grin before he tucked it away.

Embarrassed, Emery focused back on the exercise rider. He couldn't be older than sixteen, likely a cousin or son of one of the trainers. Some poor kid forced to ride when he'd rather be playing video games or chasing girls. Did they still call it that? "Tell me what's the trouble. You're tense and the horse knows it."

The boy glanced from Clark to Trip, then finally to Emery. "He threw Mike Black yesterday. Talk said Mike couldn't even get out of bed today. That's why I'm covering for him."

At that, Clark started laughing again. "You're a fool, boy. Mikey's going to hit the races today and bet away his wages for a week. Mark my word."

"So, he wasn't thrown?"

Trip patted Craving Wind. "Ah, he was thrown all right, but he got back up. So will you. We've all been thrown a few times. Rarely does anybody get injured. No one's been put in the hospital. This year." He winked at the boy, whose attention was on Emery.

"But you were thrown, weren't you, Ms. Carlisle?"

Emery felt all the blood drain from her face. For whatever reason, she'd never expected anybody on the farm to mention her injury. She knew everyone in racing knew about it. Heck, it was the Kentucky Oaks and she was a front-runner for the Derby. That kind of thing didn't go unnoticed. But how could she explain to this boy that she wasn't afraid of getting thrown or even being trampled—she was afraid she'd lost her touch. Lost her talent. Lost herself.

She'd opened her mouth to reply when Trip cut in. "Well, I think I'll show Emery around the rest of the farm. We'll check in with you later," he said to Clark, who nodded. And then, with the relief of a cup of water on a scorching day, she followed Trip back out, ignoring his curious stare. There was no doubt he had opinions, and that was fine. That was perfectly and completely fine. He could keep his opinions. As long as he kept to their agreement and let her race, she didn't care what he thought of her. So there!

Only, as she watched him walking toward the stables, his head slightly down, she knew she was lying to herself.

Trip led her around the stables and back to a small white house with navy shutters, planter boxes full of vibrant flowers below each window, and a red door. They stepped through the door without knocking and into a small kitchen with a breakfast nook just to the right, facing the pastures, with a clear view of the rising sun. A six-person rectangular oak table dominated the nook, a metal light with a rooster on it hanging down over the table, like it was ready to steal your food if you came in a minute late.

Emery glanced around, feeling better with each passing moment. From the orchard print shades over the windows to the rug below the sink that read "Southern Soul," it felt like she'd entered her grandmother's house back home. "I thought you were showing me the rest of the farm?"

Just then a woman appeared from around the corner, all gray hair and Southern curves and a smile that said she knew Emery down to her bones even before she'd heard her name. "Trust me, honey, this is the most important place on the farm. Especially first thing in the morning." Then she wiped her hands on her apron and gripped Emery's shoulders gently before leaning in to kiss her cheek. "You must be Emery. I'm Vivian Marshal, but everybody around her calls me Mama V." She winked over at Trip. "Omelet and bacon?"

Trip grinned. "You know me well." He pulled out a chair for Emery and nodded for her to sit before taking the seat across from her.

"Mama V keeps us fed," Trip said with a smile. "It's a twenty-four-hour kitchen in here."

Mama V laughed. "Well, not all day. But yes, before I started cooking for them, they'd go all day without eating. Riding those horses, training, talking business, then turn to the races. They'd go sunup to sundown, all of them turning into skin and bones and embarrassing the family. Couldn't have that." She cracked an egg into a frying pan, the sizzling sound filling the silence in a comfortable way. Then she flipped it and threw in peppers and onions, and Emery wrinkled her nose in disgust.

"Now, now. What's that look for, lady girl? I'm sensing some high-and-mighty judgment falling my way."

Mama V spun around, her wooden spoon out, and under her stare, Emery straightened and smiled. She distinctly remembered her grandmother spanking her with a wooden spoon—on more than one occasion. Something told Emery Mama V wasn't against using her spoon either.

"Nothing. I was just . . . Nothing."

Trip leaned in. "Let me guess; you're a simple, egg-whites-only kind of girl?"

Emery blanched. "Lord no. Well, unless I'm watching my weight for a race. But I never understood why anybody had to mess up a perfectly good egg by throwing vegetables into it."

"Is that right?" Trip asked, smiling.

"Yes; the only thing that belongs on eggs is cheese. And maybe salt and pepper. Onions and red and green peppers?" She made the universal yuck noise, and Mama V laughed loudly from where she stood by the stove.

"Honey, you're going to be a lot of fun around here."

Then she came over and placed a steaming omelet in front of Emery, cheddar cheese melting from its center. Emery's gaze snapped up. "How did you know?"

"Oh, Mama V sees all," Trip answered for her, before digging into his own plate.

Mama V glanced between the two of them, a small smile on her face. "Indeed I do."

The fog had completely cleared by the time they finished eating, and though Trip itched to take Emery riding, to watch her in her element, he knew she wasn't ready. He could see it on her face when the boy had called her out on her injury. A part of him wanted to talk to Clark, warn him to make sure no one else on staff brought up her accident, but he didn't think that was the best thing for her. She needed to face what happened, her fears. He just wasn't sure how to help her get there without pushing her away.

"Want to see the rest of the farm now?" he asked, reaching for her arm. Damn, he wasn't sure why, but he couldn't seem to be around her without touching her in some way.

Her blue eyes dropped to his hand on her arm, her eyebrows threaded with doubt, but he knew Emery well enough to realize she would have barked some feminist remark if she didn't like it at least a little.

"Um, sure." Her gaze lifted, and the intensity in it made Trip want to reconsider his agreement with himself to be good, to keep their relationship professional. He ached to pull the stubborn, broken woman to him and put her back together again one long, mind-blowing kiss at a time. He thought of the last time his lips were on hers, the kiss full of urgency and the good-bye he couldn't say, and wondered if it would be like that now, or if they would take it slow, relish in each other more.

Shaking himself from his thoughts before his jeans got any tighter, he asked, "Okay if we ride?" Her back went rigid, and he felt her pulling away, burying in on herself, when he realized what she thought he meant. "In the cart." He pointed at a golf cart parked by the stable, and she released a breath, smiling with relief, and he couldn't help feeling pride that he'd put that there. Damn, he was in deep, and she'd only been back in his life forty-eight hours. By this point, he should have already introduced her to the rest of the staff, passed her off to one of his assistant trainers, and gone on his way. Instead, he was giving her a personal tour of the farm. His brothers would laugh their asses off if they saw the way he was fawning all over her. Or maybe they'd be fawning, too.

The thought brought on more jealousy than he had any right to feel.

He slid into the driver's seat of the golf cart and patted the seat beside him for Emery to join him. He kept waiting for her to ask for the cane, to limp, or at the very least to show some hesitation with this much walking, but she never let on. Which either meant she genuinely didn't need it or she was too stubborn to show weakness. Both possibilities seemed equally probable.

Emery slipped into the golf cart, her hands at her side, until her left brushed against Trip's thigh, and she jerked back, placing them in her lap, then folding them together, back in her lap, and then finally crossing her arms like she needed to hold her hands down to prevent them from behaving badly. He smiled inwardly, enjoying the way she reacted to him—how she became so easily rattled. Was it possible she still had feelings for him, too?

Too?

Trip put the cart in drive before his brain could unpack that little disastrous thought, and they made their way around the farm, Trip pointing out barns, trainer quarters, training rings, and everything in between. Finally, they reached the track, and Emery drew a shallow breath, stepping out of the cart even before it was fully in park.

"You have your own track?"

Trip walked up beside her, standing far too close to be appropriate, but he couldn't help himself. When he set out to open Hamilton Stables, he told his father he wouldn't cut corners. He wanted the finest facilities on-site, and if Carter gave him those facilities, he promised to make the Hamilton brand a household name. The track went in six months later, and that year Trip had a horse in the money in two of the three legs of the Triple Crown.

"It's a seven-furlong track. I had it put in a few years back. Nothing overly grand, but it helps with training."

"You have your own track," she repeated, this time with a sense of awe and longing in her voice. "I begged Daddy to put in a track back home, but he said it wasn't necessary with so many tracks available to us."

It was a fair way of thinking, but Trip prided himself on knowing the traditional ways of training and then elevating those methods to create a more modern approach. Some of the older trainers mocked him early on, but winning was winning, and soon they began implementing Trip's methods at their own farms.

He glanced over at Emery and hesitated, unsure how much he should push her. How soon. He knew she had enough drive to get over her fear, but her eyes weren't lit with excitement. They were round with terror. He treaded carefully. "Emery, you know you can—"

She cut him off quickly, the fear winning out. "What do your brothers do around the farm? Nick and Alex, right?"

Trip stared at the track, sure staying there with her fears straight ahead would make Emery uneasy, but maybe that was what she needed right now. A visual to remind her why she loved racing. He considered asking her to race right now but knew she would pull away from him again, and he wanted her close. Too close for any good to come of it.

"Nick works for Hamilton Industries, the business side of the Hamilton brand. And you met Alex, right? He mentioned a minor assault at Patty's?"

She cringed. "I wouldn't call it *assault*. I just forcefully dragged him away from our table . . . by my fingernails. There was no blood or anything. Did he say there was blood?"

"No, no blood," Trip said with a laugh. "Though now you've got me wondering."

"He was about to tell Patty that I worked here, which would mean a direct gossip path to Daddy's ears. I couldn't let that happen."

Trip drew a breath and cut his eyes over to her. "You've got to tell him the truth eventually. You know that, right?"

"*Eventually* is a very long word. So back to Nick and Alex."

"Right." He pushed away the nagging questions in his mind— why she'd come to him, what Beckett would say if he knew, where he thought she was that second—and went on about his brothers. "Like I said, Nick works for Industries, and Alex . . . well, Alex is Alex. He does what he wants, still trying to figure out his passion. But he's recently started managing the breeding side of Hamilton Stables, working the foaling and mare barns. Keeping up with requests, talks with our staff vet, the health of our broodmares. Stuff like that. So far so good, but with Alex you never know." Trip thought of his brother's adventures over the years—backpacking through Europe, a summer in Australia, climbing Mount Everest. He reminded Trip of a colt he'd tried to train a few years back, only to realize the horse would never race. Too wild and independent. Just like Alex.

"I didn't realize you'd ventured into breeding."

Trip shrugged. "It made sense. One-stop shop and all that."

She nodded slowly, and Trip wondered if she was thinking about Carlisle Farms, and their move from training to breeding. If Beckett would view this as yet another reason to be angry at Emery for working with Hamilton Stables. They weren't the only barn to offer breeding and training services, but they were certainly the best.

"So you're the only one who trains?"

Trip adjusted his stance, memories pouring in of the first time he knew he wanted to be a trainer. "When I was little, I used to practically live at the track, taking in every detail. It amazed me—the science of it, the structure, the thrill. I knew my passion by the time I was eight years old, and so I've spent most of my life learning, watching, paying attention to what works—and what doesn't. Especially to what doesn't. Before long, I went from assistant trainer at Wyncrest Farms to starting Hamilton Stables. I've loved every minute of it. I can't imagine doing anything else."

He glanced over to find Emery watching him intently, her eyes so blue in the morning sun they appeared like something out of a fantasy. A gust of wind blew around them, causing her hair to glide over her face, and without thinking, he reached over, gently tucking the wild strands back behind her ear. She drew a slow breath, her gaze never leaving his, and Trip thought how differently this moment would go if she were anyone else. He would thread his fingers into her hair and lean in, press his mouth to hers, and take her the way she deserved to be taken. Show her she was still the woman she had once been. But then, he hadn't felt this spark with any other women. Eight years, and not a fifth of the intensity he felt around Emery.

Now, she was here, back beside him, the fire between them enough to light an entire city, and he couldn't do a thing about it. She worked for him now—an *employee*. Even having these thoughts was unethical and against the very foundation of Hamilton Stables. What the hell was he doing?

He pulled away and shook his head, clearing away the temptation, though he knew he couldn't keep it at bay for long. He needed to separate himself from her before he made a mistake he couldn't correct. "So, yeah, that's the track."

Emery faced forward, her eyebrows drawn together at the coldness in his voice. "It's great. Thanks for showing it to me."

"Sure thing. It's my job. I'll get you back to the stables now."

Trip headed to the cart, hating the tension between them. All his old feelings for her had resurfaced, clouding his logic. He needed to think, to focus, but his focus kept drifting to her dark, tight jeans, the way they hugged her legs. He wondered what those legs would feel like wrapped around his—*Dammit all to hell, dude! Pull yourself together!*

He took a long pull from his water bottle as they parked the cart by the barn and peered over at her to find her staring at a bay being brought in from his morning exercise. "Water for your thoughts?" He held the bottle out to her. They could do the friend thing, right? Nothing wrong with friends.

She laughed, but the sound didn't hold the warmth it should. "Just . . . remembering."

"Well, you know the good thing about remembering?" Emery glanced over, and Trip had to order his brain to be good, because dear God above, those eyes of hers made him want to do very bad things. "It's never just the bad stuff. If we let ourselves remember, we can remember why we made the choices we made in the first place. Remember why you love racing, Emery. And never forget it."

CHAPTER TEN

Wearing blinders

"Only one more box," Annie-Jean said triumphantly.

They'd spent all morning setting up Annie-Jean's booth at Triple Run's annual fall festival. Each year, Annie-Jean baked dozens upon dozens of her specialty cookies for the festival, and each year, she begged Emery to man the booth with her. The first year—four years ago now—Emery agreed, only to find herself stuck for eight hours, handing out cookies, smiling away, Annie-Jean like a hardcore drill sergeant, refusing to let her leave, even to go pee. Never again, Emery had said—until now.

She told herself it had nothing to do with the possibility of running into Trip. Nothing at all. He was probably out of town anyway, or at the stables, or handling any one of a thousand things trainers handled. But she couldn't get the feel of his fingertips brushing her hair from her face out of her mind. Couldn't stop the warmth spreading over her when she remembered the intensity in his stare.

"Remember, presentation is everything. Does the tablecloth look okay?"

Emery grinned as she peered down at the white cloth, with Annie-Jean's logo—AJ's Creations—printed across the top. She went all out, a characteristic she shared with her brother, Beckett Carlisle, whether she wanted to admit it or not. "It's perfect, Annie. You're worrying too much."

Despite it being early morning, the temperature was comfortable for fall. The trees all around them bore green leaves with yellow tips, the start of their change to the deep reds and oranges of the season. Emery loved fall, loved the feel of excitement in the air for football and festivities. Loved all the craft shows and baked goods, so long as a certain person's name didn't pop up.

"Yeah, well, this festival helps keep the lights on, so I don't want to miss anything. Plus, Patty's going to be here, and you know I can't let that traitor show me up."

And there it was—Patty, aka the traitor.

Emery used to ask Annie why she insisted on coming to this festival when there were others in the South, including the massive Yellow Daisy Festival in Stone Mountain, Georgia, and every time Annie claimed she came because she liked Triple Run's people. But really, it was because she wanted to see if she could outbake Patty. Prove she was the stronger cookie maker.

"Are you going to make me buy some of her cookies?"

Annie shot me an incredulous look. "Foolish girl, no."

"So you're not?"

She went about arranging her cookie display, all pink boxes and cute ribbons and glittering swirls. "I'm going to have you buy one of her Bundt cakes *and* some of her cookies." She winked. "But we'll wait an hour or two. See what's been bought up the most. The favorites, ya know?"

Emery shook her head. "No, I don't know, you crazy old lady."

"But you'll do it anyway 'cause you love me. Now, sit down and look pretty. People are already here." Her gaze landed squarely on Emery, then she peered around the table, under it, then back at Emery. "Where's your cane?"

Shoot.

"Oh, I—" Emery's words caught in her throat as she took in the man walking toward her, a crooked smile plastered across his face. Rugged jeans hung low on his waist, flannel shirt and Braves baseball cap firmly in place, like he slept with them on—or had no other clothes. She thought of his first days at Carlisle Farms, how he'd tried to impress her daddy with smart-looking outfits and overly combed hair, only to have Beckett all but laugh in his face. Then Trip was all nerdy T-shirts and worn jeans, his hands always a little callused, that smile of his always there. No wonder she fell so hard, and if she wasn't careful, it was going to happen all over again.

"Hot damn, is that him?" Annie-Jean made no effort to hide her excitement, nudging Emery continuously in the side until Emery felt sure she'd have a bruise.

"Yes. Now stop before I kill you," Emery said through clenched teeth. "He's coming over."

"Actually," a deep voice said, "he's already here."

Emery's eyes lifted to find Trip standing in front of their booth, his arms crossed, the sexiest smile she'd ever seen on his face. A fine layer of stubble covered his jaw, making him appear even more rugged than usual. God, why couldn't he have aged to look like Mr. Sampson? Or act like most trainers? Or drink a lot, so he had a beer gut? Something, anything. But this man standing before her wasn't like most trainers—or most people, for that matter—which made it all that much harder to ignore the connection between them. She wondered if he felt it, too, or if it was all in her head. She'd had that thought a lot the weeks and months after he left, doubt giving way to depression. Until she herself became an adult and realized he'd done the adult thing. He'd taken a job, an amazing job with Wyncrest. How could she fault him for that? Her mind couldn't. Her heart? Another story . . .

"I didn't think I'd see you here." She fidgeted her way through the lie, sure she was going to hell any second, the fast track on a path paved by her lies.

"Really?" He cocked his head, fighting to smile wider. "So, the *sponsored by Hamilton Stables* didn't give you a clue?"

Emery followed the direction of his nod to find a large sign hanging at the entrance to the festival, the Hamilton Stables logo visible for all to see. Chicken on a stick! She'd been here all of twenty minutes and she'd already stuck her foot in her mouth. She glanced over at Annie-Jean for help, but she only shrugged, then stood and reached out her hand.

"I'm Aunt Annie-Jean." She flashed a flirtatious smile and stroked Trip's outstretched hand like it was a loveable tabby cat. "*You* are something else. Do all Triple Run men drink from the same water as you?"

Good God. Was all her family this embarrassing? Yes, yes they were.

"Annie, I think he'd like his hand back."

Annie-Jean's smile broadened as she held his hand for another second. "Right."

Trip's knowing eyes fell on Emery, and her cheeks burned still brighter. "Is there a comment somewhere in that smirk?" she asked with a little too much sass. But she couldn't help it. She didn't do well with people mocking her.

He laughed. "There's lots of comments, but I'll hold my tongue."

"I'd like to hold your—"

"Annie!"

She looked over at Emery innocently. "What?"

Emery drew a long breath. Was nine a.m. too early to start drinking? "I need to grab another box. Want to help me?" she asked, hoping to save him before Annie jumped over the table and straight into his arms

"After you, lady girl."

"Why do you call me that?" she asked once they were away from the crowd.

Trip shrugged. "It fits the you I see in my head. The before and the now. A beautiful woman on the outside, a spunky girl on the inside."

"You think I'm beautiful?" He'd once told her she was the most beautiful girl in the world, but eight years had passed, and with it brought age and scars and a lot of things that made Emery feel anything but beautiful.

"Everyone on the planet thinks you're beautiful. Me? I think a lot of things about you. But don't worry, most of them are completely inappropriate." He winked, and a laugh broke free from her lips.

"Something tells me you shouldn't be admitting that to me. Or anyone else."

Trip tucked his hands into his pockets. "You'd be right, but I promised you once I'd always be honest with you. See no reason to start lying now."

Emery felt his gaze drift over to her as they continued on to Annie's Suburban, but she refused to look over. She didn't trust her face to hide her thoughts. The truth was, she didn't feel he'd been honest with her at all. If he were honest and upfront, he would have told her about Wyncrest before he accepted the job. Instead, he'd kissed her cheek and walked away, never to call or return again. A part of her wondered if she'd sought him out just to see if he'd flinch the first time he saw her again, but she couldn't deny he was the best, and feelings aside, her career needed him . . . even if her heart received a little damage along the way. She told herself she could handle it, but with Trip a foot away, the sentiment didn't hold like she'd hoped.

Once at the ridiculously large SUV, she opened the back cargo doors, but the box had slid to the farthest spot from where she stood. She peered into the endless abyss, knowing she couldn't reach it without crawling inside. Her foot tapped against the gravel road as she tried to think of any way around it. Just when she'd decided there was no way she was crawling into this truck with Trip outside, staring at her ass, she heard a soft chuckle.

"Well, go ahead. Do you need me to lift you up? Or maybe I could fetch you a step ladder?"

She glared at him. "Funny how you giants all act like it's so, so hilarious when we short people can't reach something."

"Honey, I'm not sure you count as short. Maybe we should call you mini. Mini Emery. I like that." His grin widened, taking over his face, perfectly white teeth flashing at her, with the exception of the front incisor, which had a small chip in it. She didn't remember the flaw being there before and felt it suited him just fine.

"Let me guess," Emery said, pointing at the tooth. "You pissed off the wrong lady and she decked you?"

Trip full-out laughed, the sound so intoxicating Emery forgot momentarily why she was so agitated. God, she missed their flirting—missed him. Sadness clamped down on her heart, and she bit her lip to keep from showing just how much he affected her.

"True enough. Though she didn't deck me so much as toss me into a fence. We're still friends, though."

Emery's frown curved into a smile. "Wait. You were thrown from a horse?"

He leaned in closer. "I'll tell you a secret: everyone's been thrown. Many times. Part of the job. The question isn't *if* you'll get thrown, it's *if* you'll get back on. What about you, lady girl? Will you get back on?"

Her heart slowed down, beating in time with his breaths, their eyes locked, and she could swear he felt it, too—that intense pull in her gut that urged her to press her mouth to his and see if he tasted as good as she remembered.

She thought of how perfectly they used to fit together. Their hands laced. His arms around her. And then the sweetness in his eyes as he slipped inside her for the first time—her very first time—and she was gone. So far gone she didn't know it until she reached the sky, and then he left her with no way to get back down. The fall back to reality after he left had broken her heart. Did she really want to trust it with him again? Was he worth the chance?

The moment drew long, and Emery thought maybe, just maybe, he was going to take the risk, but then he looked down and ran his palms over his thighs. "Um, I'll do it."

"Do what?" she asked, unable to hide the desire in her voice.

"The box. I'll grab it."

"Right. The box. Sure, thanks."

God, she needed an antianxiety pill or six if she hoped to survive her time around him.

Grabbing the box, Trip followed Emery back to the booth, but the easiness between them had shifted to something darker. "All right, then. Good seeing you, Emery. I need to . . ." He motioned toward the rest of the booths. "Check around, make sure everyone's good."

She nodded. "Of course. See you tomorrow, then."

He hesitated, like something else—more—was on the tip of his tongue, then sighed. "Yeah . . . tomorrow."

Clenching her eyes shut to gain some distance from him, she reopened them to find Kate sitting at the booth beside Annie-Jean. "Um, hey. What are you doing here?"

Kate crossed her legs and grinned, pointing over to the Hamilton Stables sign. "I heard the Hamilton boys were sponsoring this event, and I wouldn't mind seeing a certain Hamilton brother again."

A few customers came by, and Emery scooted out of the way, taking a seat on the ice chest between Annie and Kate. "What about Chris or Matt?" Or hell, anyone else. The last thing Emery wanted was her best friend shacking up with Alex Hamilton. Her life was complicated enough as it stood. Add in Alex the player breaking her friend's heart and she would have yet another reason to turn her back on Hamilton Stables. She couldn't do that—not now, when she was so close.

"They're just . . . I don't know. Not the right fit."

Emery reached for a white chocolate macadamia nut cookie from the sample tray, only to have Annie swat her hand. "For customers."

"I'm a customer."

"You are paid help," Annie said, pushing the tray out of Emery's reach.

"Since when have you paid me?"

Annie sighed. "Fine. I'll buy you both drinks at Rudy's after the festival."

"So, let me get this straight—I sit here for eight hours and you buy me a five-dollar drink? Something's not right here."

Annie stared pointedly at her niece. "Yes, you're right. Something's not right here, and it don't have a thing to do with me or cookies. Though I guess that depends on what you kids call it these days."

Shaking her head, Emery turned back to her friend. "And Alex is the right fit?"

"Not sure yet, but with an ass like his, I'm willing to find out."

Annie hit Kate's arm, and both women peered up to see a mother in front of them, her hands cuffing her son's ears, a goofy grin on the son's face.

"Cookies?" Emery asked innocently.

The boy pointed at Kate. "I'll take her, please."

Trip rushed through the central annex of the festival, eager to get out of range of Emery and her tempting mouth. It took every bit of willpower he had to step away from her.

He remembered the year he worked under Beckett, learning from his expertise, and then a thousand secret moments with his daughter. At times, Trip thought of telling him, asking permission and praying he said yes. But then Trip had been twenty to Emery's seventeen. What decent father would approve?

He blew out a long breath and had started around toward city hall to check in with Mayor Phillips when he heard his name called from behind.

The day had warmed up, not a bit of wind blowing through the trees, making it all that much easier to smell Patty's perfume even before she made it in front of him. He fought the urge to cough as she took yet another step closer, her white bob shaking as she beamed up at him from an overly made-up face.

"Trip, sweetie, I thought that was you."

Trip knew he had no choice but to speak now, forcing him to also take a giant whiff of Patty's candy-floral-God-knew-what scent. "You were right. What can I do for you, Patty?"

She sweetened her smile and placed her hand on his arm. "Well, you're on the town board, so I wondered if you knew of any new businesses coming to town? A new bakery, perhaps?" She peered around in disgust, her gaze landing decidedly close to Annie-Jean, who seemed to notice her gaze and took it upon herself to give Patty the finger.

Trip choked out a laugh before he could stop himself, because old ladies flipping each other off was funny any way you slice it, until he caught sight of Patty's glare, now pointed at him. The expression *if looks could kill* might very well have been modeled after Patty Tanner and the look she was using on Trip that very second.

He'd lived in Triple Run his whole life, leaving only for the various jobs and apprenticeships he'd taken over the years to learn the ins and outs of training. So, he'd known Patty a long time, and he knew he had all of thirty seconds to back out of that laugh or he would be stuck here for twenty minutes, listening to her dissect its deeper meaning. But Trip was a guy. He didn't have deeper meanings to pretty much anything.

"You know, I'm glad I ran into you, Patty. Mama V asked me to pick up one of your Bundt cakes. Did you make the white chocolate raspberry this year?"

Patty's face switched from anger to pride so fast you'd have thought it were programmed. "It so happens I did. How many did you say you needed? Two?" She gave Trip a look that said he would pay for his laugh in expensive cakes and cookies.

"Right . . . two. I'll swing by in a few minutes, then. I just have to talk to Mayor Phillips." He started away, but clearly not fast enough, because Patty was back at his side.

"One more thing, Trip, honey. Was that Emery Carlisle I saw you with earlier?"

Trip blinked. "Sorry, what?"

"Out by the road. I saw you with Emery Carlisle. What was that about? She came by the shop a few days ago. Is she in town now? Is she visiting the stables? Is she working for you?"

He shook his head and took a step back, unsure how one small woman could ask so many questions without her head spinning. "Sure, that was Emery. If that's all, I need to—"

"I saw him with her, too."

Trip drew a breath to calm himself and turned to see Hayden Christian leaning over his jelly and jam booth, accidentally knocking one of the jars to the ground and shattering it into pieces. Several people passing back jumped out of the way of the red glob and glass, but even that didn't keep Hayden from watching Trip for a reaction.

"I . . . yes, that was Emery, but I'm not sure how that's—"

"But what's she doing here?" a third voice asked, and Trip prayed to the Man above to give him an ounce of patience before glancing over to the booth on his left. Charlotte Myers had her hands on a rack of handmade purses and hats, but her eyes were fixed on Trip. Suddenly the warm air felt downright scalding. He needed an escape route, fast.

Just then, he felt someone's hand on his forearm and swung around, sure the whole town surrounded him now, only to find Emery standing impossibly close, her face lit with humor.

"Hey there," she said, squinting into the sun. "Annie-Jean asked me to fetch your muscles for some lifting. You up to it?" She winked, and Trip thought that might be the best thing he'd seen all day.

He peered around at Patty and Hayden and Charlotte, and now even Mayor Phillips was outside town hall, suspenders fastened tight to his pants like always, scratching his head like he'd just seen the most peculiar thing imaginable. "I'm going with yes," Trip said, pressing his hand to the small of Emery's back to lead her away. "Though of course you realize you just made this worse, right?"

Emery lifted her gaze to his. "What is *this*?"

"Our affair."

"Our what?"

"Yeah, they're plotting out the details right now. Half the town saw me help you with that box, and then you came over and flashed me that smile. It's done now. Might as well hold my hand. Give them a good show, ya know?"

"Wait a sec." Emery stopped walking, her hands on her small hips, her face all scrunched up in anger. Trip couldn't help but grin. Even mad, she shined. "How did I supposedly smile at you?"

Trip leaned in close, catching the faintest scent of vanilla on her neck, before whispering in her ear, "You know, like you want me." He pulled away with a smile of his own, and her face flushed Red Hots red. From embarrassment or rage, he couldn't be sure, though he had an inkling she erred on the rage side these days.

"You're impossible."

His grin widened. "Impossibly right."

"Ugh, forget Annie-Jean; I'd rather pull a muscle than ask you for help." She stormed off, but Trip's long legs caught up in no time.

"Settle down, lady girl. It's been a long time since I've been able to mess with you. I've missed it."

She flashed him a cocky smile. "First beautiful, now missing me? Damn, I must have done a number on you."

Trip stared down at her, not a hint of humor on his face. "No denying that."

They stopped in front of Annie's booth, Emery's expression unreadable, as her gaze went past him, her eyes going wide. She said something under her breath he couldn't quite make out and ran a hand over her face. He almost laughed until he turned around to see what had stirred her up and his eyes landed on his brothers, now almost to them.

"Shit."

"Glad to see it's not just me who finds this awkward." Emery started away as Trip reached for her hand, stopping her. And damn it all to hell. Warmth spread through him, every nerve ending at full attention, attuned to the feel of her hand in his, its softness, the scab on her palm that had yet to heal. His eyes flicked down and then up to hers, and he knew he needed to pull away, but he couldn't bring himself to let go.

"Don't go," he whispered. "You should meet them formally."

"Why?" Emery asked, and despite her facade, he heard the hitch in her voice. Was she feeling what he felt? Like eight years of pent-up emotions had burst free, refusing to stay contained another second.

"Because, I—"

"Hey, brother," Alex said, smacking Trip on the back just enough to cause him to lurch forward into Emery, her forehead connecting with his chest.

"Ow." She stepped back, rubbing the spot, which sent Alex into hysterics.

"Dude, you hit his chest. Not his head or even his chin. His *chest*. What are you, four-eight?"

Nick, the forever nice guy, reached out to her. "Are you okay?"

But her eyes were on Alex. "Five-two and a half, thank you. What are you? Five-ten instead of six-two or -three like them? I bet you needed psych sessions as a kid to boost your self-esteem, didn't you?"

Alex grinned over at Trip. "I like her. You can keep her."

Emery started to bark out a retort as Trip stepped between them. "All right, then, show's over. Emery was just asking me to help her aunt lift something heavy."

But when they all turned toward Annie-Jean's booth, it became apparent that their little exchange had an audience. A large audience. Trip peered down the long row of booths, and every one of them had a town resident half-hanging over his or her table or just straight in the path, readying their gossip.

"Christ Almighty." He sighed heavily and eyed his brothers. "Go, please, before they publish an article in the morning *Tribune*."

Alex smirked, then spread his hands out like he was showcasing a news headline. "Sexy jockey gets it on with the Hamilton brothers. Full story on pages six and nine.'"

Emery's face lit with fresh rage. "Cute. You know, you really are a piece of—"

Trip gripped Emery's hips and spun her around, easing her toward Annie-Jean's booth. "Yes, yes, he is, but you saying it out loud with Pastor Reagan in earshot won't change it." Then he focused on Nick, pleading with him to help.

"Okay, we've had our fun," Nick said, grabbing Alex around the neck and steering him away. "We're heading to Rudy's for the game. Come on by when you're done."

Trip waved good-bye to his brothers, then stepped up in front of Annie-Jean expectantly. "All right, Ms. Annie-Jean, what did you need me to lift?"

Annie-Jean smiled brightly as her gaze traveled between Emery and Trip. "Sorry, what did you ask?"

"You said you needed Trip to lift something, Annie. Where is it?" Emery said.

"Sorry," Annie-Jean replied, still grinning. "I must have been mistaken."

CHAPTER ELEVEN

Dead ringer

"I can't believe you didn't call me."

Emery sighed heavily. "He was there for all of five seconds. I couldn't just whip out my cell to call you. But do we really have to go in here?"

Kate had Emery by the arm, dragging her toward Rudy's like a kid to a dentist appointment. "Yes! They said they were going to watch a game, and Annie promised us drinks."

"That was hours ago. There's no way they're still here."

But by the looks of the bar as they entered, it was entirely possible they were there—along with every other person in town.

"I'm sure they didn't go straight here. They probably looked around the festival and then came here after, like us."

Just inside the bar, Emery tried to spy Trip. At the very least, maybe he wasn't there. But as she followed her friend toward the bar, she realized she wasn't so lucky.

Perched on three stools in front of one of the widescreens sat Nick, Alex, and Trip. Thankfully, their eyes were all locked on the game, so maybe she and Kate could slip in without—

"All right, just look natural," Kate said, taking a seat all of two bar stools away from the men.

"Could you be a little more subtle?" Emery whispered.

Kate eyed her innocently. "This *is* me being subtle."

Before Emery could argue with her friend, a man from behind the bar stepped up in front of them and pressed his elbows into the bar, leaning toward them. "What can I get you fine ladies?" He had a nice smile and clearly spent a lot of time in the gym, but he also had that I-screw-anything-that-walks vibe.

Kate grinned, and Emery thought she needed to get her friend a decent boyfriend before she hooked up with every guy in her path in search of the right one. "Corona with lime. Two," Kate said, motioning between herself and Emery.

"Coming up."

The bartender left, and Emery started to ask Kate how many drinks they had to have before they could leave, when she noticed Kate's attention had shifted to the Hamilton brothers. "Who's that?"

Craning her neck so she could see, Emery took in the pretty blonde standing beside Trip, her hand resting delicately on his arm, a flirty smile on her face. Then she leaned in closer to the bar, pushing her arms closer together and, in effect, exposing more of her cleavage.

A sharp pang of jealousy shot through Emery's chest, so intense she wasn't sure exactly what it was until she caught Kate's expression.

"Oh, Em."

"No, I'm not—"

"We talked about this. He's not an option."

Emery's gaze shifted back to the woman and Trip's grin back at her, and she thought she might break down right there. But then the bartender brought back their beers and returned to his leaning position directly in front of Emery. "I know you," he said.

"You do, huh?" she asked, telling herself she could flirt with someone else, too. She didn't need Trip. Taking a long pull of her beer and setting it back on the bar, she matched his lean.

"Yeah, I'm a big fan."

She smiled, but before she could reply, Trip stepped up beside her. "I'm sure you have something else you need to do. Right, Gage?"

Gage straightened, a hint of worry on his face as he took in Trip standing far too close to Emery. "Right." He smiled once more between Kate and Emery. "Y'all give me a yell if you need something else."

"I'll let you know if they need something."

Emery glared at Trip once Gage walked way. "What the hell was that?"

He shook his head. "What?"

"I don't need you running interference for me."

"Actually, with Gage you do. Unless STIs are your thing; then by all means, carry on."

"What's your problem?"

"Depends on the day, but right this moment it's you."

"Me?"

"Yes, you. Sitting over here with Gage. You think that's the way I want one of my jockeys behaving?"

Rage rocketed through Emery and she stood up, getting in Trip's face. "You don't get to stand over there flirting with Ms. Blonde and Perfect and then pass judgment on me for talking to someone."

He leaned into her, lowering his voice. "I wasn't flirting. Sam is an old friend and—"

"Right, I know just what kind of friend you mean. It's nice to know you haven't been lonely the last eight years."

Trip's eyes flashed with anger. "You don't know anything about what I've been through."

"*You've* been through? You—"

"I have been a half self. Breathing, but not living. Experiencing, but not caring. I have woken up every single day with one woman's face in my mind, only to know I couldn't do a thing about. Don't sit there and act like you know what's in my head. You don't know. You don't have the first damn clue."

Emery blinked, trying and failing to calm her breathing. "I . . ." She bit her lip, and Trip's gaze dropped, holding there like it took every bit of his willpower not to take over the job. She wanted to tell him that she'd missed him, that it had broken her in two when he left, that she was seventeen and yet that hurt had remained with her like it happened just yesterday. But they couldn't do this—be this. Whatever *this* was.

"Hey, Trip, I was just . . ."

Trip and Emery both looked over to see the blonde standing next to them. Her eyes shifted between them, and that was when Emery realized just how closely they stood together—their bodies nearly touching. She swallowed hard and took a step back, her gaze finding the floor. She didn't want to see Trip with this woman. With any woman.

"I'm sorry. I didn't mean to interrupt," she said.

Trip cleared his throat and sat back onto the bar stool behind him. "You didn't. Samantha Watson, this is Emery Carlisle."

Emery started to say hello when Samantha's mouth fell slack, and she stared for a long time before returning to Trip. "Emery, as in . . ."

"Yeah," Trip said, his tone hard, but below the surface lay something else. Something like hurt—but *he* left *her*. He didn't get to feel hurt. He left. She stayed and waited and longed for him to return, only to have him never call. Not even after the accident. Not once did he act as though she meant anything to him, so what was this? Some mind game to pull her back under only to run away again?

Frustrated, Emery turned back to ask Kate if they could leave, only to find the stool beside her empty. Dammit! She scanned the bar, hoping to spot her red-haired friend, and came up empty.

"It's really nice to meet you. I've heard a lot about you."

Emery's head snapped up. "Sorry, what did you say?"

Samantha offered a warm smile, and Emery felt guilty for thinking such horrible things about her earlier. It wasn't Samantha's fault that she was tall and blonde and too pretty to be real. "I said I've heard a lot about you." She looked to Trip, as though to make sure it was okay she said that, but he just tossed up his hands and called down for Gage.

"What's up, man?" Gage asked.

"My regular. Then whatever they want." Trip motioned to Emery and Samantha, like they were all friends, but nothing about the moment felt natural. Samantha clearly knew Trip, but how well? Were they friends or more? She wanted to ask but didn't want to come across as the jealous ex-girlfriend, especially when she'd never technically been his girlfriend. Her heart ached at the truth in her thoughts.

Gage flashed the women his best smile, which received a prompt glare from Trip. "What?"

"I'll have another Corona, please," Emery said, interrupting before Trip went all alpha on them again, and Samantha asked for the same. Silence fell over them, each second more awkward than the last. Then, unable to stand it another second, she faced Samantha. "So, how do you know Trip?"

Samantha stared at Trip, clearly at a loss for what to say, and Emery's stomach seeped into the floor. "Oh . . . right," Emery said. "I really should . . ." She glanced around the bar again. Where the hell was Kate?

Trip's cell rang then, saving them from continuing down this path of hell, and he peered down at it, then back at the ladies. "Sorry, I need to take this." He eyed Emery. "Are you okay?"

"I'm fine; go."

He nodded to her, then walked outside to take the call, and Emery considered making a quick exit herself, when Samantha took Trip's seat. "We never had what you had, if that's what you're wondering. I don't think he's ever had with anyone what he had with you."

Emery searched the bar for Kate again, cursing her for leaving Emery alone with this mess. Of all the conversations in the world, this had to make the top five most awkward.

"Yeah, well, we weren't . . . he didn't . . . it was a long time ago."

Samantha cocked her head. "I don't know." Her gaze traveled to the door, where Trip stood, his eyes locked on Emery. "It doesn't seem so long ago to me."

Emery tried to swallow and failed. What she wouldn't give for that to be true.

He reached them, then, his soapy scent hitting her full-on, mixing with the alcohol, making her want to take chances she shouldn't take. "Can I talk to you for a second?" he asked.

The bar buzzed with life now, packed from wall to wall, every seat filled. There was no place to go, and Triple Run liked gossip as much or more than Crestler's Key.

"I don't want to talk in here."

"Then come for a walk with me."

Emery glanced to the door. "But, my friend, Kate, she'll worry. She's—"

"She's fine. See?" Trip guided Emery's face to the left, where Kate sat with Nick and Alex, shouting at the widescreen right along with them. She couldn't help but smile. Kate had been raised with three brothers, all very athletic, so she'd grown up wearing cleats instead of ballet shoes and helmets instead of crowns. It felt nice to see her in her element.

"All right, then."

"Okay?" He stared down at her, his eyes full of warmth and memories, and she wanted to tell him she would go anywhere he asked, anytime. Just say when and show the way. But she couldn't afford to put herself out there like that. Not again.

"Lead the way."

* * *

The streets of Triple Run were quiet for the early evening, the shops all closing down around them, the air cool but not cold—just the way Trip liked it. He'd spent years working out what he'd say to Emery if he had her alone and the moment was right, and here it was. A clear night with a nearly full moon, empty sidewalks, and the quiet rustling of trees in the wind their only song. This was his opportunity to tell her everything—why he'd left, why he didn't call, why he wanted to and why he hated himself for not being brave. But nothing about the timing felt right.

Emery hadn't even ridden yet. She'd just started working for him, and she hoped to re-launch her career under his name. How could he complicate all that by telling her he'd never once forgotten her?

He couldn't, so instead he went with the truth. "I like having you here, but at the same time, it's . . ." He trailed off, shaking his head.

"It's hard."

"Yes. I had no right to step in when you were talking to Gage, and I'm sorry for that. But I wasn't wrong—he's the last guy in town you should date."

Emery grinned over at him. "Then who should I date in town?"

He smirked back. "No one. Of course."

She laughed, swatting his arm, and without thinking, he took her hand, threaded his fingers with hers. They fell into silence as they walked, a thousand words in the air that refused to settle into logical thought. He shouldn't be here with her, yet he couldn't stay away, and the thought of her with someone else, especially someone in town, made him want to break something—or fall apart. He'd spent so much time trying to forget her that he'd never stopped to realize that maybe you never forgot your first love. Maybe that person stayed with you for the rest of your life.

"You said you wanted to talk," Emery said as they reached the bridge overlooking the Cherokee River. "What do you want to talk about?" She turned to face him, leaning up against the bridge's railing, and hell if he didn't want to take her right there—scoop her into his arms and say screw everything else. Just let them be together and he'd figure out the rest. But he knew that wasn't reality, not for him and not for her.

He took a small step toward her and lifted her hand, running his thumb slowly over her palm, careful to trace each line. "I don't want to talk. There are a lot of things I want to do with you, but talking isn't one of them."

She smiled a little at the compliment and tilted her head up so she could look into his eyes. "Yet something tells me you need to talk to me."

He nodded. "I do, but I don't know what to say, so how about for tonight I just walk you to your car and say good night? The rest can wait."

"Wait for what?"

Trip ran his hands down her arms. "For it to make sense. Right now, this, us . . . it's . . ."

"Complicated."

He stared at her, allowing himself to get lost in those big blue eyes that had taken him under their spell all those years ago. "Yes."

They stopped beside her Jeep, Kate outside the bar, watching them. She lifted her hand to wave her friend over, and then gave Trip one last look. "Good night, Trip."

Shutting her Jeep's door, he backed away and tucked his hands into his jeans. "Good night, Emery," he whispered.

CHAPTER TWELVE

Head start

Emery slumped down in her chair, ignoring the sidelong look from her best friend. "What?"

"You tell me what," Kate said. "We have fresh lemon poppy seed muffins with lemon glaze in front of us, yet you've got a frown on your face. How can you frown at these muffins?" She took a bite of hers. "Yum. I swear, if you don't start eating yours soon, I'm going to eat it for you."

Emery slid her plate across the table toward Kate. "Have it."

"Em. Seriously. What's the matter?"

"It's been two weeks." Two weeks since their walk out by the Cherokee River. Two weeks of thinking about his eyes and his hair and the way his voice sounded when it dipped down, the words spoken just for her.

Two whole weeks with no hint of more from Trip and, to add salt to the wound, she was no closer to riding Craving Wind.

"What's holding you back?" Kate asked.

"With which problem?"

Kate's brows went up. "Right. Well, let's tackle one at a time. Easiest first. Why can't you ride? Are you afraid?"

Emery stared around the bakery, watched old Mrs. Gertie wringing her arthritis-ridden hands together, like somehow the bakery held the answer. The same light blue floral wallpaper covered the walls that had been there when Emery was little. The same tables and chairs. The same people there every morning like clockwork. But Gertie had gotten too old to keep up with business. What she needed was a partner.

Someone who understood baked goods, but who was energetic and could bring some life back into Crestler's Key's favorite breakfast spot.

And she knew just the person.

"I don't think I'm afraid to ride anymore. At least not fully afraid. I'm afraid to disappoint Trip. I can tell he's expecting something major, my old times. It's intimidating." Emery eyed Mrs. Gertie again. "But sometimes you gotta ask for help if you want to get back to what you love. By the way, what happened with Alex?"

Kate frowned. "Nothing. Absolutely nothing. We watched the game, he patted me on the back, and said 'bye. Like I was one of the guys." Her expression darkened. "Why do I always end up being one of the guys? I mean, they act like they want a girl who's into sports, but then they date girls who wear nothing for clothes and talk in text language, like that's how people actually speak. It's ridiculous. And sad . . ."

"Aw, K, it's just about finding the right guy."

Just then, Matthew Bridges came in, small glasses in place as he glanced down at the paper in his hand. Emery kicked Kate from under the table.

"Hey! What was that for—?"

"Kate?"

Kate's neck could have broken off for how fast she whipped around. "Matt. Hey. What are you doing here?"

Matt Bridges, aka Kate's high school love, though they'd never even been on a date. They'd been in to each other since high school, but Matt was Kate's oldest brother Charlie's best friend, so neither would act on their feelings. There seemed to be a lot of holding back going on in Crestler's Key. But it was time for a change.

"Here," Emery said, pushing out from the table. "Take my seat. The place is buzzing this morning, and I've got somewhere I need to be."

Kate's eyes went saucer wide, but Emery just shook her head and mouthed, *You're fine.* And then she set out to force another person in her life to stop holding back. Others first, then she'd work on herself.

Emery pulled down Annie's long gravel drive and closed the door to find her mama's car parked in front of the house. With trepidation, Emery went up the steps, knowing she couldn't just leave without them noticing. She went through the screen door, letting it hit loudly as she entered.

"Hello?"

"Back here!" Annie called from the kitchen. Like always.

But when she circled into the expansive room, she caught her mama dabbing her eyes with a tissue and peered over at Annie with concern.

"Is everything okay?"

Her mother then went on to wipe the tissue over her neck, unbuttoning the top button of her blouse and patting her chest. "Yes, child. Haven't you ever seen a person burn from the inside out?"

Here we go.

"This blasted menopause is going to kill me. Kill me. I can't even—" Then she burst into tears.

Annie and Emery went for her at the same time, but she'd crossed over to the crazy side. There was no coming back. And asking if she was okay always resulted in a sharp look. Then, if they said nothing at all, they didn't care. There was no winning in the battle of menopause.

"It's fine. I'm fine. I need to get back to the farm."

Emery wanted to call Daddy and warn him that the storm was coming, but then she risked him asking where she'd been. Again. And her excuses got lamer and lamer with each question.

A part of her thought Daddy would understand. He shared her passion for racing, and he would never have given up if he'd been in her shoes. And Daddy liked Trip, respected him and spoke of him fondly. But now she'd lied to him numerous times. How could she admit to working with Trip, the boy he trained, over him?

She couldn't.

Grace Carlisle left after another long cry, and that was when Emery noticed the kitchen. Or, more appropriately, the demolition site. Flour covered everything visible, including Annie-Jean, who looked as though she'd entered a paintball fight, but instead of paint for ammo they'd used flour balls and . . . chocolate chips? "Annie, what happened in here?"

She tossed her hands. "If Patty thinks she's got the patent on Bundt cakes, well, she can think again. I can make one, too. And better than hers!"

Emery's eyebrows lifted as she motioned around the kitchen. "All of this. For just one cake?"

Annie shot her a look that said she'd better watch her mouth or Annie would find a switch out back. Emery grimaced at the memories of Granny switching her legs when she was little. "A cake!" she corrected, faking a giant smile. "That's so great. How did it taste?"

Annie's face fell. "I'm a failure. I spent all night baking and only have one worth eating."

Emery started cleaning up the kitchen. "No, you're not. You just need more space, and I know just the place." Then she went into everything about Gertie, Annie's face unreadable throughout her spiel. She continued pitching the idea until the kitchen sparkled, and then faced her aunt. "So what do you think?"

Annie wiped up the last of the flour and dusted her hands on her apron. "I think I'm going to buy Gertie's bakery."

Emery squealed with excitement. "I thought work there, but yes, buy it!"

Annie grinned as she rushed for her keys. "I'm going to do it."

"Woah, wait, where are you going?"

"To Gertie's. Come on, Em, keep up."

"Um, Annie." Emery scanned her aunt's face, apron, even her fluffy socks were coated in flour and yuck. "You might want to shower first."

Annie laughed. "Right. Shower."

The track buzzed with life even at six thirty in the morning. Such was the way at Santa Anita track. Normally, Trip would have one of his assistant trainers manage the morning workout for their horses, but on race days, he liked to have a hand on each of them. Make sure there were no avoidable surprises. But while all those things were the truth, today he needed a distraction. It had been more than two weeks since he'd walked hand in hand with Emery, since he'd agreed to hire her, and still he hadn't seen her race. Hadn't even seen her on a horse. And while it wasn't unusual to introduce a jockey and horse on race day, this was different. Emery hadn't ridden since her accident. His emotions aside, this was a problem. A huge fucking problem.

His thoughts drifted to the meeting with his family the day before, how easily the lie had rolled off his tongue when his father asked about her times. Trip knew he had to get Emery back in the saddle, and fast. He just wasn't sure how.

The first wave of horses hit the track, and Trip leaned against a nearby rail, watching, analyzing. And then his gaze lifted to the riders on their backs. Exercise riders. He realized then that he'd rarely paid them any attention. He talked to the ones on his staff, but beyond that, the riders weren't important. The horses were important. Which was exactly what Emery needed. An idea took shape in his mind. What if Emery could ride without expectation, without anyone paying attention to her form? She'd already told Beckett that she was an exercise rider. So why not make her one?

He knew part of her fear lay in the memory of being trampled, the pain of her bones crushing, but another part—maybe even a larger part—was afraid she wouldn't be the same rider. Winning the Kentucky Oaks two years in a row was no easy feat. In a short time, she'd had others standing up and paying attention. Which was why everyone who was anyone knew about her injury. The weight of expectation must be killing her. If he took that weight away, then maybe, just maybe, she would ride again.

He crossed his arms and watched the horses he'd trained circle the track, his mind on Emery and how similar she was to the colt she so desperately wanted to ride. And just like that colt, Emery was destined for great things. She just needed a little confidence boost, and if Trip's plan worked, she'd get a lot more than a little boost. Of course, convincing her could be the greatest challenge of all.

Trip pulled his cell from his pocket and surfed through until he found Emery's new number, then stared at it for a good ten seconds before deciding to stop being a damn coward and just call her. The phone rang twice, three times, then, "Hello?"

"Emery? It's Trip."

He heard a car door close on the other end. "Yeah, I kind of figured by the name on my caller ID."

He grinned. Damn, was she ever feisty. "Are you always this coiled up, or do I bring out the best in you?"

He was rewarded with a laugh, and for a moment he couldn't speak, lost in the soft sound. Clearing his throat, he pressed on. "Can you come by tomorrow morning? I have an idea that I want to run past you."

She went silent again, and Trip wondered how many hearts she'd broken over the years by that silence. How many men between the Emery he left and the Emery of today? Desperate men eager to hear that rich voice and instead were met with a void. Had any of them made an impression? Was she dating someone now? He hadn't thought to even ask. Then he cursed himself, because what right did he have to ask?

"Um, sure. What time?"

"Sorry what?" he asked, then, realizing what she'd said, added, "Is five too early?"

"No . . ."

"I'd say tonight, but I'm out of town."

Her breath hitched. "Out of town? Where?"

"I'm in California at the Santa Anita."

He could almost hear the excitement work its way through her. "There's a race tonight?"

"Yes. You should have come."

"With you?"

Trip turned away and walked down the path before him, unsure where he was going both in his walk and the conversation. "With me."

"Trip, this is getting—"

"Five it is, then. Be there, okay?"

She released a slow breath that slid through Trip's chest, soaking his heart in the sound. God, he was in trouble. "See you at five."

Trip tapped his phone on his thigh, then turned around only to find an attractive woman and a photographer behind him. It wasn't unusual for the press to show on race days to get photos of the workouts, but Trip wasn't in the mood for an interview. Nor was he comfortable with someone following him around.

"Hello, Mr. Hamilton. I'm Nancy Blake with *Racing Today*. I wondered if I could get a shot for an article I'm working on about the Santa Anita?"

Trip was running behind, and he didn't like how close they were to him while he was having a private phone conversation. But angering the press was never a good idea. "Sure, just the photo, please," Trip said.

The photographer motioned for Trip to move so the track ran in the background, then began snapping photos. It didn't occur to Trip until a second or two had passed that the woman—the journalist— was jotting down notes. He hadn't said anything, so what could she possibly be writing?

"Mr. Hamilton, I couldn't help overhearing you on the phone before. I could have sworn you said the name Emery. As in Emery Carlisle?"

Trip's back went rigid, his eyebrows drawing together. "I think that will do," he said to her and the photographer.

"Is she working with you?" the journalist pressed. "Is she riding in the Kentucky Oaks this year? The conversation sounded intimate. Are you two together now?"

Trip walked away, the journalist still shouting out questions, but there was only one word on Trip's mind—screwed. He needed to warn Emery before the article about the Santa Anita suddenly became an article about her.

CHAPTER THIRTEEN

Leg up

"**O**kay, you have me here," Emery said as she walked into the stable. "What are you planning to do with me?"

Trip's lips twitched, a smile fighting to break free. "There's a lot of things I'd like to do with you. *To you*, if we're being specific. But this isn't really about me."

She smiled, instead of giving it to Trip like she wanted—like she should. Of course, even that would have been for show. Because while she hated men who thought they could sexy talk their way into your pants, she couldn't deny that she liked it when it came from Trip and those delicious lips of his. Her anger became flattery. And her grimace all too often became a grin. Damn him for making her fall for him all over again.

They'd kept their interactions to cute banter and mild flirtation, nothing more, but she could feel it building inside her, a voice telling her to take it further. There was no denying she wanted him, but this was six shades complicated with a deformed cherry on top.

She thought of his days at their farm all those years ago, watching her daddy with such awe and intensity. While she watched him with the same look of awe. Back then, the three years between them meant he looked more man than boy. His shoulders strong. His voice deep. His hands callused. Only when he laughed did she remember that while he wasn't a teenager, like her, he was still young. Both in mind and body.

Now, everything was different. They were both adults. It should be easy, but their situation couldn't be further from easy.

Her gaze met Trip's. The same amazing eyes, but where they once held a world of hope, now they held wisdom. That boy she once knew wasn't the same man standing in front of her. Success had changed him. She just didn't know yet if it was for the good or the bad.

Mama V came rushing into the stable, two cups of coffee in hand. "Hey, darlin'," she said, passing a cup to Emery and once again kissing her cheek. "Thought you could use some liquid strength today."

Emery glanced, confused, at Mama V. "What do you mean?"

"The riding thing. Trip said you were riding today." Emery started to argue as Mama V gripped her hand. "I want you to know how proud I am of you. Getting back on a mount. That isn't easy stuff. No matter how you do today, be proud."

Emery couldn't respond. All she could do was stare daggers at Trip, who seemed suddenly very interested in the notebook in his hand. She waited for Mama V to leave, and then stormed over and pushed him in the chest with her finger.

"So not only have you talked about me to everyone here, but you decided today, without even telling me, that I'm riding?"

Trip set down the notebook and turned slowly. "Look, I get how you work. I get that you walk the line between sweet lady and raging warrior every day, and that I've got you deep into rage territory right now." Emery's face went scarlet, her eyes on fire, but he held up a hand to cut her off. "But we both know you aren't going to ride until I force you to. And I'm sorry, but I'm not your daddy. You are a contract employee here, which means you work for me."

Emery's entire body shook with anger. She put her hands on her hips and took a step back, huffing, unsure of what to say next. She wanted to tell him he could shove the job up his perfect ass. She quit. But then she saw Craving Wind stick his head out of his stall, and all the hot air sucked right out of her.

Taking slow steps, she made her way to the horse and gently stroked his mane and neck, letting his strength be her strength. She closed her eyes and drew a breath, the scents of hay and horse and stable all around her. She could almost picture them inside the starting gate, Craving Wind ready to earn his name.

The gates open and they break free, gaining early momentum. Then they soar around the first turn and it's neck and neck, but Craving Wind's stamina wins out, and he pulls ahead, one length, two, and then they're across the finish line, the crowd roaring in the grand-

stand. The winner's circle. The feel of collective celebration from
every person who worked to get them there. Because it isn't just the
trainer or the owner or even the jockey. It's a stable's worth of people,
all dedicated, all full of pride at the win.

Her heart sped up as she opened her eyes and stared into the
colt's. "What do you want me to do?" Emery said, her voice low.
"Tell me what to do, boy."

Trip walked up and covered her hand with his, urging her to look
up. "I don't want to force you to do anything. But it's time, Em. It's
just you and me, and I need you to trust me. Trust that I know you,
and I know you're ready. But see, the thing is, maybe you don't know
yet, so I had an idea. I think part of the fear is in expectation. You
know your old times, you know what you want to do now. Let's take
that away for a moment. Maybe to begin, you could help with the
morning workouts, just like you told Beckett. You don't even need to
ride Craving Wind. We'll put you on Blank Space or another filly.
Start there. Just exercise 'em. No times. No worries. Just ride."

Emery let the idea settle over her. No times or pressure. No making sure she connected with Craving Wind, like she wanted to. She
knew other jockeys considered her way of racing a joke. Talking to
her horses, riding them well in advance, getting to know them as
friends. This wasn't how it was done. But their opinions didn't matter, and it was never about them anyway. Her daddy had trained some
of the best racehorses in the last thirty years, and then he retired from
training and became a successful breeder—and owner—of many of
the top champions over the last ten years. He'd hired Mr. Sampson to
train, and so it became very easy for Emery to grow attached to the
horses she rode. They were right there.

She knew this was part of the reason she'd been so hesitant to ride
for Trip—there wouldn't be that familiarity or comfort. She could
ride the horse, but it wasn't the same as seeing that horse all the time.
Still, she did know Craving Wind, felt the same connection she'd felt
with Firecrest. This was her horse, her champion.

She peered back up at Trip. "Just ride?"

"Just a little exercise. Nothing more. Clark has Blank Space at the
track. The cart's just outside."

For the first time in forever, a thrilling feeling coursed through
Emery, igniting her insides, waking her up. "All right. Let's ride."

They slipped into the golf cart and started on, the morning air chilly as it swept past them. Her left leg jumped continuously, unwilling to relax. And just when she decided to cross her right leg over it in hopes of settling it down, Trip reached out and lightly squeezed her thigh, and suddenly her spazzy left leg went still. She glanced down at his hand, then at him.

"It's okay. You know that, right? I'm not going to let anything happen to you here."

Emery drew a short breath, unable to handle the kindness in his voice. The intimacy. There was something happening between them, but she knew it had to stop now. She had to focus, and there was no focusing to be had around Trip if she allowed herself to do the things she wanted to do. Feel the things she wanted to feel.

"Trip, we should talk," she said, but then they were at the track, the sun still hidden away, trees cradling them in, warming the moment. She peered over, and he pressed his finger gently to her lips.

"I know. I know everything you're going to say. But you're overthinking it. Someone's gotta be there for you, lady girl. Might as well be me."

Their gazes held, and she thought how much better she liked his face worn, like it was now, age making him so much more than simply attractive or hot. He was unbelievably sexy. From those chocolate eyes to his wavy hair to the way he knew she needed him. Just like the first time she'd lost, when she was sure she'd win. He taught her so much back then, and she felt sure if she let him, he could teach her even more now.

"Okay."

"Okay?"

"Fine, but you're not allowed to stare at my ass when Clark gives me a leg up on the mount."

He grinned. "I make no promises."

Trip parked them close to the track, and together they walked down to meet Clark and the exercise boy from a few weeks ago. They both said hello to Emery as she fastened on her helmet, but she barely listened. Her heartbeat was the only thing she could hear, pounding away in her ears as she neared the roan filly.

She lifted her hand and ran it down the horse's mane, patting her easily on the neck. "So you're Blank Space? You're a beautiful thing," she said. "Now, I'm going to take you around a few times. Think you can be good for me?" She patted the horse again and peered over to see all three of them watching her.

"Stop staring already and help me up," she ordered, causing Trip to laugh.

Clark started over, but Trip held him back. "Let me."

Emery gently pulled down her stirrup, so as not to agitate the filly, then grabbed the left rein and pulled it around the back of the saddle, made a half cross, and took a lock of mane. With her right hand on the pommel, she peered back at Trip, his chest too close, his soapy scent overwhelming.

"You've got this," he said, giving her a leg up.

She held her breath as she settled into the saddle and then released it slowly, relief washing over her. It was like breathing after being underwater for too long. Like drinking after a forgetful afternoon in the sun. *Like coming home.* Tears welled in her eyes, every emotion bubbling to the surface.

"You all right?" Trip called.

She drew another breath, staring out at the track, then peered down. "It's . . ." She swallowed before her emotions overcame her. "I'm perfect."

He stared back at her and patted Blank Space. "Yeah, you are. All right, then. Give her a go."

Emery trotted to the center of the dirt. "Hear that, girl," she said. "He likes me." She smiled once more and then, pushing away her fear, she started down the track, building from trot to canter to gallop, getting out of the way of the horse, letting her be the magnificent animal she was born to be. Adrenaline burst through her, excitement and happiness, a thousand moments rushing back with each whip of wind past her. Memories poured in of her first time on a track, in a race, her first win—all the reasons why she loved this sport. Why she risked her life again and again. Why she refused to eat chocolate or anything with the word *cream*. The speed. The unbelievable magic of the Thoroughbred horse. She loved racing, and like the horse below her, she was born for this.

Her time had come.

CHAPTER FOURTEEN

Across the board

Trip pushed through the door to town hall, eager to get his meeting with Mayor Phillips started so it could hurry up and end. The town hall building was all classic brick on the outside and hardwood floors and tan walls on the inside. He wasn't sure if they'd ever redecorated since it was built thirty years ago, but Trip liked it all the same.

He inhaled once, and then pressed on, trying to prepare himself for whatever came at him. Mayor Phillips liked to talk like the rest of the world liked to breathe, and Trip wasn't in the mood to answer the questions he was sure were coming. He'd managed to avoid most of the town the last few weeks, with various trips to the races and sales. Add in his work at the stables, and he'd rarely been in town at all. But he knew the time would come when he would have to explain why Emery Carlisle hung around so much—he just didn't know how he would answer.

On the outside, it was simple—Emery worked for him. She came by the barn to ride. Forget that none of his other jockeys came to his farm. Forget that he hadn't so much as spoken to half of his jockeys in the last month. Still, she'd contracted to ride for him, so she could be there. It made sense.

What didn't make sense was his complete inability to get her out of his mind. Or that he let her ride any horse she liked now and had for weeks, except the one she was supposed to ride. He'd lied to his father in the last three meetings, all to protect Emery, who either didn't understand the shitty spot she put him in or didn't care. On top of all that, Trip was dying to see her on Craving Wind, whose times were already so much faster than every other colt he had. Trip knew a champion when he saw one, and from Craving Wind's near perfect conformation to his stamina and speed, this horse was destined to be the next Derby winner; hell, maybe even the Triple Crown. He was built so similarly to Secretariat that it could happen. Trip could see it happening.

With the right jockey.

And there wasn't a trainer alive who would put Emery on Craving Wind in an important race. Trip thought the horse was ready for a maiden race to see how he performed with other horses fighting it out alongside him. But he knew Emery wanted to be the one to ride him, and every time he tried to get her on the mount, she shut down. Well, he was done waiting.

"Trip, come on in," Mayor Phillips said, waving from just inside his office. He ran a sunspot-ridden hand over his face and peered around. "You'll have to excuse the little mess."

He stepped into the mayor's office and thought the word *mess* was as much an understatement as saying a tornado was a little wind. In fact, it looked like a tornado had overtaken the large space. Papers were scattered everywhere. Two small trash cans sat sideways, their contents strewn across the floor. "What happened in here?"

Mayor Phillips lifted his hat and ran his hand over his nearly bald head, then returned the hat to its resting place. "A little misunderstanding." He was using the word "*little*" far too often for the misunderstanding to be anything but little.

"It doesn't look *little*, Mayor. Is there something I can help you with?"

"Oh, no, just a little misplaced document."

Suddenly the mess became clearer. "Misplaced document?"

"You know, a zoning thing. Jefferson Place is claiming that Triple Run's historic cemetery is in their town limits, not ours. They want to tear it down."

"But surely there are state documents that prove otherwise. Something that shows the dividing line?"

Mayor Phillips's face turned red then, hints of sweat on his brow. "There are indeed. But then the area was rezoned to Jefferson Place, and Jefferson Place's mayor, Frankie Carter, and I signed an agreement to keep the zoning the way it had always been. But I cannot find the blasted document."

Trip nodded slowly, wondering why he'd even asked. As a member of the board of trustees, he had an obligation to attend the monthly meetings, but since Mrs. Phillips had passed away a year ago and the mayor had refused to come out of his bedroom for a month, Trip had taken on the job of checking in to make sure nothing was missed— like a zoning agreement signed by two old men who likely had no idea what they were signing.

"Have you called Frankie to ask if he has a copy or if he's willing to sign a new agreement?"

"Of course, but he claims the document never existed!" The mayor threw his hands in the air, then held them, thought for a moment, and went to the filing cabinet against the left-hand wall. He opened the bottom drawer and proceeded to pull out all the files, only to huff loudly and return to his desk. "Not there. See, this is all over that Scrabble match two weeks ago. He lost and now he's punishing me."

Trip walked over to the desk and began stacking papers. "I can call him, if you'd like." He knew Frankie to be a difficult man, but this went beyond simply being difficult and straight into asshole territory. Mayor Phillips didn't have a mean bone in his body, so Trip knew he wouldn't stand up to Frankie like he should.

"No, no. I'll find the agreement, and then I'll make flyers of it and post it all over Jefferson Place's town square. That'll show him."

So much for no mean bone. Trip shook his head, knowing there was no arguing with the man. "Right . . . that'll show him. Well, let me help you track it down."

They spent the next hour searching every inch of the office, and before long, Trip wondered if maybe Frankie was right and there'd never been an agreement.

"So, Trip," Mayor Phillips said from his desk chair. Come to think of it, he'd spent most of that hour sitting and directing Trip on places to look. "Are you going to open up about that little secret you're hiding at the barn?"

"And what secret would that be?" Trip asked as he glanced out the open office door to find several office workers near the doorway, listening in.

"Emery Carlisle."

Trip's stomach clenched at the name, warmth spreading through him. "What about her?"

"We've noticed her in town from time to time. She refused to go into Patty's and instead bought cobbler from the cafe. No one eats the cobbler at the cafe."

"So let me get this straight—she didn't buy a Bundt cake from Patty and now she's on the town's blacklist?"

"Now, now, we wouldn't *black*-list her. But it would sure help if we knew why she was here . . . and if she'd be hanging around a while. Some are saying you two are . . . close."

"We're as close as the moon over an ocean."

Mayor Phillips leaned back into his chair. "Yet the moon affects the tides, and something tells me Emery Carlisle's had an effect on you, son."

Trip's hands paused while sorting the papers. The mayor was right—she'd definitely had an effect on him. It was the past repeating itself all over again. He just didn't know how to stop it. Maybe less time around her, though the thought of her leaving made him feel sick to the core. He wanted more time around her, wanted to hear that laugh of hers, that sass that put him in his place like no one else dared. He realized that he craved her attention like an addict craved his next fix. It was a sick, sick problem. And the more he thought about it, the angrier he became.

"All right, I think we're done here. I'll see you in a few days," Trip said, starting for the door.

Mayor Phillips stood then, removed his glasses, and set them down on his desk. "Nothing wrong with feeling something, Trip. Some people go their whole lives without feeling. I'd hate to see that for you. I might have lost myself for a while after Elizabeth passed, but I don't regret a second of loving her. Those were the best days of my life."

Trip sighed, wishing it were easier. "I'll keep that in mind. Thanks, Mayor. See you next time."

The sky had darkened outside by the time Trip left town hall, clouds moving in, threatening to storm. Thoughts worked through Trip's mind in harsh bursts, all the reasons he wanted Emery—and all the reasons he wasn't allowed to have her. He thought of the women he'd dated, how not one held a bit of the spark he'd felt with Emery. How not one made him want ridiculous things like *forever*.

None of this was fair. Mr. Sampson ordering him to leave all those years ago. Her coming back now, making him want her all the more. Lying to Beckett. Lying to his father. All for what? She wouldn't even ride the damn horse!

He threw his truck into park outside the stables and slammed the door, heat radiating off him in waves. And that's when he saw Emery's Jeep, parked there like she could come and go whenever she liked. Like this was her barn, not his. Rage shot straight from his heart to his head, and he stormed inside, spotting her outside Craving Wind's stall, petting the horse and whispering kind words. Then her head swung his way, those large blue eyes pinning him to the spot, and for a moment, all he could do was stare.

"Hey, stranger," she said, smiling wide. "I was hoping to find you here. I—"

"Clark!"

Emery jumped at the harshness in Trip's voice, and instantly he wanted to apologize, but he pushed that away. He was a trainer, and he was damn good at his job. He didn't do emotions and weakness. He didn't fall for jockeys and employees. He didn't *do* any of this! They were done, a thing of the past. Why couldn't he keep her there?

Just then Trip's assistant trainer made his way toward them, his gaze shifting nervously between them. "You called?"

Several other stable hands came around to see what the commotion was about, which did nothing more than frustrate Trip further. He didn't want an audience, and he knew that was the last thing Emery needed, but enough with the delays. "Bring Craving Wind to the track. Emery's running him."

"Now?" Clark asked, looking over to Emery. "Are you sure?"

Trip whipped around. "She doesn't need to be sure. I'm sure. Bring him down. Now." Then he stormed from the stable, jumping in the cart and taking off before anyone could say another word. Anger pulsed in his chest, this time at himself. What the hell was he doing? He told himself he did his job, but he knew that wasn't the truth. He punished Emery for things that were in no way her fault. His feelings were just that, his. Complicated and stupid and stubborn to the bone.

By the time he circled around to check with Alex on a few broodmares scheduled to foal any day and then made it to the track, Clark and Emery were already there, Craving Wind saddled and ready to run.

The darkening sky went from navy to black, clouds moving so

fast the rain could start any second, but the weather wasn't calling for rain, so Trip hoped the clouds would pass by without a threat.

Emery fixed her helmet into place, refusing to look at Trip, and his heart sank into his stomach. He was an asshole. A jerk-filled, piece of shit asshole. But while his reason for doing this didn't fully make sense to him, a part of him knew he needed to push Emery more than he had.

She gripped the reins, and Trip went over to give her a leg up, but she pushed him back. "No. I don't want your help." The bite in her words made Trip want to punch himself in the face.

"Look, I didn't mean—"

"Clark, can you help me, please?" she asked, focusing on the assistant trainer.

Uneasy, Clark glanced from Trip to Emery. Poor man; he had no idea what he was in the middle of here. "Um, sure."

He gripped her left leg and helped her up, and Lord if Trip didn't feel a stab of jealousy that he wasn't the one touching her, helping her. He hated himself more and more each second, but there was no undoing this. He knew Emery too well. She would ride Craving Wind now if for no other reason than to spite Trip, and maybe that was a good thing. If she never spoke to him again, at least it would be worth something.

She nodded thanks to Clark, then trotted away, her expression unreadable, but he could see the fear in her eyes, the tension in her back. The horse would sense it, too.

"Emery?" Trip said, but then she was off, bringing the horse to canter, letting his muscles warm up; then they ran at full gallop, and suddenly the pounding in Trip's heart had nothing to do with guilt. They sped around the track, less running and more flying. The horse had speed and stamina unlike any horse Trip had ever seen. His mouth fell slack and he waved Clark over. "Are you timing this?"

"One step ahead of you, boss," Clark said, his eyes fixed on a stopwatch in his hand as Emery came back around to them and started a second set.

They continued to watch in amazement as Craving Wind showed off, barely appearing to work at all. He ran like he was born to run— and damn if he wasn't doing it well.

Emery finally slowed him down in front of them, the smile on her face so bright that Trip had to fight to keep from taking her off the horse and straight into his arms.

"Did you see that?" she squealed, slightly out of breath.

Clark held out the stopwatch to Trip, and he slowly walked over to her, knowing somewhere in that smile lay a woman ready to go off on him. "See for yourself, lady girl."

Emery's eyes fixed on the watch and then she burst out laughing, her excitement bubbling over, water in her eyes "Is that for real?" she asked, her gaze on Clark. She might be excited, but she wasn't forgiving him for the episode back at the stables.

Trip started to say he was sorry, but then the sky opened up, pouring down on him, and he called for Clark to get Craving Wind to a small stable they kept near the practice track.

"Come with me!" he shouted to Emery over the rain, and he could see she wanted to argue. "Look, I get that you're pissed, but you can continue being pissed once we're dry and inside. All right?"

Rain dripped down her face as she took him in. "Fine. But you should know I don't like you right now."

A smile tugged at his lips. "Duly noted."

CHAPTER FIFTEEN

Neck and neck

The cold air, coupled with soaked clothes, had Emery shaking down to her bones, but she still couldn't pull the smile from her face. She'd been riding for Trip for weeks now, running fillies and colts, allowing herself to remember why she loved riding. But she had purposefully avoided Craving Wind, knowing that ride would mean so much more than the others. Trip would form his opinion of her as a rider by that one run, and she wanted to be more than impressive. She wanted to meet his challenge and prove she was the best jockey, woman or man, to ride Craving Wind.

She'd proven that today.

The excitement was almost enough to make her forgive Trip for his attitude, for bossing her around and making her feel like a child. But something else was going on in Trip's head. She could see it, and nothing angered her more than receiving someone else's beating. She started to ask him who'd stolen his Halloween candy when she noticed he'd driven past the main barn, cutting around the training building and heading deeper into the woods.

"Where are you going?" Emery shouted over the rain.

He shot her a look that said it should be obvious, but Emery had never been to this side of the farm.

"Trip, where are we going?" she repeated, just as he turned down a right-hand road, not slowing down despite the warning rumble of thunder overhead. Then, when she'd officially decided he was the most infuriating man she'd ever met in her life, he pulled into a short driveway that led to a ranch house with a three-car garage. She had only enough time to think the garage was as large as the house itself, and how very Triplike that was, when he hit a button on the cart and the garage door closest to the house surged open.

He pulled inside the garage, and then before she could open her mouth, he spun on her. "You're drenched and the storm's only getting worse. You can't drive home in this. Come in and change. Stay until the storm clears. You can scream at me the entire time if that makes you feel better." He flashed a grin that would normally have her smiling back, but she was still too angry at him to play nice.

A crack of lightning struck behind them, causing Emery to jump, and Trip reached out for her arm, only for her to jerk back. "Don't."

He released a slow breath. "Look, I know—"

She got out of the cart and started for the closest door without asking him if it were the door into the house. She needed distance from him, so even a closet would do. "No, you don't know. You don't know anything."

Emery jerked open the door and stepped inside, realizing a little too late that she was still dripping wet, and immediately slipped on the tile in his utility room. Trip caught her by the arm, steadying her, and she thought about how safe she'd once felt in those arms. How badly she wanted to feel them around her now. How she couldn't think of anything else. And then how horrible she'd felt when he'd gone off on her at the stable, right in front of Clark and the rest of the staff.

She pushed away from him and continued on into the house, without stopping to take off her boots. So there!

Trip flipped on a light in a small hallway, and then in the great room, giving Emery a chance to peer around. The house had all the look and feel of a lodge. A large trophy elk stuck out from above the fireplace mantel. The walls were all a warm tan, the floors dark hardwood, and the stone in the fireplace deep grays and browns. The only pictures in the room were a few on the mantel, all of champion horses, likely all trained by him. Her gaze dropped down to a massive bearskin rug and—crap! She cringed at the mud on her boots, now caked into the rug.

"Oh! I'm . . ." She stepped off the rug and kicked off her boots, but it was no use. The black rug now had Emery-sized mud and grass boot prints across it. "Shoot." She huffed loudly, aggravated that she even cared, given how he'd treated her, but she knew how much these things cost, and if Trip had shot the bear himself, it wasn't just the expense. The trophy was irreplaceable, and she'd ruined it.

Her gaze lifted to Trip, and he shook his head, his hands on his hips. She couldn't tell if he was about to go off on her again or laugh.

Instead, he took a step toward her, words pouring out quickly. "Look, I'm sorry about earlier. I had no right to talk to you that way. But you are driving me crazy!" He threw his hands into the air. "The memories were enough to kill me, and then you walk into my world, flinging everything off balance."

"Hey! I'm not the one—"

Another step. "You boss everyone around and give opinions way before you're asked."

"Wait, now, I didn't—"

Still closer. "And you walk into my house like you own the place."

"You were the one who—"

He was to her now, a foot away, a breath. "Then, when I think I know what to expect from you, you're on the verge of tears for ruining a rug I could give two shits about." He lifted her chin and pushed her hair from her face. "I feel like I'm losing my mind every time I'm around you, and yet . . . I can't get enough."

Emery was too shocked to respond, and then his hands were on her hips, his eyes dipping down to hers, and suddenly there were no words. Only action.

His lips crushed into hers, stealing away her worry and doubt, erasing each fear with his warm touch. She leaned into the kiss, gripping his shirt, securing him to her, and parted her mouth, inviting him in. Trip released a soft groan, and the kiss intensified, heat spreading from her chest out, coating her in it like a blanket, sparking each nerve from her head to her toes. All these weeks, all the tension, built up to this moment, this kiss, and Trip wasn't the only one who couldn't get enough.

Her fingers threaded into his hair and then he lifted her up, wrapping her legs around his waist and walking over to the sofa. He sat down and fixed her to him, her straddling his waist, their lips never separating. She left his mouth to explore his neck, his ear, tasting each bit of skin, enjoying the feel of his breath on her face, the way his body reacted to her touch. It was addicting.

Finally, Trip pulled away, and she had to fight the urge to pout. He laughed, running a thumb over her lips. "No frown. But you're shivering, so I think we should get you into warm clothes."

Her shivers had nothing at all to do with being cold, and the last thing she wanted was warm clothes. In fact, she wanted to get out of the ones she was wearing and help Trip out of his to see if they could find a different way to keep warm.

He lifted her up and set her beside him, then stood and reached out for her hand. "I don't have any lady clothes here, but I'll give you one of my T-shirts and pajama pants. They'll drown you, but at least they're warm." He fetched a change of clothes from his bedroom while she waited, and then showed her to a guest bathroom. "Take as long as you need." His gaze found hers, and she wondered if he would kiss her again, but instead he backed away and ran a hand through his hair, causing it to curl out in a thousand directions. Sweet Jesus . . . "I'll be out here if you need me." Then he disappeared back down the hall, and Emery pressed her forehead to the door.

What had she done?

Trip couldn't decide if he wanted to punch a wall or shout or knock on the door and carry Emery to his bed, tucking her into his sheets and his world. This was a dangerous game he was playing, and there was a lot more at stake than feelings. This was his reputation, his family's reputation. Already, the journalist from *Racing Today* had zeroed in on them, and that was from a phone conversation. What would the press say when they saw them together?

The thought made him want to puke.

The rain had slowed, and as Trip went to his room to change he thought through the implications of his actions. He could handle the gossip about him, but it wasn't fair to drag his family into this. And that's what this would mean. A media circus for the entire family.

What was he thinking?

Clearly, he wasn't. He thought of his mother's death, and how hard it had been on everyone. She and Alex had gone to eat lunch that day, and he'd told them she'd complained of a headache but refused to go back home. While eating lunch, her headache worsened, so Alex helped her out to the car, prepared to take her back home so she could rest. He'd opened the passenger side door for her, helped her into the seat, and by the time he'd made it around to the driver's side, she was all but gone. She'd spent three days on a ventilator before Carter made the impossible decision to send her to God.

As the oldest, Trip had stepped up, made sure his dad and brothers were okay. That's what he did. And now he was risking so much without even consulting them. But what was he supposed to do? Take it to a vote at the next meeting?

Why couldn't this be easier? If only he could take back his offer for her to work with him, set her up with a new trainer, and claim her as his the moment she agreed. But that wasn't what she wanted, and arrogant to admit it or not, he was the best. Craving Wind was the best. He couldn't turn his back on Emery now. Her career mattered more than his attachment to her. Frustrated, he was shoving his arms into a shirt and pulling it over his head when he heard Emery clear her throat from the open doorway.

"We can't do this . . . can we?"

Trip poked his head through the shirt opening and glanced over at her, all chaotic damp hair and warm smile. His too large T-shirt hung off her ivory shoulder, drawing his attention there. What he wouldn't give to kiss that spot, lick a trail up her neck, but he knew he needed to be more responsible. To think with his brain instead of his . . .

He walked over and ran his fingertips over her exposed shoulder—unable to stop himself—and then took her hands and pressed a kiss to her palm. "I want this. You have no idea how long or how badly I have wanted this. But this is your comeback. It's important. Plus . . ." He didn't want to make it sound like he wasn't willing to risk his career for her, because it wasn't all about him.

"Your family."

He bit his lip as he peered down at her and nodded slowly. "It would be a press disaster without you working for me. But now . . . we can't just jump into this." He tucked her hair behind her ear, and she leaned into his touch. "As much as we both want to."

The storm blew away, bringing with it clearer skies—and clearer thinking. Trip knew this was the right decision. So why did it feel so wrong?

She ducked her head, and Trip wished he could ask what she was thinking, but truthfully, he was afraid she would say something to crack his resolve, and it took every ounce of effort to keep from sweeping her into his arms and taking her to his bed. Screw everything and everyone else. It was so close. He could almost see her in it now.

After a long pause, she tilted her head up, the strong Emery he knew before him. "I understand."

"I'm not ending this. I'm just . . ."

"Ending it," she said. Then she took a step back. "Do you think you could take me to my Jeep? It looks like the storm has passed."

Trip sighed and tucked his hands into his jeans, hating the sadness in her eyes. She could put up a strong front, but her eyes gave her away, and right now they were deep oceans of disappointment. Damn it all to hell.

He grabbed his keys. "Sure. I'll take you now."

They were in the cart, heading to her car, before he remembered her clothes. "Your things are back at the house." He started to turn around when she touched his arm.

"I'd just like to go."

Trip sighed and continued on to the stables, despising himself more and more with each passing moment. He pulled up to her Jeep, the silence too much to bear. "Emery, I . . ."

She stepped out of the cart before he could continue. "I get it; I do. It's fine. Really."

But nothing about it was at all *fine*.

He thought of begging her to come back to his house, to talk. Anything. But he wasn't sure what he'd say, and he had no right to ask her for anything anyway.

So, instead, Trip sat still and watched as her taillights disappeared down the road, farther and farther away. And then he turned back for his house, more alone than ever.

CHAPTER SIXTEEN

Pony up

"Now come on, I need you," Annie said, reaching out a long ivory hand to Emery. She'd known from a young age where she had gotten her very fair skin—and her feisty attitude.

"I'm not stepping foot out of this car," Emery said, crossing her arms, sure she looked like a five year old, but she didn't care. Why Annie insisted on coming to Triple Run to check out Patty's bakery was a mystery to her. She had everything all set up with Gertie back home. She didn't need Patty, but it was funny how need and want weren't always the same thing, especially when it came to the heart.

Emery thought maybe Annie just wanted to show Patty that she had her own place, and how would she do that without coming to tell Patty personally?

"Okay, fine. I'll give you the house in my will."

Emery's ears pricked up. She loved that house, had always loved that house, and Annie knew it. "You're playing low now."

"Woman's gotta do what a woman's gotta do. Why are you fighting me on this anyway?"

Emery stared out the passenger window of Annie's Suburban, her thoughts back to standing in Trip's doorway, a wealth of excitement and possibilities bubbling up inside her. Until he turned around and she could see it. The fear, the regret. And nothing made a woman feel worse than seeing regret on a man's face. Lord, she had been so foolish. She'd let her guard down and walked Trip straight into the depths of her heart—again. For him to let her down—again. The trouble was, she liked him, liked being around him. Liked that crooked smile and those warm eyes. Liked how he wore flannel every day and never apologized for himself. And, God above, could he kiss! But now that was all over and they were what—friends?

The word made her want to burst into tears. How had she screwed this up so royally? They were fine, and now it was a plate full of awkward with no silverware around to cut it into manageable bites.

"Oh, honey . . ."

Emery peered over, unaware that her aunt was watching her.

"When did it happen?"

"What?"

Annie huffed loudly. "When did you fall for that hot trainer of yours? I saw the sparks back at the festival, but I thought your sensible side would keep your feelings at bay. At least until after the Derby. Now you've got half a year or more to work with this man, all the while nursing a broken heart? Luck don't get much worse, sugar pie."

Yeah, well, tell her something she didn't know.

"I just need to forget it. It was one kiss. You can forget a kiss, right?"

Annie patted her hand. "Depends on the kiss. Some stay with us for a lifetime."

Fantastic.

Emery glanced out the window again, remembering the feel of his hands on her cheeks, his breath on her neck. But she wasn't the kind of woman to get stirred up in emotions. She was driven and focused and had goals that silly things like feelings couldn't get in the way of. The truth was, Trip had done her a favor. She didn't need the distraction. If only she'd been the one to turn him away, or at the very least had told him she agreed with him, but instead she'd showed every bit of her hurt. Stupid, foolish woman!

"Are you okay?" Annie asked, which did little more than anger Emery. Of course she was okay! She didn't let some man ruin who she was, wreck her mood, and leave her sobbing for days. That didn't happen. Female jockeys had enough problems playing in what was very much considered a male sport. She'd learned to tuck away her sensitive side ages ago, and she had no intention of letting it fly free today.

She pushed out of the SUV and stared through the now open door to her aunt.

"What are you doing?" Annie asked.

"I'm going into Patty's. Are you coming or aren't you?"

"Coming!" Annie scrambled from the SUV and patted down her hair, adjusting her purse twice, before nodding to Emery that it was okay to go inside.

Of course, this was Triple Run, Kentucky, not some major city like Atlanta. Patty and whoever she kept on her staff stood at the store's window, watching this entire encounter. Fabulous.

Emery held open the door, motioning for Annie to go on ahead of her, but Annie wanted no part of that and they ended up practically fighting to see who would be forced to go in first. Emery spun out of Annie's grasp right as her aunt gave her a small push into someone inside the store. Jesus in heaven! Emery closed her eyes and shook her head in embarrassment, then flashed a smile and peered up, prepared to give a good Southern, "So sorry about that," when her gaze locked on the person she'd nearly taken out. Suddenly, a thousand ways to kill Annie-Jean for forcing her there raced through her mind. Forget the house; she'd never speak to her aunt again.

"Hey there, lady girl."

Emery straightened, very much aware that Trip's hand was still on her arm, initially there to keep her from falling, but now there with no purpose, sending tingles through her, reminding her of how very good those hands felt on her skin.

She swallowed and with effort took a step away from him. "Hey yourself," she said in her most even voice, though even to her own ears it sounded small. Damn her for getting herself into this mess.

Trip glanced around at the four other women in the store—all of their eyes on Trip and Emery—then back to her. "Do you think . . . can we talk outside for a second?"

Emery couldn't think of anything she'd like to do less than have a conversation with Trip out in the open in Triple Run, where anybody could listen in as he recounted just how much he didn't want her. "Um, I'm here with Annie. She——"

But somehow Annie and Patty were already having their own little exchange, and phrases like backstabbing and confection stealer were being thrown around like snowballs in the middle of a January blizzard.

"Annie?" Emery started over before her aunt's attitude turned to punches. Surely women in their fifties didn't actually fight? But by the daggers coming from Annie and Patty, she couldn't be sure.

Trip stepped beside Patty and Emery beside Annie.

"I didn't steal your recipe, you old bat!" Patty called, ignoring the sidelong looks from the two other patrons in the bakery.

Annie's hands clenched into fists. "You'd never once mixed cranberries and white chocolate, and now you act like it's your signature. Bundts, cookies, cupcakes, all with my recipe inside!"

Patty had placed her hands on her hips and opened her mouth to argue when she readjusted her weight and shook her head. "This is about Blake Williams, isn't it? You were broken up, Annie, and that was more than thirty years ago. I wouldn't have told you if I thought you'd get this angry."

Blake Williams? Who—oh, no. Emery remembered Annie talking about her first love, the smile on her face that lasted long after the story had ended. She said he'd disappointed her, and Emery thought she'd meant by going to Notre Dame, but maybe there was more to the story.

"Do you think it matters how long ago it was?" Annie halfscreamed. "You were my best friend and he was my first love. You knew that." The pain in Annie's eyes made Emery reach for her hand, but Annie would have no comfort right then and pulled away.

"It was one kiss, when you first got together, before he became your first love. It was a mistake, Annie, which was why we never told you."

"Yet somehow you felt the need to relieve your conscience twentyfive years later? Do you think I really needed to know at that point?"

Patty shook her head. "You asked about that day and I told you. You were my friend, Annie. I thought it was the right thing to do."

"There's no kindness in that."

"So you'd rather I lied?"

"Yes! I didn't want to know it and now I can never unknow it. Some things don't need to be known. Some things don't need the complication. You can live life and go on your way without hashing out every single detail. Live the magic of the moment and go on. I want my moment back, but now it's gone." Annie dropped her head, and Emery thought her heart might break in two.

Trip's gaze lifted to Emery and she knew what he was thinking. They'd shared a magic moment, and just like with Annie . . . it was gone.

She reached out for her aunt, and this time Annie took hold of her hand, grasping it tightly like she needed a little of Emery's strength to go on. Even after all these years, Annie's heart was still broken, the wound still fresh. "Come on, Annie. I think we're done."

Annie nodded slowly, and wiped her hand over her eyes as though a tear had fallen. Maybe she was all cried out. "All right, honey. Let's go. We're done here."

They started away as Trip called out Emery's name, and she peered back at him, wishing they could turn back time and make a thousand different decisions. Instead, they were here, in this moment, and there was no going back.

"Wait, please," he said.

"It's like Annie said . . . we're done here."

CHAPTER SEVENTEEN

Off to a flying start

Trip found himself standing outside Craving Wind's stall, staring at the horse that had started everything, searching for some answers in his eyes that would surely never come.

"You like her, too," Trip said to the horse. "I can tell. You relax more around her. Like she puts you at ease." Trip ran his hand down the horse's nose. "She puts me at ease, too."

The sound of a boot shuffling against ground hit Trip's ears, and he peered over to find Emery a few yards away, watching him, her expression unreadable. Clark stood behind him, refusing to look at Trip, and he knew they'd heard every word.

"So, today's the day," Trip said, pushing away from the stall. It was the first race for the colt and Emery's return to the racetrack. They'd had the horse stabled there two days prior, giving him an opportunity to run on the track a few times before the actual race. It was a maiden race, and the perfect one to launch Craving Wind into racing while still gaining exposure. And they needed him to win.

The track's backside began filling up then, caretakers and trainers and jockeys doing their jobs. Trip's gaze dropped to Emery's colors, Sarah Anderson's colors, and he felt a sense of pride seeing them—an extension of himself—on her. He wanted to ask her if she'd talked to Beckett yet, told him she was racing today, and that she was racing for Trip instead of for Carlisle Farms. He had no idea what story she'd concocted, but there was no denying that if she and Craving Wind won this race, Beckett would hear about it. And he would know she'd betrayed him.

Trip hoped she'd had the conversation before now and wasn't holding out that the race was too small for it to reach her daddy, because they both knew he followed nearly every race in the country. Always had. Still, right now wasn't the moment to bring it up to Emery. Right now, she needed to conjure that tiger inside her and let it loose—let it carry her first over the finish line.

"Ready?" Trip said to her, wishing he could do more than simply ask her the question. He wanted to hug her close and whisper reassuring words in her ear, but she wasn't his to whisper to, and it had been weeks since their kiss, all with awkward moments between them and stilted conversations. Whatever they had—friendship, attraction, whatever—was gone. But maybe winning today would be the start to bringing it back. Because the truth was, he wanted to be a part of her life, in whatever way she would allow it. He knew he couldn't explore something more with her, especially not now, with her career relaunching under his name. But he also knew that if he ever made another move it would have to be the final move—no testing the waters, all in, no looking back. And he wouldn't do that unless he knew there would be no consequences to her or his family.

The announcer called for riders to the paddock, and Trip gave Emery one last look. "Good luck."

She held his gaze, and he could almost hear the words on the tip of her tongue. She was excited but also nervous. "Trip . . ."

"You've got this, lady girl," he said, reaching for her hand. "Trust yourself. I do."

She nodded once and then he gave her a leg up, and the sight of her on Craving Wind, dressed in colors, looking like she belonged right there and nowhere else, made him momentarily forget all the complications of their relationship and enjoy the sight of the woman he cared about doing the thing she loved most.

He watched her leave, adjusting his tie, needing room to breathe, and started to go up to the grandstand when he heard his name called from behind. He turned to see the same journalist from Santa Anita walking toward him.

"Hello again, Mr. Hamilton. I wondered if I could ask you a few more questions."

Trip squared his shoulders. "I think you asked enough the last time we met, and the race is about to begin."

He turned around as she called, "Just one: How long have you been in a relationship with Emery Carlisle?"

Several people around stopped what they were doing, watching the exchange.

"I told you before, Emery and my relationship is strictly professional."

Then, before she could ask something else, he headed for the grandstand, ignoring the stares from those who'd heard the conversation. Dammit! This wasn't good. He wondered how long before the journalist wrote the story without factual information to support it. He needed to tell Emery.

Nick and Alex were waiting for him when he reached their seats in the grandstand. The crowd buzzed with energy, everyone excited to see who would win—which horses would become contenders for the Kentucky Derby.

"You look like you're ready to deck someone," Alex said.

"Reporters," Trip said as answer, wishing he were in his normal jeans and flannel shirt instead of the suit. Suddenly, the tie strangled him, his jacket far too tight around his shoulders.

"And since when are they a problem?" Nick asked, then lowering his voice added, "Is it Emery?"

One look from Trip confirmed he was right, but the horses were in the starting gate, the race about to begin.

A surge of fear hit Emery's stomach as she entered the starting gate, her teeth clamping down at the sound of metal grinding together and then the clang of the lock, securing them inside. There was no going back now, no escape. For a moment, she felt like a little girl on a roller coaster, forced into the coaster's car by her parents, them telling her to be brave, her on the verge of crying. And then the coaster rose up, up, up until it was at the top of the first giant drop, and the girl felt sure her parents must hate her; why else would they force her to do this? The sound of something releasing echoed in the air, and then the coaster soared down, the girl's stomach in her throat, and then—

"Breathe."

Emery jolted upright, causing Craving Wind to stir. She glanced over to see the jockey beside her nodding encouragingly, his eyes warm.

"Remember, it's only two minutes. We can do anything for two minutes."

Her head bobbed. "Right, two minutes."

And then the magnets holding the gates closed were turned off and the gates flew open and her breath caught in her throat, air whipping past her as she rose up, Craving Wind gaining early momentum. She held the reins close, unwilling to let up. Not yet. She knew Queen's Revenge and Groundbreaker were closers. They would find their stride any second, any second, any—

She held her breath, feeling the horses close in as she rounded the first turn. She had to maintain pace, had to know when to break free without causing Craving Wind to tire before the race was over. Her nerves coiled up, doubt and excitement waging war in her head, her hands shaking so badly she wasn't sure how she held the reins. Craving Wind would be the dark horse of this race, the colt no one expected to win but everyone should have had faith in. His worst time was seconds faster than either of his competitors' best reported times. He was ready, born for this, and she refused to let him down.

Forcing herself to take a slow breath, she loosened the reins and leaned forward, readying herself for the burst of speed she knew would come. *Don't be afraid, don't be afraid.* She told herself to close away her memories, the pain she still felt in her leg whenever it rained. Like the weather held all her worst experiences. This was it. Ready? "Go, boy!" she screamed.

And he did.

They made their way into the backstretch, gaining on Groundbreaker, until they were side by side, neck and neck, and then, like Craving Wind grew bored with toying with the horse, he took off. Queen's Revenge in sight, he sped toward her. If not for the sounds of his hooves on the dirt, she would think he flew. Because while he didn't have wings, there was no denying they were flying, faster and faster, blowing past Queen's Revenge. One length. Two. Five. *Oh my God.*

Happiness replaced fear and determination replaced doubt, and for the first time, Emery allowed herself to feel this moment. The speed, the raw power, the thrill that would remain with her for the rest of the night. Because that jockey in the starting gate had been wrong—this wasn't two minutes. This was hours and days, months and years of preparation. Countless staff members' sweat and tears and hope and fear. One race never told the whole story, but it was a start. And this start she intended to win.

She shouted one more command to Craving Wind, reminding him to keep going, to stay strong, and then, in a blink, they sailed over the finish line. Emery's chest clenched tight, tears brimming in her eyes as she lifted her hands into the air, the grandstand erupting in cheers as the announcer said the three precious words Emery was dying to hear: *Craving Wind wins!*

The world slowed down all around her, each second passing in sharp detail. The announcer's energy. The flashes from photographers. The calls from the crowd. Emery blinked, allowing her tears to fall, and dropped her chest down against Craving Wind, hugging the horse she loved close. "Thank you," she whispered. "Thank you so much."

They made their way to the winner's circle, and Emery could almost feel the moment Trip walked up, Sarah Anderson right beside him, but somehow Emery could only see Trip, her eyes locked on his, some unspoken celebration passing between them—words too private for others' ears.

"You did it," Emery said, smiling down at him.

He shook his head and peered up at her. "No, you did."

Emery's heart *beat, beat, beat* in her chest, in her ears, the sound almost foreign. Had it always sounded so loud? She didn't know. But one thing she knew for sure—she would never forget this day.

CHAPTER EIGHTEEN

Smart money says

Emery walked into the hotel's restaurant, her hands gliding down her dress. She'd chosen a black cocktail dress that hit above her knee. Classy but attractive. Her hair was pulled back into a messy bun, her makeup and jewelry were simple. She wanted the staff and people attending Hamilton Stables' celebratory dinner to know she wasn't embarrassed to be a woman. She'd won.

Trip stood as she neared the table, dressed in a dark navy suit tailored to perfection. His eyes drifted down her body and then back up. "You look amazing."

She smiled. "You look pretty great yourself."

They stared at each other, her heart speeding up in her chest, and then someone cleared his throat and Emery's attention shifted to the table, all eyes on them.

"Here, allow me." Trip pulled out her chair and she sat down between him and Alex.

Sarah Anderson grinned over at Emery, her once-blond hair now white with age, making her icy blue eyes almost scary if not for the warmth of her smile. She raised her glass. "To our winner of the evening, Emery Carlisle. May this be the first of many."

Emery returned a gracious smile, and then the table started in on the race: who looked strong, the competitors, the disappointments.

"Good job, slick," Alex whispered to her.

Emery shook her head. "What is with you Hamilton boys and your nicknames?"

Alex glanced over at Trip. "Ah, probably has something to do with so many women and our inability to remember all of your names."

"Ignore him," Nick said, leaning over his brother. "And congratulations. Your time was impressive."

"Thank you. I think you may be my new favorite Hamilton."

His eyes widened a touch and his gaze shifted to Trip, who seemed very interested in his wine.

"It was a joke," she whispered to him.

"I got it."

Emery took a long sip of her own wine, wishing they could go back to before, when their relationship was all flirtation and easy banter. And then they kissed, and everything became messy.

"So, Alex, I heard you're a big college football fan," she said, hoping to lighten the mood.

"How? Oh, Kate. Yeah, I played in high school and walked on when I went to Virginia Tech."

"Were you any good?" Emery asked, taking another sip of wine, then, realizing she should pace herself, set it back down.

Nick laughed. "I'd say Alex thinks he's the best at everything he touches."

"There's no thinking about it." Alex winked. "I *am* the best."

"Kate's a big fan, too." Emery hoped she didn't sound as obvious as she felt, but Kate hadn't stopped talking about Alex since their last date. Though, apparently, Alex never once called it a date. He'd invited her over to watch a game but had spent the entire time talking and acting like she was only a friend. He hadn't called her since.

Alex cut into his steak and took his time chewing. "I know. She's a cool chick."

Cool chick? "Yeah, she is."

Trip stood up then and walked over to speak to someone at another table. Emery stared after him, wondering if she'd said something she shouldn't have, as Alex leaned in close. "You should cut him some slack. He's just doing what he thinks is best."

"I'm not doing anything."

"Really? He's sitting right beside you and you've yet to speak to him."

Emery patted her mouth with her napkin and returned it to her lap. "I don't know how to talk to him, okay? And this isn't really any of your business."

Alex laughed sarcastically. "Trust me, with Trip and his mood, it's everyone's business. He doesn't want to mess up."

"Is that why you're refusing to really go out with Kate? I can tell you like her."

He pulled away, returning his attention to his plate. "That's . . . complicated."

"I hear that word a lot these days. . . ."

Alex set down his fork. "Trip's trusting me to focus on breeding, to grow the business, and to help cement our name as one of the best breeders in the country. This is the first time my family has ever taken me seriously. He's giving me a chance, and I have no intention of blowing it."

Emery shook her head. "But you can still date. You can have a career *and* a life."

"Really? Do you?"

Trip returned to his seat, and they fell into an awkward silence, until finally the meal was over and everyone said good-bye. The Hamilton brothers and Emery all shared an elevator up, and as they reached her floor, Emery contemplated asking Trip to come back to her room, to talk, to work through the mess they'd become. But then he held the door and said, "Good night, Emery," and she felt her heart drop.

"Good night."

Once back in her room, she lay down on her hotel room bed, allowing her fingers to spread out over the feather duvet, and recounted the race from earlier. A laugh burst from her lips. She'd won. The feeling of crossing that finish line, knowing she'd won, made her want to scream out in excitement and laugh and jump and call everyone she knew. But that was the problem with the way she'd done this. She couldn't call the one person who would be the proudest of her, the person who would feel the same level of joy at her accomplishment. Her father.

He still had no idea she rode for Trip, but she had a feeling he would know after this race. Not only had she won but Craving Wind's time had impressed. The press had surrounded her immediately, asking question after question, and then a pretty blonde had asked her the hardest question of all—how did it feel racing for Hamilton Stables instead of for her family? She'd wanted to ignore the question, call her father and explain everything, praying the win would be enough to make him understand—to make him forgive her. But Beckett Carlisle wasn't a forgiving man. Now she had no choice but to tell him, but she didn't want to do it over the phone. He deserved more from her.

Guilt punched through her gut and she felt the rising buildup of tears, exhaustion, and worry taking over her happiness. She'd done this all backward.

Just when she'd decided to drown her sorrows in the hotel's large whirlpool bath, a glass of wine in hand, she heard a soft knock on her door. Unsure if she wanted to see anyone, she hesitated, but the knocking came again.

Peeking through the peephole, she snapped back. She pulled open the door, unable to keep the smile from her face. "Hey there."

Trip adjusted his weight from one foot to the other, then, seeming to remember he'd brought something, held out a bottle of wine to her. "I thought maybe we could talk." He peered over at her, his expression guarded, and she realized he was nervous.

"Sure." Stepping back, she waved him inside. "It's a mess. I was a little out of sorts this morning, so yeah, my hotel room received the brunt of it."

He laughed, and Emery closed her eyes, enjoying the sound far too much, only to open her eyes and find him watching her.

He reached for her hand. "Have a drink with me."

The room became very warm, the silence noticeable, her heart the only thing she could hear. "Is that a good idea?"

He walked over to a nearby table and uncorked the wine, then poured them each a glass. "No. But here I am." He passed over a glass and their fingertips touched lightly. Unable to stop herself, she took a step toward him, needing to feel his closeness, smell the combination of soap and the outdoors that was only Trip. She expected him to back up, but he didn't. Instead, he set down his glass and took her hand, running his fingers easily through each of hers, his gaze so concentrated on the effort she wondered what he possibly could be thinking as his eyes lifted.

"You were amazing today. Perfect. Everyone's talking. There's mention of the Derby."

She smiled at the compliment. It wasn't every day a trainer like Trip complimented a rider. "Well, it wasn't me. He's made for this, craves it. His name fits. He *does* crave wind."

"People were asking for you downstairs at the bar."

Emery took a step back, refusing to look at him. "I'm tired."

"I don't doubt it, but that isn't why. You haven't told Beckett."

"I just . . . I don't know how. You don't understand."

Trip walked around so he stood in front of her again. "I do. I spent a year working for your father. I saw how much he loved you and how much pride he had in you, even then. He deserves to hear this from you, not some half-written article that doesn't know or understand the full details. Does he even know you're riding again?"

"Not exactly. I told him I was an exercise rider, so he assumes, but he hasn't seen me ride."

"Why are you keeping so much from him? Beckett's a good man. He isn't going to yell or disown you."

"I think either of those would be better than what he'll do."

"Which is . . . ?"

Emery walked over to the window and peered down at Saratoga. "I'm not worried about angering him. I can handle the anger. But I can't handle the disappointment. You may think he'll be pleased that I'm riding again, but he won't see it that way. He'll think I betrayed him, and the truth is . . . he's right. I'm surprised only one reporter brought it up."

"What do you mean? Brought what up?"

Emery sat down at the small table and took a sip of the wine. She needed liquid courage for what she was going to do. "In the winner's circle. That one blonde reporter? She asked how I felt riding for you instead of Daddy. Was he hurt when he heard the news? And you should have seen her face when she realized he didn't know. It was horrible."

Releasing a long breath, Trip slumped into the other chair, taking the glass of wine and drinking it down. "That's my fault."

"What?"

"That journalist has been questioning me for weeks about you and me and our relationship. I planned to talk to you about it after the race. She's claiming we're together."

"What?" Emery jumped from her chair and started pacing around. "When will the article go live?"

"With social media so prevalent, it might already be online."

Oh, no! She quickly reached for her phone and Googled her name, but there was nothing that linked her and Trip. Yet. Grabbing her carry-on, she stuffed all the clothes strewn around the room in the bag, then was starting for the bathroom for her toiletries when Trip stopped her.

"What are you doing?"

"I'm leaving. What does it look like? Her article isn't out yet. I can get to him before he hears anything. I can—"

Trip took her hands. "You can't. There's no way you'd get a flight back this late. And even if you did, he'll hear who won the race. Likely already has. He doesn't need to read an article, lady girl. Beckett follows the races. He knows."

Emery glanced up, broken. All she wanted was to get back on a mount, to ride again, to make him proud. Why hadn't she realized the first two wouldn't mean anything without the third?

"What should I do? What should I tell him?"

"The truth."

CHAPTER NINETEEN

Dark horse

Emery pushed the key into the front door lock, her heart screaming for her to turn around, avoid hell for another day—or year. But she could almost feel the tension oozing out of the house. She couldn't bring herself to check for an article that morning, but she could tell by Trip's face over breakfast that it had released. The world now knew she worked for Hamilton Stables—which meant so did her father.

She felt like a sixteen-year-old girl again, acting without thinking, seeing only what she wanted to see. How had she been so stupid? Knowing she couldn't avoid it any longer, she turned the knob and stepped into her parents' foyer, the old hardwoods creaking with each step, letting them know she was home. Ready for her punishment. But the house sat eerily quiet for early afternoon.

The sounds that made the house her home weren't there. Mama's dog rushing to the door, her screaming for him to be quiet. The dishwasher running. The vacuum. Anything. A sinking feeling washed over Emery as she made her way down the long hall to Daddy's office. The door was closed, so he might not be home. A part of her found relief in the idea, but then, putting this off wouldn't make it any easier.

Dipping her head and saying a silent prayer for forgiveness and that he'd go easy on her, she knocked on the door.

"It's open," Daddy called, his voice so small she nearly broke into tears right then.

Opening the door, she folded her arms and tried for confidence, failing miserably. He faced away from her, bent over his laptop. "Hey, Daddy," she said. "Have a minute?"

"I suppose I do." He pushed away from the laptop and spun around, exposing what was on the screen. In large letters, the top read: Emery Carlisle, Hamilton Stables' newest star or Trip's latest conquest?

Emery gasped, her eyes widening more and more with each horrible word. "It's a lie."

"Which part? Tell me the truth, Emery. That's the least you can do now."

Emery felt like Baby in *Dirty Dancing*, out on the wide deck, her father in a rocking chair, tears in both their eyes as they revealed how deeply they'd disappointed each other. Because the truth was, her father had disappointed her, too. Never once had he told her he believed in her recovery, that she was ready. Never once had he trusted her to know her body, to know herself when she was ready. Instead, he'd hovered over her, reminding her again and again of what had happened—of how close she'd been to dying. Frustration surged up inside her, and for a moment she wanted to scream all those things at him, but she wasn't a teenager, like Baby, ready to go off to college. She was an adult who'd lied to the person who loved her the most.

"You deserve so much more than the truth. I'm so sorry, Daddy. I should have come to you immediately. I thought . . . I don't know what I thought. But what I do know is that I'm a good rider, and I'm not living unless I'm riding. I know you worry that something's going to happen again. I know what it did to you when I fell. How you blamed yourself. But this is my life, and being a jockey is my career choice. Not yours. You didn't force this on me. I chose it. And I love it. I should never have lied to you, but I won't say I'm sorry for racing again. I'm too good to sit in the grandstand, watching others do what I'm born to do."

She stared at her father, waiting for him to reply, but he wasn't even looking at her, instead focused on something behind her. Turning to see what had caught his attention, her gaze fell on a framed photo of her sitting tall on her first horse. She looked so little then, so fragile, and that was when she realized he still saw her as that little girl. His little girl.

"Daddy?"

He refused to look at her, his attention fixed on the photo.

"Daddy, I'm not that little girl anymore."

Finally, his eyes lifted to hers, all the pain in the world in them. "No, you're not. My little girl wouldn't have lied to me. I don't know who you are anymore. Now, if you could please leave. I have work to do." He spun back around in his chair and clicked off the Web site.

Tears welled in Emery's eyes, her body shaking from the effort not to cry. She opened her mouth to say more, but there were no words left to say. She'd broken his heart.

She left her parents' house and walked down the path to the guesthouse, eager to soak in a hot bath, but when she walked up the front steps and put her key in the door, she found it wouldn't turn. She tried again, jiggling the knob, but it still wouldn't budge.

She walked around to one of the windows and peered in, curious to see whether someone had tried to break in or something. The locks had definitely been changed, and why else would her father have changed them unless—

Oh, no. Her phone buzzed in her pocket, and she pulled it out to see a single text from her father.

Quit Hamilton Stables or find yourself a new home. I have the new keys waiting for you when you've come to your senses. Until then, you aren't welcome here.

Unable to hold it in any longer, she slumped down onto the front porch, staring out over her family's farm, her arms wrapped around her legs as tears rained down her face.

Trip sat down in his father's conference room. He was fifteen minutes early, something that never happened for him, but his father had called the meeting after Emery's win on Craving Wind, and Trip was excited to hear what he would say. Trip was proud of Emery's performance, but he could almost feel the guilt weighing her down in the winner's circle. It was bittersweet, winning without Beckett there beside her.

Twiddling a pen against the table, he barely noticed Nick and Alex come in and sit in front of him.

"Trip."

He glanced up to see them both looking at him. "What?"

"This meeting. It's—"

Just then, their father came in, clapping his hands together. "All right, let's chat."

Trip's father set a folder in front of him, and Trip opened it to see photos of Emery . . . and Marcus, the Hamilton Stables logo above the shots. "What is this?"

"There's a lot of publicity buzzing around Emery's win, but we have to remember it's the horse people are betting on, not the jockey."

"Can you get to the point?"

Carter's eyes narrowed. "I think Marcus should ride Craving Wind in the Derby, and Emery can ride a filly of your choosing in the Kentucky Oaks."

"Marcus is an asshole."

"Perhaps, but he's a winner, and he's the best shot we have of winning the Derby."

Anger rocked through Trip. "No. She's worked too hard for us to pull her from Craving Wind."

"A female jockey has never won the Derby, Trip. Be reasonable here. We have an obligation to Sarah Anderson, don't forget that."

"Yeah, well, you let me handle the owners. After all, I'm the trainer, not you. And I say she rides Craving Wind until she gives us a reason to doubt her. I won't doubt her now."

His father leaned back in his chair, clearly not expecting this reaction. "What is your connection to this woman? Why do you care?"

"I hired her. It's my job to make sure she crosses that finish line first. You let me worry about getting her there." Then he turned his rage on his brothers. "You knew about this?"

Nick shook his head. "We just found out."

"Emery wins or she's done. Do you understand?" Carter Hamilton said, his tone hard.

"You don't make that call," Trip said, pushing out of his chair and tossing the folder on the table. "I do. I'm the trainer here, not you."

"Yes, but you're not Craving Wind's owner. You are his trainer. And I've already spoken with Sarah. She agreed that Emery is a risk. A risk she's not willing to take unless Emery continues to perform. One slip, and Marcus is Craving Wind's rider."

Trip threw open the conference door and stormed out. His father could screw himself. *He* was the reason people came to Hamilton Stables. *He* was the reason their name was synonymous with winning. They needed him more than he needed them. And he wouldn't let his father take this from Emery. But his father was right about one thing—he was at the mercy of Sarah Anderson. He couldn't force her to allow Emery to ride, and though she trusted him, he couldn't risk the family's business if Emery stopped performing.

He couldn't let that happen.

Needing to do something, he jumped in his truck and drove in silence, unsure where he was going until he found himself in Crestler's Key, driving down Main Street, not sure how he would find Emery but knowing he had to talk to her. First her father, now this.

Crestler's Key looked astonishingly similar to Triple Run, like the filly version to Triple Run's colt. Cobblestone streets through downtown, small shops on each side of the road. But where Triple Run had a slight masculine vibe, Crestler's Key boasted flowers and vegetation everywhere you looked. The stop signs were wooden, but with floral detail cut into the posts. Triple Run was charming where Crestler's Key was beautiful.

He'd get kicked out of his town if he ever uttered those words aloud.

Parking outside GP Bakery, he went inside, hoping to find a familiar face, though he only knew three people in town. The bakery brimmed with life, every chair full, and he thought maybe he'd get lucky and spot Kate when instead his eyes landed on someone else. He smiled wide and started over.

"Color me surprised. What are you doing here, handsome?" Annie-Jean said as she put out fresh pastries.

He thought of all the reasons he'd come there, but the truth was, it all boiled down to one thing. "I need to see her."

She nodded once. "I think she needs to see you, too. Here's my address." She jotted it down on a Post-it Note and passed it over.

"Why isn't she at Carlisle Farms?"

"Beckett asked her to leave after . . . well, you know."

Trip's chest tightened in hurt and anger. Beckett was a stubborn man, but this? "Right. And she's there? At your house?"

"She hasn't left since it happened."

The thought of her falling to this level made Trip want to punch something—his father, Beckett, anyone for driving her to this low. But that wasn't what she needed now. She needed someone to remind her that she was an amazing rider, to remind her why she kept racing a secret from Beckett in the first place. It wasn't to hurt him—it was because she needed to prove to herself that she could get back on a mount without her father standing by with skepticism.

He went for the door as Annie called out, "What are you going to do?"

"I'm going to remind her."

"Of what?"

"Of exactly who Emery Carlisle is to the racing world . . . and to me."

CHAPTER TWENTY

Hands down

Emery pulled the rubber band from her wrist and wrapped it around the mess of hair piled on her head. She hadn't showered since the hotel back in Saratoga, and though she probably smelled like a horse by now, she didn't care.

All she could think about was her father's expression as he stared at the picture of little Emery, like he wondered where he'd gone wrong. She reached blindly for another doughnut from the half-eaten box on the coffee table and eyed the TV, tears building in her eyes as she watched Meg Ryan and Tom Hanks walking toward one another in the park, "Somewhere Over the Rainbow" playing in the background. They finally reached each other and a hiccupped cry released from Emery's lips.

"See, this is what love should be like," she said to the empty room. Then, realizing how pathetic it was to talk to herself, she reached for a tissue from the various half-crumpled bunches surrounding her on Annie-Jean's couch. She'd been that way for more than a day, watching romantic comedies and eating doughnuts and . . . crying. Because while the movies always got their happily ever after, Emery knew with certainly she wouldn't get hers. At least not a full happily ever after.

She might win, but what was winning without the people she loved around her to celebrate? And then there was Trip, the only man to make her heart dance and scream, and he'd turned her away. Told her no.

She imagined him coming to her now and saying he was wrong,

sweeping her into his arms, her long hair flowing behind her as he pulled her close and took ownership of her mouth, then her body. So what if her breasts were a little larger in the fantasy, her thighs a little slimmer, her hair a little fuller? It could happen . . .

A fresh wave of self-pity washed over her as she realized, no, it couldn't, and she was wondering if there was any ice cream in the fridge she could dip her doughnuts in when she heard a knock, followed by the doorbell ringing. Crap fire. She was in no way presentable enough to take a delivery from Annie's obsessed mailman, who hadn't quite gotten the hell-no memo Annie'd sent him.

Deciding to ignore it, she turned up the volume on the TV. *Marty could leave it on the front porch.* But the knocking persisted, and finally she had no choice but to wrap her grandma robe tightly around her and trudge to the door.

Without looking, she threw it open, prepared to let the mailman have it. This crush of his was interfering with Emery's miserable afternoon. "Look, Marty, she's not home. You can—" But her words cut short at the sight of the man before her. So not short and stocky Marty.

Instead, she took in the tall, lean frame. The loose jeans hung low on his hips, the flannel shirt rolled to his elbows, the Atlanta Braves cap containing a mess of wavy brown hair. Her hands went to her own messy hair, her worse-than-no-makeup face. Had she even brushed her teeth today? Yes, she thought—she hoped.

"This is not at all how I pictured this moment."

A smile played at Trip's lips, and he reached down for the tie to her robe, gripping each end in his hands. "How did you picture it?"

"What?" Ah, crap, she hadn't realized she'd said that out loud.

"Can I come in?"

Emery peered down at her yucky robe and bare legs because she couldn't be bothered to put on pants, only a T-shirt and the robe.

"I'm not really . . ." she trailed off, her eyes finding his. Bless the gods of warm chocolate eyes.

"Please."

"Um, okay, sure. Come in."

She led Trip into the family room and sat on the couch, crossing her legs up under her as he took in the tissues, the doughnuts—the romantic movie paused on the screen.

"I'm assuming Beckett didn't take it very well?"

Emery offered a sarcastic laugh. "If by well you mean calling me a liar, telling me he didn't know me anymore, and kicking me out, then yes, he took it splendidly well." She reached for another tissue, but Trip got there first, sitting beside her as he dabbed her eyes.

"Why are you doing this?" she asked. "Why are you here?"

He opened his mouth twice before speaking, as though he wasn't quite sure himself. "I have something to show you." He walked over to the TV and peered around the sides, then, seeming to spot something he'd hoped to see, grinned and returned to the couch to sit beside her. When she didn't argue at his nearness, he pulled out his phone and clicked on the Roku app, then searched until he was on YouTube.

Glancing over at her with his penetrating stare, he said, "I know you feel lost right now. I know without Beckett beside you, you're questioning why you're doing this, what it all means. But it was never about Beckett. This has always been about you, your gift, and you've earned the right to see it through. You can't quit. Not now. You're too good to quit." Then he typed in the search field and clicked for the video to start.

Music filled the air, and then she was watching her first race, her first win, the first time she'd crossed the finish line at the Kentucky Oaks. Race after race appeared on the screen, her heart bursting with each second. She leaned in closer to the TV, captivated by the athlete she'd once been. And then the final race filled the screen, the Saratoga maiden she'd just run, and her chest heaved with emotion. Because this race, her first race back from the dead, had beaten her best time from before, the year she'd considered the best of her life until the accident. Part of that was Craving Wind, who by all accounts was a machine of a horse that might function as well with any jockey. But maybe not. Maybe she was a piece of the winning puzzle.

The final race replayed, and then the video ended and she caught the words *Hamilton Stables* below the video, and suddenly her heart soared for different reasons. "You did this?" She turned to him, her feelings out of control. Her thoughts out of control. All she knew was that she wanted to kiss him, long and hard, until he knew how much this meant to her. But she couldn't—he'd said no. Why did he have to say no?

"I needed you to remember who you are. Who you were born to be." He cupped her face, trailing his thumb over her cheek, sending a zing through her body that felt a lot like hope. "Who you are to me." And then, before she could question what he meant, he covered her mouth with his, all the want they'd felt for each other taking over, refusing to let go. The kiss skipped sweet and went straight for holy-God-above-I'd-die-happy intense, and Emery's body responded, heat pooling low in her belly, sinking lower until she was sure she'd explode.

She rose onto her knees and he pulled her into his lap, straddling his waist, her robe falling open, nothing between her and the rigidness of his jeans but a thin strip of silk panties and a T-shirt. He gripped her hips and tugged her closer, allowing her to feel his need as his hands wrapped around her ass, and then in one quick move, he had her on her back on the couch, him over her, one hand bracing himself up while the other explored every reachable inch of skin.

She ran her hands under his shirt, gently stroking the sharp contours of his abs, his pecs, and then he released the sexiest sound she'd ever heard when her fingertips went across his nipple, and she thought, *forget the risk of heartbreak.* She wanted this man, right here and right now. No more delays.

"Emery . . ."

"Don't stop. Don't you dare stop."

All the prompting he needed; he lifted her up and eased off her robe and shirt and lay her back, taking in her naked chest, then her face, holding her gaze. "Damn . . . you are so beautiful."

She stopped her work at unbuttoning his shirt, growing frustrated by how very little she had on when he was still fully clothed. After all, she'd seen *her* body. It was his body that filled her dreams.

"A little help here," she said, gripping the shirt, "or I'm not sure these buttons are going to survive the afternoon."

Trip's lips quirked up. "Do you have a room here?"

She motioned to the hall running beside the TV. "Third door on the right. It's—" But before she could continue, he swept her into his arms and started down the hall, shutting the door behind him, the shirt off so quickly she wondered if he'd ripped it off. And then he was there in front of her, bare chest cut to absolute perfection, jeans unbuttoned, a wicked look on his face, but she had to be sure. Lust could make a person make mistakes, and she didn't want to be his mistake.

"You said we couldn't do this," she said, fighting to keep from drooling as he pushed his jeans to the floor and stepped out of them.

"I actually said we *shouldn't*." He slowly strutted toward her, taking her hand and kissing her palm, then the inside of her wrist. "But I've never been good at doing what I'm supposed to do. And I'm tired of pretending when I'm around you. Talking when I want to be doing this." He pressed his lips to her neck, trailing up to her jaw.

"And your family?"

Trip pulled away to look at her. "Have you changed your mind?"

"I have wanted you since I was seventeen years old, long before you were *the* Trip Hamilton, manly horse whisperer. I want this. But I need to know you aren't going to regret me in the morning."

Trip took a step away from her and peered down. "I don't make mistakes, Emery. I make decisions, and then I handle the consequences of those decisions, but I never make mistakes. And certainly not with you."

"But—"

"Do you remember when your dad first got Broken Fence? You were sitting in a nearby pasture, watching, your hands clasped together in excitement. You'd been with him at the auction. I still remember your smile when Beckett won him, and I knew then, staring at you instead of the horse, that there would never be another woman like you. I've never seen another woman the way I see you."

"But you left."

Trip hesitated.

And it was then Emery knew that he hadn't wanted to leave. Something had happened. "Tell me."

"It doesn't matter now."

"Please . . . tell me."

He hung his head. "All right, but you should know you have me in a pretty vulnerable state here." She smiled, so he continued. "Mr. Sampson asked me to leave. Said he would tell Beckett if I didn't go quietly."

She sucked in a breath. "He . . . I . . . but that wasn't his decision to make."

"You were seventeen and I was twenty, working for your dad. Worshipping your dad. He taught me everything I know. I couldn't let him find out like that. So I left. But you never left me. You were always right here." He tapped the space over his heart. "Eight years, and not a day went by that I didn't wish I'd stayed. Don't make me stay away now."

Emery took a step toward him, closing the distance he'd made. "Your reputation . . ."

"Is just that—mine. Let me worry about it." When she didn't say anything, he ran his fingers through her hair, gently tugging the ends so her head tilted back. "I don't want to talk anymore. Do you?"

She shook her head, and he swooped in, pressing her to him, unable to get close enough. He lay her back, staring down at her once again, the wicked look in his eyes enough to make her explode right there, but then he was over her again, kissing a trail up her legs, stopping to press a hard kiss to her mound over her panties. "I'm taking these off now." The words were not a question but a statement of ownership. For that moment, that day and night, she was his.

She closed her eyes, drawing a long calming breath, and heard the crinkle of their protection, then she gasped as he drove deep inside her. She expected it to turn fast, rough and controlling like the man inside her. But instead his gaze locked on hers and they moved in unison, enjoying each slow thrust, careful to watch for what made her tense and what made her moan with pleasure. It was then she knew Trip was more than a skilled lover but a man who cared for her—as she cared for him.

The realization nearly knocked the wind out of her, and seeing the change, Trip sped up, both of them no longer able to handle the emotions swirling through them, all around them, taking them into this dangerous unknown.

Emery clung to him as they came together, and then Trip pulled her to him, her face pressed against his chest, listening to the sound of his heart, her own aching as she realized her feelings weren't merely feelings. Not at all.

They were love.

CHAPTER TWENTY-ONE

Homestretch

Trip woke to the feel of a warm body pressed against his chest, the same warm body who'd been pressed against him for days now, and he was enjoying every minute of it.

But the day was already long begun, and he had a list from here to California that wasn't going to handle itself. He shifted, gently pulling his arm out from under Emery, and stared down at her asleep in his bed, looking like she belonged there.

Then the memory of their last race hit him, and a sinking feeling worked through his gut. They'd won—barely. Craving Wind's times were getting slowly worse with each race, and though he was still a contender for the Derby, he was no longer the favorite, slipping to second, even third on some of the more prominent sites.

He continued to think about it as he showered and got ready for the day, worry weighing heavy on his shoulders. Trip's father hadn't said anything yet, but he knew it was coming, could feel it in the air, which was why he'd avoided him at every turn, staying busy working the other horses, getting them ready for their own races or coordinating transfer to the track if he thought the horse could compete. He could handle his father, but he couldn't force Sarah Anderson to use Emery if she was against it. He worked for her, not the other way around.

In short, one part of his life shone with happiness and the other had taken a nosedive. But maybe the worst part of it all was the sadness he saw in Emery's face every time she took the mount before a race, the long look as she glanced around, like she hoped Beckett would be there, even though they both knew he wasn't and wouldn't be. Beckett hadn't spoken so much as a word to Emery since the fight over the Saratoga race, and though Trip had picked up the phone to call him a hundred times himself, each time he set it back down.

Family was family, and he had no right to interfere unless she asked him to. Plus, he still had far too much respect for Beckett to call him out on his behavior, even though he felt he was being a royal dick about the whole thing. So she lied? She did it to protect him as much as anything. Why couldn't he see that? She knew that his seeing her back on the track would hurt him, so she did it without him having to see. In her own twisted way, she was saving him from the pain. But Beckett could only see the betrayal—her racing for Trip . . . instead of him.

"Hey there, where are you going?" Emery asked, her voice still foggy from sleep. Trip leaned down to kiss her, pulled back, then kissed her again, closing his eyes and enjoying the feel of her lips on his.

"I have a meeting with Mayor Phillips."

Emery nodded, and though he could tell she wanted to ask more, she didn't. It was one of the things he loved most about her. *Wait . . . what was that? Love?* The word hit him so suddenly he nearly missed it, and as he retraced his thoughts, he found himself turning away, his heart creeping into his throat. Shit. When did that happen?

"Trip?"

He cleared his throat, but it'd gone as dry as the Sahara Desert and wasn't thinking of working anytime soon. So he forced himself to look her in the eye, because he was a man after all, not a coward, and this was only a word—it didn't mean anything. They hadn't said anything. There was no risk of marriage or disappointment— or losing her.

He thought of his mother dying and the brokenness of his father, then Nick losing Brit, and Mayor Phillips being unable to get out of bed for all those months, and Trip thought he might pass out right there. He'd made the commitment to focus on his career, never letting anyone in, never exposing himself to the pain he saw all around him. Yet Emery had broken through his walls all over again, curled right up against him like she fit there—was meant to be there, and damn if he didn't want her to stay.

With a long sigh, he kissed her again. "Hang out as long as you need. I'll be back later this afternoon." Then he turned from the room before he did something really asinine. Like say the word out loud.

Trip parked outside town hall and went on in, unsure exactly why Mayor Phillips had called the emergency meeting, but since there had been that one true emergency last year and he'd skipped it because of all the fake ones, he'd vowed to be here when the good mayor called.

He waved to a few of the office staff and then continued on to the conference room to find the rest of the trustees already there, all of them staring his way like they'd been waiting for him. Hesitating at the door, he peered from one to the other, stopping at Mayor Phillips. "Is there something I should know?"

"Hello, Trip. How are you today?"

"Um . . . fine. What's this about, Mayor?"

Mayor Phillips leaned in, his hands laced on the table, his expression serious. "We were hoping you could run interference."

"On . . . ?"

Mayor Phillips turned over a piece of paper in his hand and pushed it toward Trip. "Annie-Jean Carlisle has opened a bakery in Crestler's Key."

Trip cocked his head, like he was missing something important. "All right. And how does that involve us?" Or, more accurately, him, but he knew better than to call that out. To the people in that room, Triple Run was one giant family, one joined community.

"She's seeking to expand into Triple Run, which has Patty in fits."

"Plus," Hayden Christian added, his forehead crinkled from over-thinking, "how would we know where to go in the mornings if there were two bakeries?"

The rest of the group agreed, and Trip wondered if he had slipped into one of those old sitcoms. "So, let me get this straight," he said, taking a seat in front of them. "This is the emergency? Two women feuding over a small misunderstanding from more than thirty years ago?"

This time it was Agatha Saint who spoke up. "It isn't small to them, Trip."

True enough. "What are you wanting me to do?"

"Well, we were hoping you could talk to Emery and have her ask Annie-Jean to stay in Crestler's Key. Patty will stay here, and everything will be fine."

He shook his head while everyone around the table nodded. "But why would Emery listen to me?"

All eyes found the table except the mayor's. "Well, because of your relationship, of course. Or has that ended? Charlotte—" He glanced over to the woman, who seemed to find her necklace very interesting all of a sudden. "Um . . . we *heard* you were still together. Is that the case?"

Trip couldn't believe an emergency town meeting had been called to discuss his relationship. An emergency! He opened his mouth to chastise them for this silliness, but then he caught the concern on all their faces, and though these meetings drove him crazy, though the town drove him crazy, he loved it—and all the quirky people in it.

What the hell? Trip jumped up, his heart in his throat. Dammit. There it was again. That word. Like it was placed in his chest by the devil himself, eager to drag Trip down to his personal hell.

"Are you okay, son?" Mayor Phillips asked, but Trip was sure he was seeing stars at this point, sweat building at the base of his back.

Freaked out on more levels than one, Trip spun around. "Sorry, I uh, I have to be somewhere."

He started for the door when Hayden called out, "But what about the bakery?"

"Set up a meeting with Annie-Jean and Patty. It's time they hash this out."

"But what about you? Where are you going?"

Trip stopped inside the office and peered back around at them. "I just . . . need a little air." And a heart transplant, apparently, so he could stop all this *loving* before it buried him.

CHAPTER TWENTY-TWO

Heavyweight

Emery stared down at her phone, watching as her mama's name continued to appear, torn between answering and ignoring it. Like she had the last three times she'd called. The problem was, they'd already had this conversation—twice. And Emery didn't think she had it in her, today of all days, to have it again.

The crowd buzzed with excitement, chatter carrying down to where she stood in the backside, waiting on Clark to call her to mount Craving Wind. It was her fifth race, and though she loved every second of it, she felt herself only 90 percent in it. Like she couldn't quite reach that full level of happiness, and because of it, she found herself holding back. She always lost herself when she raced, disappearing in the speed and adrenaline, allowing the thousand-pound animal below her to take over while she became nothing more than a feather on his back, guiding when she needed to but otherwise staying out of his way.

But somehow she couldn't do that now. She was thinking the whole time, overthinking her commands: when to use the stick, when to hold back, thinking, thinking, thinking. And all that thinking had nearly cost her the last race.

Ducking her head, she walked away and clicked to answer the call. "Hey, Mama."

"Emery Jane Carlisle. This is the third time I've called you and yet the first time you've answered? Is there a reason you're ignoring me or, or . . ." Emery heard her mother's voice rising and knew she was on the verge of another menopausal meltdown. She had to intercept it before she was responsible for all of Carlisle Farms enduring her mama's wrath.

"No, ma'am. I'm at the track about to race."

"Which one?"

"Billington."

Her mother went silent, and it was as though she had transferred a giant helping of guilt through the phone, dropping it right on Emery's shoulders. "Mama?"

"He should be there," she whispered. "This just isn't right."

Daddy.

Emery's bottom lip wobbled, so she clamped it down with her teeth, then drew a breath. She knew people were watching her—cameras snapping shots. It'd been relentless since her first win in Saratoga, and she didn't need to give them anything they could fabricate into a story about her. Her family didn't need that. She'd done enough.

"I wish he was," Emery managed to say, then she saw Trip walking toward her, Clark on his heels, and hurriedly added, "I love you, Mama. And I'm sorry. I've said it a thousand times, and I'd say it a thousand more times if it'd change anything. I'm sorry."

"Emery . . ."

"I've got to go. The race is about to begin."

"All right, honey. Love you, too."

Then the call was over, and Emery turned away from Trip and Clark, her hand pressed into a nearby wall, steadying herself. She thought she might break down right there, until Trip reached her and slipped in front of her, pulling her to him, ignoring everything and everyone around him. How amazing it must feel to never become affected. To never waiver. She wished she were more like him.

"What happened?"

"Just my mother, and the reminder of what I've done to Daddy."

Trip took a moment to consider this before responding. "I know it's hard for you. I can see it in your eyes, but I need you to put it out of your mind. For two minutes, I need you to forget. Can you do that?"

"Yes." *No.*

He cupped her cheeks and pressed an easy kiss to her lips, though even that felt a little too businesslike. She realized then that she liked the Trip at home a lot better than the Trip at the track. "Ready?"

"Yes."

Just then, the announcer called the riders to the paddock, and Emery went on, her heart anywhere but at that race.

And then she was inside the gate, listening to her breathing, and somehow she couldn't stop hearing it. Her breath came in and went out, slow, then fast, then slow again. It sounded unnatural, so loud in her ears that she couldn't hear anything else. Then the gates flew open and Craving Wind broke free. But Emery couldn't focus, couldn't lose herself, couldn't stop thinking about how miserable she was there, riding without her family in the grandstand. Sensing her unease, the colt fell back, but he was a closer. He'd find his pace. And then, suddenly, Emery was suffocating, her colors too tight, the strap of her helmet cutting into her chin. God, breathe, breathe. *Just help me breathe.* Her lungs burned and her hands tightened on the reins, and unsure what to do, Craving Wind fell back again, a length, then two, more and more horses zooming past them, and then they sailed over the finish line and panic ripped through her. No! It couldn't be over yet. They'd just started. She had time to fix her delay, she could . . . *oh my God.* It was over. She didn't need to see the time or hear who was in the money to know that she wasn't.

Her heart felt so heavy she wasn't sure how Craving Wind still held her up. Tears pricked her eyes and she pushed them away, standing tall despite how very, very small she felt.

She'd lost.

Emery sat quietly in the passenger seat of Trip's truck the next day, staring out the window, unwilling to look at him. She knew he wouldn't return her stare anyway. He'd barely said two words to her since the race, the disappointment all over his face, and she wondered how the hell it was possible to so fully disappointment everyone she cared about. The thought packed a fresh pound of misery on her chest and, angry, she lashed out, jabbing at the radio.

"I'm tired of this crap."

"It's Sports Talk Radio. What'd it do to you?"

She glared over, and he glared right back. "The constant crackling is giving me a headache. Who listens to AM anymore anyway?" She turned back to her window.

"So now it's the radio station's fault?"

"What did you say?"

"You heard me."

Fury rose so quickly in her chest she thought she'd explode. "Pull the damn truck over. I can walk from here."

Trip gripped the steering wheel tighter. "No."

"Pull over!"

He stared forward. "No."

"You, you—"

"What? Let me guess—now it's my fault? Go ahead, throw the bucket at anyone but yourself, Emery."

And then it hit her what he was talking about. He blamed her for losing the race and thought she didn't want to accept fault. Little did he know she had no trouble blaming herself. She'd spent all night awake, replaying what had happened, trying to find a way to learn from it, but it all came down to her. There was no one else to put this on, no one else riding Craving Wind and completely falling apart with each passing second. She remembered her inability to breathe, to focus, all the decisions she'd made and all the pain she'd caused washing over her until she was so close to a nervous breakdown it was a miracle she'd made it across the finish line at all.

"You blame me," she finally managed, the words hurting more than they should. More than she should let them.

Trip leaned back in his seat, his jaw set, all the answer she needed, and she felt herself losing it all over again, but this time not in anger but sadness.

They pulled into Annie-Jean's and Emery slipped out, Trip refusing to look at her. She started to shut the door, then paused and swallowed once so she wouldn't lose it as she spoke. "I'm sorry I let you down."

Then she shut the door and disappeared into her favorite house, praying Annie had a fresh batch of cookies in the oven. She'd need a few dozen to soothe this heartache.

CHAPTER TWENTY-THREE

Tight race

Trip pulled into his garage and dropped his head against the steering wheel, so angry at himself he contemplated driving back to Annie-Jean's and begging Emery on his hands and knees for forgiveness. He'd done exactly what he'd fought all night last night not to do, and the shit of it was, it had nothing to do with Emery losing and everything to do with *why* she lost and the repercussions of that loss.

Beckett had all but tied a weight around her, dragging her down. It was a miracle she hadn't lost sooner. Then her mother called, and it was done. He could see it in her face, but he thought the strong, feisty woman he knew would put it aside to race. But that Emery wasn't the real Emery. Inside, she aimed to please, craved it, and without Beckett's approval and support, she'd slowly and painfully become a half version of herself. He should have seen this coming.

What's worse, he already had three missed calls from his father. He knew he'd seen the race, knew he'd talked to Sarah Anderson and already put it in motion to have Marcus ride Craving Wind instead of Emery. The thought hit him so hard he felt breathless. How the hell had he lost control so completely?

Feeling like avoidance was the medicine of the hour, he pushed out of his truck and into his house to find a game playing on the widescreen and his brothers both kicked back on his leather sofa.

"Get out," he said, ignoring them as he made his way to the shower, hoping he could burn away some of this guilt.

"Now, now," Alex said, standing. "We brought beer." He went into the kitchen, and Trip heard him crack open a can, then return and pass it to him. Still fuming, he gripped the beer and nearly threw it against the wall.

Nick was to him then, always the calm brother. "Dude, when did it happen?"

Trip's heart clenched tight. "What? Don't tell me they already fired her."

Nick shook his head. "Nah . . . not yet."

Trip cursed, walking away for fear he might lose it. He lived and breathed by a certain life order—control and patience and intellect cured all. But he couldn't talk his way out of this, couldn't order someone to do something, couldn't think of a single damn way to save her from this misery. And the realization nearly broke him in half.

"Damn."

Trip glanced over to find both his brothers staring at him, Nick with sympathetic eyes, Alex with a touch of disgust. "What are you two barking about? Spill it already."

"You love her," Nick said, his voice low, like he was revealing a secret.

"I . . ." But all Trip could do was trail off, because he knew with certainty that he didn't simply love Emery Carlisle. He worshipped her, needed her to breathe, to feel whole. And now he wasn't sure how to be the man he'd always been. Who was Trip Hamilton? The old him was nothing, emotionless and closed off. He didn't want to be that man anymore, yet he knew he'd not only lost Emery's trust but as soon as she heard she wouldn't ride Craving Wind in the Kentucky Derby, she'd never speak to him again. She'd blame him. And she'd be right.

His gaze fell helplessly on his brothers, the two people in the world who understood how hard this was for him. "What do I do?"

Alex opened his mouth, likely to spout out something smart, but Nick hit him in the chest before he could continue. "Hey!"

"Well," Nick said. "No one needs your opinion." And then he turned to Trip. "You tell her. You open your heart wide and tell her. And then, when you're done telling her, tell her about Craving Wind before someone else does. Because we tend to forget all the reasons we have to forgive someone when we're at our worst."

"Will she hear me out? Will she forgive me for not telling her sooner?"

Nick shrugged and took a long pull from his beer. "No clue. But you'll never know standing here talking to us."

Trip hesitated, and Nick took a step closer. "Look, I know we messed up your love life for you. Screwed up the way you see it."

"Hey!" Alex called for the second time, but with one look from the brothers, his shoulders fell and he sighed. "All right, fine. So I'm not exactly the poster child for relationships."

"Understatement." Nick laughed. "But here's the thing, Trip, at least we're trying. I know I lost Brit, but I'd do it all over again if I could. So would Dad. We don't regret falling in love just because we lost the ones we loved. Talk to her, man. You'll regret it for the rest of your life if you don't."

All the convincing he needed. Trip grabbed his keys off the counter and started for the door as his cell rang. Most of the time he'd ignore it, but Mama V rarely called him. He hit Answer on the phone as he jumped into his truck. "Hamilton."

"Honey, are you home?" she whispered.

Trip's eyebrows drew together. Mama V spoke in one tone—loud. For her to whisper, something had to be wrong. Very wrong. "What happened, V?"

"You need to get down to the barn. Fast."

"Can you explain?"

"Just . . . hurry."

He threw the truck in reverse and sped down the road, a thousand thoughts going through his head. Had something happened to one of the broodmares while foaling? Had something happened to his father? No. She would've called his brothers, too, and she wanted him down at the barn, which could only mean one thing.

Stepping on it, he made the last turn toward the main barn, spotting Emery's Jeep parked outside, and then his gaze fell on the scene—Mama V wringing her hands. Clark and half the others on the farm standing around, tense. And Emery and Marcus standing off, shouting at each other, their faces so close it was amazing no one had thrown a punch yet.

Dammit!

Trip threw the truck in park and jumped out, slamming the door and racing over. "What the hell is going on?" he shouted as he reached them, and then Emery turned, her face full of pain. She knew.

He took a step back, the weight of her stare too much for him to stand in, but she deserved more than a coward. He opened his mouth to say he was sorry, to ask her to come talk—anything—when she tossed up her hand.

"Don't. Don't you dare." And the hurt combined with the words, so close to the ones she'd used when they were together, sent him reeling.

"Emery, please."

"Guess screwing the boss didn't get you very far after all," Marcus said, and unable to hold his temper another second, Trip stormed him, tossing him into a stable door, ready to punch, before Clark stepped between them, urging Trip back.

"Stop. Take a breath," Clark said.

Trip stared at his assistant trainer, his friend, his breathing heavy, and then his gaze fell on Emery, walking away.

"Emery!" he called, but she wasn't stopping. Not for anybody, certainly not for him. He reached her and skidded in front of her, his arms out to stop her. "Please, listen . . ."

"Did you know?" she asked, a hint of hope in her eyes. "Tell me you didn't know."

Hanging his head, he stepped back and put his hands on his hips, sure if he didn't put them somewhere they'd betray him and reach out to the woman he loved. Damn, how had he messed this up when he'd just gotten her back? With incredible will, he lifted his eyes, pushing aside the need to protect himself. This wasn't about him. "Yes."

She spun on her heels. "That's all I needed to know."

"No, let me explain. Sarah Anderson, she—"

"I lost one race, Trip. One! You're the trainer. They hire you, not me. They listen to you, not the other way around." Her eyes found the ground, her teeth working at her bottom lip, and God if he didn't feel like the piece of shit he was. "Did you even try?" Tear-filled eyes found him. "Did you fight for me?"

He tried to draw a breath and failed. "I . . ."

"That's what I thought."

And then she was in her Jeep, and all he could do was stare as she drove away.

CHAPTER TWENTY-FOUR

Jump the gun

"Darlin', you're gonna have to move to another drug. Vodka, maybe?" Annie said, passing over a slice of freshly made peach cobbler. "I'm all out of sugar."

Emery dug her fork into the cobbler, stuffing far more into her mouth than her mama would find appropriate, and lay back on the couch, ignoring the memories of Trip and her on that very couch, everything so perfect. Why couldn't it stay that way? The two of them lost in each other, her heart floating somewhere high above.

"I can get behind some vodka." Kate pushed her own fork into the cobbler and moaned loudly as she slowly enjoyed the dessert. "Annie, you've got a gift. Did you sell your soul or something? Nobody makes desserts like this."

Annie beamed over at them, until her gaze landed on Emery, staring at the TV but not at all seeing it. "Heavens, child, you're going to make *me* cry, and I vowed to stop crying in 1995."

Kate slumped against her and wrapped her tightly in a hug. "We just need to find you another trainer, another horse."

The thought made Emery want to sob, because it wasn't about the Kentucky Derby. She wanted to ride Craving Wind . . . and she wanted Trip to feel she was the best rider for him, that no one else could ride Craving Wind the way she could ride him. Instead, she'd lost one race and he'd turned on her completely.

"I think I'm ready for that vodka now." Emery held out her empty plate to Annie, and with only a moment of hesitation, she shrugged and disappeared into the kitchen, returning with drinks for each of them. "Okay, but no puking on this rug. It's new."

Kate passed Emery a glass and then sat back against the couch beside her. "I don't want to make it worse, but what happened at the track, Em? Why did you lose?"

"You can't win every race."

"No, but something tells me it's more than that. I'm not asking why someone loses. I'm asking why *you* lost."

Emery closed her eyes, remembering the way her helmet strap had cut into her chin, her shirt tight against her chest. Air had flown past her, yet she couldn't seem to find a breath. "I just . . . I felt like I was suffocating. I kept thinking about Daddy, and how hard he's worked for me all these years. He helped me become a rider, taught me how to race. He's the reason I won the Kentucky Oaks two years ago, and why I would have won it a second time if not for the accident. He believed in me." She choked on a sob, emotions rising from her chest. "And what sucks the most is, I turned my back on him only to ride for Trip, who clearly never believed in me. And to think I thought I . . ." She shook her head, not wanting to admit it out loud now that things had changed so completely.

"Thought what?" Kate asked, setting her glass on the coffee table.

Emery stared down at the phone in her hand, the three missed calls from Trip and two text messages asking her to call him. "Thought I loved him."

"Oh, God, Em . . ."

"It's okay, really. It wasn't meant to be."

Kate hiccupped, then took another long sip of her drink. "Just like me and Alex."

"Oh, no." Emery gripped her hand. "I thought you went out again and it went well."

She blew a stray red curl from her eyes. "Yeah, if well means a guy patting you on the back and saying, 'See you next time, champ.'"

"He didn't."

"He did. He champed me."

Emery clinked her glass against her friend's. "To us, and to never falling for guys who don't love us. I mean, I probably didn't really love him anyway. You can't really love someone who doesn't love you back. Surely love doesn't work that way."

Annie leaned against the wall in the family room and crossed her arms. "You are so stupid."

Both Emery and Kate's heads snapped up. "What?"

"Of course you love him, Em. And he loves you. You could see it plain on his face whenever he was around you. And now he's called you numerous times, sent texts. I'm surprised I don't have delivery guys pounding on my door with obnoxious floral arrangements."

"But he—"

Annie tossed up her hands. "I know what he did. You've told me at least ten times now, but when you've lived as long as I have, you start seeing things in levels of importance. Seeing the truth behind actions. Don't you see? He got angry with you for the loss because he knew what it meant. He knew you'd get pulled from that horse you loved and it tore him apart, so he lashed out. Was it right? Hell no. But he's a man. They never act the way they should when we want them to. Their brains are installed with screwup software at birth."

Could Annie be right?

The clock on the mantel hit five, and Emery's heart stilled. Right now, Marcus was riding Craving Wind, breaking from the gate and feeling all the wonder of Craving Wind's ability. Emery had never ridden such a horse, and she suspected neither had Marcus. But now he would, and maybe even better than she had. And Trip would be there, ready to congratulate them in the winner's circle. Not her.

She slumped down into the couch, pulling her ratty robe tighter around her. "I need a stronger drink." Emery toyed with the phone in her hand, desperate to hear Trip's voice, for him to confirm everything Annie had said, but she knew Trip. He was an amazing trainer. He wouldn't pull her from Craving Wind unless he truly felt another jockey could do a better job.

Annie brought a fresh round of drinks, then two, then five, and before she knew it, she and Kate were two sheets to the wind, dancing along to the Dixie Chicks' "Cowboy Take Me Away," blasting from the Vevo channel from Annie's Roku. Thank God for Rokus, and the Vevo channel, and the Dixie Chicks, who knew exactly what she needed to hear. And what happened to the Dixie Chicks, anyway? Probably got screwed by some man who told them some other singer could sing about cowboys and getting taken away better than them. And who did that man think he was, telling them someone else could sing cowboys better? No one sung cowboys better than the Dixie Chicks! Even though, Emery thought, this was their only song actually *about* cowboys, but still! They did it best, and they didn't need some stupid man telling them to stop!

In fact . . .

Emery swiped her phone off the coffee table and scrolled until she found Trip's name, and then clicked the little Phone icon and then Speaker, 'cause she wasn't 100 percent sure she could hold the phone steady against her ear. The phone rang two and a half times before—

"Emery?"

"You can't tell me not to sing about cowboys."

"Um . . . okay."

"And just because they only wrote the one song about cowboys doesn't mean they aren't experts on cowboys. One doesn't mean a thing. They are experts. They're the *best* at cowboys."

"Yeah!" Kate called out for emphasis. "The best!"

"Emery, how much have you had to drink?"

"We're not talking about drinking. We're talking about cowboys, and how you men try to tell us we can't do it. But we can. And the Dixie Chicks can. And, and . . . I can." A strangled cry broke from her lips, and if not for the alcohol, Emery would have screamed at herself. But there was no stopping this. "You didn't believe in me."

Her cry was met with a moment of silence; then he said, "You're wrong. No one believes in you like I do. I can't take back what's happened, and I won't blame you if you never forgive me. But for what it's worth, I'm sorry, and no matter who you race for, no matter whose colors you wear, I'll be rooting for you."

Emery hung up before she did something stupid, like confess how much she missed him. Or, worse, how much she loved him. Because loving someone who didn't believe in you was worse than loving no one at all. And despite what he'd said, she knew how he really felt. She set her phone down and peered up to find both Annie and Kate staring at her.

"Em . . ."

"Stop," Emery said, holding up a hand and nearly knocking herself off balance.

"Annie's right. He loves you."

Emery fell back against the couch, her eyes on the Dixie Chicks, her mind on only one cowboy. "No. If he loved me, he would have told me the truth. He wouldn't have let me find out from Marcus the asshole. I'm just a silly girl who fell for the wrong man. Twice!"

Only he didn't feel like the wrong man. He got her, understood what made her tick, and that alone was enough to make her wish to be with him for the rest of her life. But him seeing her wasn't the same thing as him loving her. Love was putting a person first, protecting her, and being honest even when it was hard.

"All right, enough of this," Annie said, wiping her hands on her apron. "I'm not nursing two drunks. Sober up. We're going out."

Kate fist pumped the air. "Yes! Let's go out!" Then her forehead crinkled and she turned to Annie. "But there aren't any bars in town."

A glint of wickedness flashed in Emery's aunt's eyes. "No. But I know of one that'll be perfect. Go get dressed."

Before Emery could argue—not that she was sober enough to try—Annie had them over in Triple Run, parking outside Rudy's. "All righty, we're here."

Emery craned her neck and then straightened in her seat. "I'm not going anywhere near there."

"Why? Trip's at that stakes race, right? He's not even in town. Plus, I know the owner, and he'll give us a deal on drinks."

Or make virgin ones without telling us, Emery thought. But the truth was, she wanted to go inside, wanted be here in Triple Run among Trip's people, like she was a part of his life, which was maybe the most pathetic thing she'd ever thought in her life.

"Come on, Em," Kate said. "It can't be that bad, and it's the closest bar to home. You won't even see anyone you know."

Emery peered back up at the sign and then down the sidewalk, but there was no one especially out, so what was the harm? Plus, she felt bad for her aunt and her best friend, doing their best to cheer her up and her being more than a little difficult. She owed it to them to put her misery aside—or at least to go along.

"All right, fine, but if Mama V's in there, I'm walking."

"Who's Mama V?" Annie asked as she opened the door to the bar, then stopped cold as her gaze landed on someone by the bar.

Emery followed her glare to see Patty there, laughing with the older man behind the bar, who Emery could only assume to be Rudy. "Uh-oh, now who's running?"

"I don't do running." Annie *wasn't* one to run, but she hadn't taken a step either.

"I heard you. But I haven't seen you move either."

Annie glared at her only niece, then pushed in front of her and strode toward the bar, and Emery thought maybe it hadn't been such a good idea to joke with her after all. Annie might be an amazing person, but like any good Southern woman, she turned into a raging bitch if pushed too far.

With a sidelong look at Kate, Emery followed her on inside, thankful Annie chose a four-top table close to the bar but on the opposite side from Patty.

People stood all around, watching a game on the widescreens around the room, the chatter making it hard to hear anyone else or pay attention to those around them. Which was why Emery didn't see Alex Hamilton until he stood right in front of her.

"Hey there," he said, flashing a smile because this was Alex, and his face was set permanently in flirt mode. She tried not to take it personally.

"What do you want, Alex?"

He started to answer, but his gaze shifted to Emery's right. "Kate."

"Yep. That's my name," Kate said.

Alex peered from her to Emery. "You're drunk."

"So, what's it to you?" Emery and Kate said at the same time, then broke into laughter. They'd always thought the same way. Clearly that particular aspect of their friendship emerged when they were drunk.

"It's a lot to me," he said, and Kate blinked, staring at him like she was seeing him for the first time. Emery rolled her eyes, wishing they'd leave and get a room or whatever, so she could drink whiskey and listen to Carrie Underwood singing about smashing in her cheating boyfriend's truck.

Finally, Alex pulled away from Kate, but the smile he'd used on her was still in place. She bet he used that weapon everywhere he went. Like Trip, he had the same tall, strong build and wavy brown hair, but his had streaks of blond mixed into it, setting off the flecks of gold in his green eyes. His jeans and shirt were a little too I-rolled-out-of-bed perfect, which made Emery think behind the carefree facade was a guy who genuinely cared what others thought of him.

Unlike Trip.

Trip was the definition of self-actualized. He knew himself, respected who that person was, and never let anyone get in the way of it. It was part of what had attracted her to him all those years ago, when she was a girl watching him learn to be the great trainer he became. Only he didn't train like her daddy trained. He'd created his own style; a mix of others maybe, or maybe all Trip Hamilton. It was like magic watching him work. Everything about him was so—

"Wow."

Her gaze snapped up to find Kate and Alex both watching her. "What?" She peered around, unsure if she'd missed something.

"I thought it was just him."

"What was just him?"

Alex's smirk rose to take up his face, and Emery thought she didn't really like him or his well-bred Southern charm so much.

"Spill it already or go on." She glared at the double shot in front of her, the amber liquid both coaxing her in and pushing her away. She couldn't hold her whiskey and she knew it.

"Damn, you sound exactly like him. No wonder he fell in love with you."

She opened her mouth to reply as she realized Annie was no longer with them. The whole town must be there now. Unable to spot her around them, she pushed off the table and stood up in her chair, scanning the room.

"Woah!" Alex called. "Get down before you kill yourself."

"Emery, seriously, get down before you fall." Kate reached out to her.

"I'm not going to fall," she said, finally locking in on Annie, and— *crap.*

Annie stood at the bar, right beside Patty, and even from here Emery could tell the conversation wasn't a friendly hello. Emery leaned forward to try to decipher what they were saying, and suddenly all the shots she'd had since she'd walked into Rudy's hit at once. The room started spinning, which Emery thought was pretty damn funny until she adjusted her feet to climb back down, and instead, her stupid high heel got caught in a wooden slat in the chair. She jerked hard to break free, throwing her body off balance, and then she was falling.

She had enough time to think *this is going to suck*, before strong arms wrapped around her, catching her in midfall.

"Let me go, Alex," she shouted, but then she drew a breath and her heart pressed against her ribs, desperate to get closer to the man who held her—the man whose rustic, soapy scent she would recognize anywhere.

CHAPTER TWENTY-FIVE

Beating a dead horse

Trip stared down at the woman in his arms, equal parts relieved to have her near him again and pissed that she was behaving so recklessly. "What the hell are you doing? Trying to break your neck or drink yourself into a coma?"

"Ugh!" Emery fought against him, but he tightened his grip.

"I'm not putting you down, so you can relax before you hurt yourself."

"You are infuriating!"

He wanted to laugh but thought it really wasn't the time. "Yeah, well, you aren't the first to tell me that. Probably not the last."

"What are you doing here, anyway?"

"I called him," Alex said to her, a hint of guilt in his voice. He was a people pleaser through and through and couldn't stand to rock the boat. "You looked a little buzzed when you got here, and nobody comes to Rudy's without leaving drunk, so . . ." He nodded to Trip. "Sorry, but he'd have killed me if I didn't call him." Then, before Emery could go off on him, he grabbed Kate's hand. "Buy you a drink?"

Kate beamed back, and Trip wanted to warn her that there was no point beaming in Alex's general direction, but it was no use. Alex had that effect on women. At least until the next morning.

The crowd seemed to thicken more and more with each passing second, and that's when Trip finally set Emery down in her chair and peered around, his gaze connecting with far too many people for it to be a coincidence. Rudy's was never this packed. Hell, they were all there for Trip and Emery—watching this showdown like some soap opera drama. It was a wonder old Rudy didn't pass out popcorn to go with the show.

Trip lowered his voice and leaned into Emery, who immediately pulled back. "I don't need your lean. I'm over your lean. Way over. Take that lean elsewhere."

He fought back a smile. Damn if he didn't love her sass. And there it was again, that word, followed by the dread in his chest that he'd lost her. Unable to help himself, he tucked her hair behind her ear. "What if I don't want to take it elsewhere? What if there's only one person I want to lean into?"

She swallowed hard, her face the picture of strength despite the glassiness of her eyes. From alcohol or emotion, he couldn't be sure. "I can't do this." Pushing to stand, she started away from him, only to sway on her heels, and once again he caught her.

"Woah, lady girl," Trip said, only to receive a sharp look that screamed *screw you*. "I can't let you leave like this. We don't have to talk about us, but you're not leaving like this."

With reluctance, he steered her back to her seat and stood in front of her, his hands still on her hips, the urge to kiss her so intense he nearly did it—even if he received her wrath immediately after. How this woman had infected him so fully was a mystery to him, but if this was what it felt like to be lovesick, he didn't want a cure. He wanted her.

"I'm sorry."

"Yeah, you said that, but it doesn't really change anything. Do you have any idea how I feel right now? It isn't about the Derby. I love Craving Wind. He is my horse. Mine. I knew he was a champion the moment I saw him." She sucked in a rattled breath and focused back on the crowd. "You took him from me. You, the person who's supposed to care about me. The person I—"

Gently, Trip gripped her hips, forcing her to look at him. "The person you what?"

She hit him with her steely blue eyes. "Trusted. But I won't make that mistake again."

Alex and Kate rushed up then, before Trip could work out the word he felt sure she wanted to say—the word he wanted to say, and he would, if he didn't feel it would make things worse.

"Y'all better get over to the bar. Annie-Jean and Patty are about to fight. Rudy's taking bets. I swear, this town'll bet on anything."

"Jesus." Emery pushed out of her chair, glaring at Trip when he tried to steady her, so he kept close, prepared to catch her if she stumbled.

They reached the bar, and sure enough, Annie and Patty stood nose to nose, fists clenched, shouting.

"Annie, what the hell?" Emery said, stopping beside her. Trip could tell she was working to sober up fast so she could be there for her aunt, and he dropped that into yet another thing he adored about her—she put others first. Always.

Annie pointed at Patty. "This lying hag is trying to out me from town!"

"This is my town, not yours. You have Crestler's Key. I left, like you told me to. I stayed away. You can't move here, too. You can't have the whole South, you selfish cow!"

"Me a selfish cow? I didn't betray my best friend." This time Annie's voice wasn't full of hate but misery.

Patty's face fell. "How many times can I say I'm sorry, Annie? I am so, so sorry. I was a child then, and you're right. I was selfish. But I'm not a girl now, and I would never do that to you again. But I'm not the only adult here, and you holding this grudge, refusing to forgive me, proves you never cared about me the way I cared about you. Because there is nothing you could have done to make me turn my back on you."

Patty reached behind her for her purse and disappeared through the crowd, Annie watching her go, all the fire in her replaced by sadness. "I want to go," Annie said.

"No," Emery said to her aunt. "We're not continuing this feud for another decade. She's sorry, Annie. How can you keep hating her when you know she loves you? When you know she's sick with guilt? Why continue hating someone you so clearly need in your life?"

Annie shook her head, like she was trying to fight off what Emery said but couldn't find a hole in her logic. She drew a breath and blew it out slowly. "Dammit. I hate when I'm wrong." Then she followed Patty's path to the door, reaching her before she slipped out. Trip and Emery watched them talk for a second, and then they hugged, and Trip had a surge of hope. If Annie could forgive Patty, then maybe, just maybe, Emery could forgive him.

But then Emery turned to Kate. "Ready to go? I'm tired." She pressed her hand to her head.

Kate eyed Alex and then Emery, chewing on her lip. "Actually, Alex and I were going to . . . um . . ."

"Oh," Emery said. Damn Alex for getting the girl without even trying. "Sure. Call me if you need me." Then she followed her aunt to the door, and Trip caught her hand.

"Stop. You can't go. Not like this."

Her expression held all the telltale signs of defeat. "I don't want to argue with you. I don't have it in me to argue."

"Then don't. You told Annie to forgive. Why can't you?"

Emery's shoulders slumped as she peered up at him. "Because what Patty did was a long time ago, when they were kids. This, you and me, we're not kids, Trip. And I'm sorry, I can't let it go. I just can't . . ." She spun around and walked slowly toward the door, and though every part of him wanted to stop her, he didn't follow. He knew there was no point.

She was gone.

CHAPTER TWENTY-SIX

Safe bet

AG Bakery brimmed with excitement as Emery stepped inside, curious to see what her favorite aunt was up to now. She spotted her mama by the front as soon as she entered and walked over, kissing her easily on the cheek.

"Hey, Mama. What are you doing here?"

She pointed to the room, a wide smile on her face, and Emery thanked God she was dealing with Sane Mama versus Menopause-laden Crazy Mama. "Didn't you hear from Annie? She and Patty are going into business together. Giving away free cookies all day to celebrate."

Emery shifted her gaze to behind the counter of the bakery to find her aunt and Patty laughing together, passing out cookies of all sorts. Her heart swelled at seeing a smile on Annie's face, someone who deserved her fair share of happiness.

She started to ask when it happened—and why Annie hadn't told her—when she found her mama watching her. "What?"

"Nothing. I just . . . I hate seeing my baby so sad."

Avoiding her mother's knowing eyes else she might cry right there in the middle of the cookie fest, she said, "I'm okay, Mama."

"The Derby's this weekend. I think you're anything but okay. Just like your daddy. He's barely left his office since y'alls' fight. Can't you talk to him?"

"I've tried. He won't take my calls."

"He's your daddy, Emery. Try harder."

Emery looked at her mother.

"We fight for our family, Em. We don't let petty stuff break us. We fight for the people we love. Life happens, stuff hurts, but as long as we have each other, we'll get through."

Blinking hard, Emery tried to keep her voice steady. "He made me leave."

At this, her mother stepped in front of her, inches shorter at barely five foot tall, but with that Stern Mama expression on her face. "Now you listen here, young lady; he was angry and acted rashly, but he would never make you leave. You chose to leave. And I understand, honey. Running is a lot easier than enduring the pain. But it's time to face the music. Your daddy loves you; stubborn as he is, he loves you. Love him enough to take the first step."

Emery sat in her Jeep outside her parents' house, waiting for some wave of courage to overcome her. She thought of all the times she'd raced into that house, calling for them, never once hesitating, never once questioning whether she was wanted there. Now her father had pushed her away, changed the locks, and turned his back on her. How could she go in there now? And if it were anyone else, she'd throw away the caring key and never look back, but this wasn't just anyone. This was her father, and didn't he deserve the right to make a mistake? A part of Emery longed for him to call her and ask for forgiveness, but waiting on stubborn Beckett Carlisle was like waiting for water in hell—not happening.

Drawing a breath of bravery, she pushed out of her Jeep and started up the steps, unsure if she should knock or not. Maybe he'd changed these locks too. But then she gripped the doorknob and pushed, her heart heavy as she stepped inside. The smells of her childhood all hit her, and for a moment, she thought she might break down right there. But she couldn't go the rest of her life without trying, so she continued on around to her daddy's office, knocking once, then opening the door, knowing he was inside and not wanting to give him the chance to turn her away without seeing her first.

He swiveled in his chair as soon as the door opened, clearly expecting her mama. His eyes locked on Emery, first showing happiness, then anger, then settling on sadness.

"What are you doing here, Emery?"

Knowing she'd lose her nerve if she didn't speak fast, she started with the truth, holding nothing back from him, for once in her life.

"I've been thinking these last few weeks, and I'm completely lost as to how we arrived here. I feel like a stranger in the house where I grew up. I thought of all the things I could say to make you forgive me, what could help, and that's when I realized there is no fix. You want me to do what you tell me to do. And I can't do that anymore, Daddy. I'm an adult now, and if I learned anything from my accident, it's that I'm strong enough to stand on my own two feet. Will I make some mistakes? Sure. But at least I'll know they're mine. And here's the thing—I would never do this to you. There is nothing in the world you could do to make me look at you the way you're looking at me." She released a breath, her eyes finding the floor. "I understand what I did, and I won't try to explain it away, but I couldn't live with myself if I didn't come here and try one last time to make amends. Because you're my hero, Daddy. I love you. And I guess that's all." She paused to look at him, giving him time to reply, to say something—any-thing—but all he did was stare. "All right, then; good-bye."

She shut the door behind herself and ran down the hall, making it all the way to her Jeep before the tears found her again. At least she'd tried . . .

CHAPTER TWENTY-SEVEN

Under the wire

Trip watched from the backstretch as Craving Wind went through her morning workout, Marcus on his back instead of the exercise rider out of Trip's insistence. So far, Marcus had yet to be on the horse without Craving Wind acting like he wanted to throw him back off, and the last thing they needed was for Marcus to be the reason they lost the Derby.

The air outside was warm but not humid, the sky so blue it blinded. People milled all around, excited for the next day, and Trip should be excited, too. He had a horse in the Kentucky Derby, a horse who had a very good chance of winning, yet all Trip could see was a world of gray. He thought of Emery riding Craving Wind, how perfectly they worked together, how the horse trusted her—maybe even more than Trip himself. She should be here, riding the horse she loved. She should be the one to celebrate this moment.

Anger coursed through him at the volatility of being a jockey—how they rarely received the respect they deserved, how they could be replaced like this on a whim, unlike trainers. Unlike him. Trip had won the Eclipse Award for Outstanding Trainer three years in a row, and with that and his series of wins, he'd become the most sought-out trainer in the world. There wasn't an owner who would turn him away, who would deny him anything.

He took a step back, the thought swarming through his mind, and then it hit him—Craving Wind's owner wouldn't deny him anything. Why hadn't he thought of this before? It was a risk, a giant risk that might ruin his career, but he didn't want a career without Emery beside him. Didn't want to stand here, watching all his success, without someone he loved to share in it. He understood now what Nick and Mayor Phillips had meant—there was no joy in life greater than being with someone you love. That was living. *Loving* was living.

He only hoped it worked.

Trip stepped away from the backside, ignoring the call from a reporter, and walked away from earshot, then called Sarah Anderson, Craving Wind's owner.

The phone rang three times, and Trip feared she wouldn't answer and all hope would be lost. But then he heard a quiet, "Sarah Anderson."

"Sarah? It's Trip. Are you at Churchill Downs?"

"I arrived yesterday."

He released a breath. "Great. I need to speak with you. Immediately. How about lunch?"

She hesitated then, "Sure. I have a few afternoon engagements, but I could meet you at eleven."

"Eleven is perfect."

They hung up, and Trip called Clark. "I need a favor. . . ."

The Derby Cafe buzzed with excitement, every table full. Several people walked over to shake Trip's hand, even Peter Grant, trainer for Lucky Cross, this year's favorite to win the Kentucky Derby. There was even talk of him going all the way to winning the Triple Crown.

Trip hoped to stop that streak with the Derby. But he needed Craving Wind on his best game, and he knew that horse would only fly for one person—Emery. They were a perfect match, and it was time they were reunited.

A hostess walked up, Sarah Anderson beside her, "Here you are, Ms. Anderson."

"Thank you."

The older woman sat across from Trip, her kind eyes lined with wrinkles. The Anderson family was well known in the racing world and had been for years, owning many champions, including the 2011 Preakness winner and the 2013 Breeders' Cup winner. She understood this sport through and through, which he hoped would help him with his case.

"Is there a problem with Craving Wind?" she asked, a hint of nervousness behind her poise. "Injury? Abscess?"

"Oh, no," Trip said. "Nothing like that. But we do have a problem.

He refuses to perform for our new jockey, Marcus, the way he performed for Emery Carlisle."

Sarah took a sip from her sweet tea. "Yes, but Emery lost her last race on Craving Wind."

Trip nodded. "She did. But anyone can lose one race. She's won every other race on that horse."

"Yes, but she hasn't ridden him *since* that loss. This would be a gamble I'm not sure I'm willing to take."

Drawing a long breath and taking a drink of his water, wishing he'd ordered something stronger, he went with his second argument—the one he hoped spoke to her. "Sarah, you grew up around horses. You've owned and loved many."

"I have," she replied hesitantly. "Though I'm not sure how that's relevant."

"Do you remember who sold you Craving Wind?"

She opened her mouth and then closed it again, her gaze focused on him now. "Carlisle Farms."

"Exactly. There's a reason he runs best for her. She's been around him since birth. He loves her, and she loves him. Marcus has yet to meet Emery's best time on Craving Wind. I need you to trust me; they won't let you down."

Sarah studied him, refusing to break eye contact. "Perhaps, but I sense their love for each other isn't the love driving this conversation."

And there it was, the thing he'd hoped she wouldn't catch, but she wasn't a fool. "You're right. Which brings me to the reason I called this meeting. Emery is the right rider for this horse. Apart from my feelings for her, she is your best chance of winning the Derby. So . . ."

"Trip, I'm an old lady who values her time. Please, can we get to the point?"

He steadied his gaze on hers, blocking out the people around them, the press who were sure to listen in, taking notes on the meeting. He didn't care. He only cared about one thing—one person now—and he'd let her down. He wouldn't make that mistake again.

"Either Emery rides . . . or you can find yourself another trainer."

Sarah's eyes narrowed on Trip as she took another sip of her tea. He watched her every move, waiting, praying this worked.

"I see you're taking a gamble as well."

Trip laughed. "We're in racing, Sarah. There's always risk."

"So there is." She studied him a moment longer, as though searching for some hint of doubt, and then smiled up at him. "I trust you, Trip. If you say she's the rider for Craving Wind, then she's the rider. I'll take this gamble with you. Once. Don't let me down."

He released a breath. "Thank you. You won't regret this."

They finished lunch, and Trip said good-bye, relieved she'd agreed, until he took out his phone for the second part of his plan. He ran through his spiel again and again, but this wasn't someone who could be easily persuaded. This was the most stubborn person he knew, a person who lived and breathed racing—and the only other person who would have done what Trip did.

He scrolled until he found the person in his contacts, hesitated, then tapped the name.

"Hello?"

"Beckett? It's Trip Hamilton. It's time we had a chat."

CHAPTER TWENTY-EIGHT

Race card

Emery walked down the aisle of shops on Main Street, trying to convince herself that she could find another trainer to work for— Peter Grant or Lynn Mack. There were others. Plenty of others. And she wouldn't complicate it this time. She would ride and do her job and keep her feelings to herself. She could do that.

Brighton waved to her as she passed Brighton's Sandwiches and Pastries, and she thought she liked sandwiches and pastries. Maybe she should forget racing and work there. Or Paula's Flowers & Gifts. Or any one of the shops in town. She didn't need racing to be happy, and she didn't need Trip Hamilton. The problem was, those were lies, all of them. But maybe in time she could trick herself into believing them.

She had just reached for the door to Brighton's to meet Kate for a late lunch when her phone rang.

"Mama? Everything okay?"

"Yes, honey. I called because you have a visitor."

"There at the farm?" Emery tried to think of who might come to Carlisle Farms to see her, and a tiny tendril of excitement coiled through her heart. Could it be? But then she remembered he'd been to Annie's and knew she'd still be there. Sadness overcame her, and she pressed her palm over her heart, hoping to massage out the pain. How had he affected her so completely? She'd protected her heart from him all those years ago, why had she failed the second time around?

"Em?"

She shook her head, pulling herself back to the moment. "Sorry. Um, can you just—"

"Your daddy's not home."

Emery tried to process this, and where he might be, if he'd gone to the Derby without her, but these thoughts weren't going to bring her anything but more pain. "All right, Mama. I'll be right there."

Ten minutes later, she parked her Jeep in the turnaround in front of her parents' house. Tears threatened her as she walked up the steps, the memories coming back once again. She'd been so lucky to grow up there, her parents nothing but supportive from the beginning. She hadn't told her mother what happened earlier, when she'd gone to see her father. The details didn't matter. All that mattered now was that she'd told him she loved him—the ball was in his court now. A part of her was still angry that he didn't trust her to know when she was ready, but then she thought it must have been hard for them to see her get hurt, to wait in the hospital through all three surgeries, to finally see her, all broken and bruised. They wouldn't be the good parents they were if that hadn't impacted them.

She reached for the door right as it opened and Clark walked out.

"Oh my God, Clark." She opened her arms to hug him, not realizing until that moment how much she missed the staff she'd spent so much time with over the last six months. "What are you doing here?"

"Emery," he said, nodding once to her. "Care to sit?" He nodded to the white rockers on the porch.

"Um, yeah, sure."

They sat down, and Emery tried to keep her hands still in her lap as she ran through reasons he could be there—all of them leading back to false hope.

Clark stared down the long driveway. "I've never been here before. It's nice."

"It is."

"Has it always been this large?"

Emery shook her head. "No. Daddy bought more of the surrounding acreage when he took up breeding." They fell into silence, and Emery, always the talker, couldn't stand it any longer. "I don't think you came to talk about the farm."

He smiled. "No. I guess I didn't."

"So what do you need? Is it . . . ?" Emery trailed off, not wanting to even think his name.

"I know things got a little complicated, and I won't pretend I know all the details or understand how you must feel. But you and I both know you were meant to ride Craving Wind in the Kentucky Derby. Well, now you've got your chance."

Emery gripped the arms of her rocker, her heart rate speeding up. "What did you say?"

"I'm saying Craving Wind's running tomorrow, and he needs a rider."

"But how? Marcus . . ."

"Trip told Sarah Anderson that it was either you or him. She chose you."

Emery tried to process what Clark was telling him. "He threatened to quit?"

"He loves you, would do anything for you. Now he needs you to love him back enough to forgive him. He's got a horse but no rider, and if you refuse to go, then Craving Wind and Trip will be disqualified. Complications aside, you love that horse, and I have a feeling you love Trip even more. The Derby's yours, Em—go get it."

CHAPTER TWENTY-NINE

Off to the races

Trip paced the backside, his nerves twisting into knots. He'd yet to see Emery, yet to hear from Clark, and at this point, his sanity had checked out. He'd registered Emery as their rider despite having no idea if she'd actually show. The tension was killing him, and if he had to answer one more question about Craving Wind and why he'd fired Marcus, he was going to turn Hulk on somebody. He didn't do well with the unknown, and this situation was slathered in unknowns, then coated in shit for good measure. The announcer would call Craving Wind to the paddock any second. Any second! Where the hell was everyone?

Scrubbing a hand over his face, he reached for his phone to call Clark again when he spotted him rushing toward Trip, a smile on his face.

"Tell me you've got good news, man." Trip put his hands on his hips to keep them steady. He might die of a heart attack before the race began.

"See for yourself."

Clark turned, and Trip followed his outstretched hand to the person walking toward them, already dressed in the orange and red and yellow silks that represented an Anderson horse. He told himself to remain still, to watch her and file away this moment into his memory, but he'd never been one to follow the rules. Before he could think about it, he started for her, speeding up until he stood over her, peering down at the most beautiful woman he'd ever seen. He wanted to say thank you, to say he was sorry, to spit out a thousand words that might mean nothing.

"Trip, I . . ."

He pressed a finger to her lips, the feel of them against his skin so good he nearly lost himself right there. "I have something to say."

She stared up at him with those blue eyes narrowed in aggravation, and then he lost his ability to think—lost the speech he'd planned out, all the things he wanted to say and apologize for, instead replaced with three small words, and he couldn't keep them inside another second.

"God, I love you." She snapped back, her angry eyes suddenly wide, her mouth fallen slack. "I feel like I've loved you my whole life, like every moment before you was dead and useless, like I wasn't really living, like I wasn't breathing. And then you came into my life and showed me all that spunk and fire, and now I can't seem to function without you. I don't care about this race. I don't care if we win or lose. I don't care if I never have another trophy on my mantel. All I care about is you."

Emery took a step toward him, and he threw up his hands, sure she was going to go off on him, but she said, "Will you shut up and kiss me already?"

A smile broke across her face, and he leaned down, pressing his lips to hers, securing her to him, promising himself he'd never let her go again.

Flashes went off all around them, and Trip pulled away to see reporters and photographers circling them, Trip and Emery still in an embrace, Clark off to the side, and Craving Wind behind them in the background. Trip smiled at the cameras, no longer caring who knew about them. If Trip had his way, she'd be beside him for the rest of his life.

"Riders up!" the announcer called.

Trip cupped Emery's face. "All right, lady girl, you ready for this?"

She smiled. "I was born for this."

Trip gave her a leg up, then took her hand and pressed his lips to her palm. "One more thing. I have a surprise for you in the grandstand. We'll be waiting for you in the winner's circle."

"We?"

"Good luck, lady girl. Show these men who's the real rider out here."

She grinned wide, and then he watched Clark lead her away, and he went to the grandstand, a sureness washing over him. He'd always been able to feel a race, to know the win was coming. Call it a sixth sense or a feeling, but it burned bright in him today.

They were going to win. They *had* to win.

CHAPTER THIRTY

Run for the Roses

Emery told herself to relax, to breathe, to ignore the butterflies fluttering in her stomach. This was it—the moment she'd spent her whole life preparing for. She smiled inwardly, proud. No matter what happened, she would remember this moment forever.

They walked out of Craving Wind's stall, and Emery took in each step, the walking ring, the two circuits to warm up. She couldn't pull the smile from her face.

"Ready, Ms. Carlisle?"

She peered over to see her escort rider smiling encouragingly at her. "I'm ready."

The trumpet sounded, and Emery's heart swelled as the University of Louisville's marching band played the traditional "My Old Kentucky Home." The grandstand was on their feet, singing along.

> The sun shines bright in the old Kentucky home,
> Tis summer, the people are gay;
> The corn-top's ripe and the meadow's in the bloom
> While the birds make music all the day.
> The young folks roll on the little cabin floor
> All merry, all happy and bright;
> By'n by hard times comes a knocking at the door
> Then my old Kentucky home, Good-night!
> Weep no more my lady. Oh! Weep no more today!
> We will sing one song for my old Kentucky home
> For the old Kentucky home, far away.

Twenty racehorses, including hers, made their grand entrance onto the track for the post parade, the song playing in the background, everyone on their feet, the crowd overflowing with anticipation—the purse well over two million dollars. The announcer introduced each horse one by one—his winnings, his owners, his trainer, the jockey on his back. And then he called number four, Craving Wind, and Emery felt a surge of excitement burst from her chest. She smiled as they walked in front of the grandstand, allowing attendees to see them, to gauge whether the horse was alert or eager or agitated. And then the setup was over, and the real point of it all was about to begin. The most exciting two minutes in sports.

Emery edged Craving Wind into the starting gate, tuning out the taunts from the male riders all around her. Talk of her fall at the Kentucky Oaks. Talk of her and Trip. And that's when she realized she hadn't told him. He'd spilled his guts to her and she hadn't said the one thing he wanted—the thing he needed—her to say back.

That she loved him, too. That she wanted him beside her for the rest of her life, that she hadn't been whole without him, how nothing else mattered but them, together. And now she was going into the race, on the very track where she'd nearly lost her life, and she hadn't told him.

Shaking, she turned around, hoping to spot Clark, someone, but it was almost time. There was nothing she could do. God, why hadn't she told him?

Then she realized the words were just that, words. She couldn't say them to him now, but she could show him. And she would. She leaned down and pressed a kiss to Craving Wind, ignoring the laughter from the other jockeys. "Let's do this, boy." And then the horn sounded and the gates opened, and they were off.

Craving Wind broke from the gate like a cannon, all strength and speed, and Emery smiled despite herself. But then Rowdy Mouth and Hemingway sped past her, and Emery held her breath into the first turn, Craving Wind breaking too sharply, nearly bumping into Rowdy Mouth. Fear licked its way through her, memories shooting up of Firecrest doing the same thing, and then the surge of pain as she was trampled.

"Come on, boy," she screamed at him, and then, like the first light of day clearing the darkness, she saw Rowdy Mouth and Hemingway running out of gas and knew this was her chance. *Please, God*, she prayed, then she loosened her hold, and it was like Craving Wind had heard her prayer, like he'd been right there with her all along, in her head, and he broke free, speeding past Rowdy and Hemingway.

Memories flooded in all at once—her first time on a saddle, waving to her parents as she trotted by. The first time she raced and lost. The first time she raced and won. Then Trip arriving at Carlisle Farms, all tanned skin and white smile and eyes that saw right through her. Weeks of flirtation, then their first kiss, and she thought her heart stopped that very second, offering itself over to Trip, never to return to her again. God, how she loved him, even then, and now he was here, waiting for her—watching and experiencing this moment with her. She couldn't get back to him fast enough.

"Take her home, boy," Emery screamed to Craving Wind as they hit the mile mark. She shook her stick in his face, commanding him to give it his all. And he did. She could feel it in her bones, the distance building between her and the field, two lengths, three, six—*oh my God*. And then they blew across the finish line, and she rose up, tears streaming down her face as she punched the air. She'd done it; they'd done it!

Emery was the first woman to win the Kentucky Derby.

Emotion overflowed as she made her way to the winner's circle, and then her gaze landed on the person standing beside Trip, tears in his eyes as she reached out to him.

"Daddy?" she said, a sob breaking free. "You're here?"

"There's no way I'd miss this." He kissed her cheek. "I'm so proud of you."

Emery wiped away her tears. "You taught me to never quit. You taught me everything. I'm here because of you."

They hugged again, and then she turned to Trip, unable to stand it another second. She jumped off Craving Wind and threw herself into his arms. "I forgot to tell you something."

He kissed her softly. "Oh, yeah?"

"You are my match, Trip Hamilton. I love you. I will love you forever."

He took her helmet off and peered into her eyes. "Care to say that in a church?"

"Are you . . . ?"

"There's no one else for me. I love you. Marry me and you'll make me the happiest man in the world."

Emery laughed with joy as chaos started all around them, reporters ordering their cameramen to get the shot. But she tuned everything out and stared up into the warm eyes of the man she loved.

The governor announced Craving Wind as the winner of the Kentucky Derby and draped the garland of more than four hundred roses over him, and then handed Emery a bouquet of sixty long-stemmed roses wrapped in ten yards of ribbon, and she couldn't help feeling she was a part of this history now, this tradition. Her name would forever live in Churchill Downs.

Sarah Anderson received her winning trophy, and reporters began questioning Emery and Trip, but she couldn't hear their questions above the cheers, above the clapping—above the sound of her racing heart.

Trip pulled her to him once more and pressed a kiss to her cheek, then her lips. "Let's go home. You're Triple Run's first champion. The town will want to celebrate."

Beckett cleared his throat from beside them. "You mean Crestler's Key's first champion."

"No, she races for Hamilton Stables . . . which is in Triple Run."

"But she's *from* Crestler's Key."

Emery sighed heavily as they walked to the backside, the debate continuing, sure to be one among many. And then the thought settled over her peacefully.

Many. She liked the sound of that.

Please turn the page for an exciting sneak peek of

WILD HEARTS

the second novel in Melissa West's Hamilton Stables trilogy

coming in February 2016!

CHAPTER ONE

Alex Hamilton groaned as he rolled over in bed, the taste of gin still on his lips, his throat cottony from a hangover he couldn't afford to have. Cursing himself, he sat up and immediately groaned again at the ringing in his ears and the pain slicing through the center of his brain. Why the hell did he drink? He'd asked himself that single question on more occasions than he could count, each one with the same answer—no damn clue. And no damn sense.

Pushing out of his sheets, he stood, stretching his long and lean body until the joints in his back cracked, then started for the shower, when his foot hit a pair of boots on the floor. Boots that weren't his and weren't male, for that matter. He lifted one very tall black boot into the air, curious how anyone managed to walk on such a high heel, but being thankful all the same, because damn he loved a woman in knee high boots. All this went through his mind without much thought as to who belonged in these boots, until he heard someone clearing her throat from behind him. Shit. *Please tell me she isn't still in my—*

"Good morning, handsome."

Alex turned slowly to find a very blond and very young woman in his bed. His first thought and worry was whether he had ever stopped to ask her age.

She stepped out of his bed, not caring to cover her naked body. There was once a time that Alex would have appreciated her audacity, but that time had long come and gone. He missed female modesty and soft smiles, the looks and actions of a Southern lady. The kind of lady his mother would have liked if she were still alive. And in two years, he'd only been with one woman who met that description, but she'd walked away or maybe he'd walked away. Still, months later he wasn't sure which of them had actually left.

Staring at the woman before him, Alex found her nakedness grated on his nerves. Of course, he too stood with nothing on, and feeling a tinge of unease about that fact, he crossed his arms over his chest and stared at the woman.

Her gaze dipped down to his lower half, still very exposed despite the whole crossing his arms thing. As if she'd read his thoughts, she said, "It's Brittany, and I'm twenty-two."

Alex didn't know if he should congratulate her or show her out. He'd never heard someone reveal her age with such pride. Again, he wondered what the hell he was doing. He had to be at the foaling barn in an hour, and knowing his brother, he was already—

Before he could finish the thought, his cell vibrated against his nightstand and he glanced over. He didn't want to take the call in front of the girl, but then he caught Trip's name flashing across the screen.

"Look," he said to Brittany. "I hate to play and run, but I've got a busy schedule and..." The phone vibrated again, supporting his story.

"Play and run?" She grabbed up her clothes and jerked her dress down over her body, hopping as she pulled on her boots. "Play and run! Who even says that? I'll see myself out." Then she stopped at the door and spun around. "And when Trip asks why I quit, just let him know I refuse to work with his jackass of a brother."

She slammed the door shut and Alex cringed, searching his mind for a Brittany who worked at the farm, and that was when he remembered his conversation with Trip the week before. New exercise rider, Brittany Light. Well, there went that.

Taking his phone from his nightstand, he texted his brother that he'd see him in twenty, then jumped in the shower to wash off the night, his thoughts on the week he had before him. Calls with two stud farms, vet checks on the broodmares, and hopefully a flight out to Ireland later in the week.

Soaring Star was ovulating, and though he still wasn't 100 percent sure that Pirate Pete was the best match for her to produce a champion, he couldn't argue with Pete's pedigree. He'd long since known that breeding was less science, more art, and he was close to finding the perfect balance. If only he could keep Trip off his back long enough to make a decision.

Wrapping a towel around his waist, he stepped out of his shower, only to hear his phone vibrate again. Sighing, he hit answer and said, "Give me ten," before hanging up and walking to his closet, throwing on a pair of jeans and a black T-shirt, and shoving on his boots. Shaking out his hair as a means of styling it, he went to work brushing his teeth, curious how the day had just begun and it was already shit. That didn't bode well for his week.

Alex ran a hand over his face as he went through the rest of his morning routine—black coffee, notepad and pencil, because he liked the quiet he felt whenever he jotted down notes. That same quiet never came when he entered things into his phone or iPad. So notepad and pencil for him.

Once out in his three-car garage, he eyed his diesel truck and Harley, shaking his head a little that his life required him to walk past both man vehicles. Instead, he hopped into a small golf cart, glad to be out of his house. Well, technically it was Trip's house, but Alex liked to ignore that fact, especially when he was pissed at Trip. And he was heading that way now.

The sky was dark in places, light in others, the day unsure of its official starting time, as if Mother Nature had hit snooze. He knew the feeling.

Mama V greeted him as he parked the cart by her house, grabbed a protein shake, then continued on to the foaling barn, where sure enough his brother's truck had been parked at an angle—proving that he ran the farm and could park wherever the hell he liked. It irritated Alex to no end, but instead of lashing out, he reminded himself that the breeding side of Hamilton Stables could more than triple the earnings of training. Alex might be the youngest Hamilton brother, but if his plan worked, he would bring in the most profit for the family business this year. And then what would they have to say? Nothing, that's what. But Alex told himself that didn't matter. He wasn't doing this to prove himself to his family. And any day now, he'd believe it.

"'Bout damn time." Trip walked out of the foaling barn, his Stetson firmly planted on his head, the same cowboy boots he always wore around the farm on his feet. A red and black plaid shirt hung loose over his Levi's, and though to some he might appear to be an ignorant hick, those in the business knew the truth—no one in horseracing was half the trainer Trip was.

Among owners, Alex felt the weight of his brother's name following him around like a dark shadow that refused to let up. He introduced himself and immediately owners asked, "Trip's brother, right?" For Christ's sake, there were three Hamilton brothers, not one.

Pushing aside his bitter thoughts, he opened his mouth to say that he wasn't late, Trip was early, but then his eyes caught the two women standing a few yards away from his brother, and suddenly Alex's throat refused to work properly.

"How are you doing, Alex?" Emery, Trip's fiancée, asked as she started over. Emery was a rider for Hamilton Stables, and her father was the legendary Beckett Carlisle. Which all meant their relationship owned the title of most unexpected match, but there they were, head over heels in love, wedding date three months away. But while all that was true, Emery wasn't the woman who'd caught Alex's attention.

His gaze landed and refused to lift from the bright redhead beside Emery, skin as fair as milk except for the occasional freckle. Her eyes were so intensely blue Alex found it difficult to look at her without his mouth falling slack. She wore a simple blue and white cotton dress that hit mid thigh, her look so out of place on the farm many women might feel self conscious, but Alex would bet this woman had never felt self conscious a day in her life. Why would she? To date, he'd never met a woman who held a candle to her.

"Alex," she said, her voice soft, a hint of modesty there that he'd never understood, but cut through him all the same.

"Kate."

Kate Littleton stared at the man she'd had sex with not eighteen months before, wondering if he still looked the same underneath his perfectly fitted T-shirt and jeans.

She tried to remember why she'd ended their dating streak, and then the memory came to her like a spoonful of vinegar. Alex had freaked out when Trip and Emery became serious, which meant that he'd had no real feelings for her anyway. But the part that had always gnawed at her was that she hadn't wanted anything from him beyond a chance to spend time with him. Despite the arrogant vibe he put out there, Alex was a nice guy. She enjoyed being around him, his laugh, the way the conversation never became stilted. He had a carefree spirit and a sharp mind. He just didn't see himself clearly. Shadowed by his brothers, he'd spent his whole life climbing a hill that only rose taller with each step.

Kate knew she'd rather turn him loose than trust her heart to keep its word to her and stay good. So one day they sat on his couch watching the Falcons play, and the next, he was a stranger. Eighteen months went by without a word, which was fine. Kate had things to do. Students to teach. Plays to plan out. Little league games to attend. She didn't need Alex Hamilton, but she did want someone. If only she could find the right man to fill the job.

"We were just heading out," Kate said, suddenly uneasy standing before a man who so clearly *didn't* want the job. "Em?"

Emery's gaze shifted from Kate to Alex and then back, her eyebrows lifting. From the age of twelve, Kate had told Emery every detail of her life, except where it concerned Alex Hamilton. She could almost hear Emery's brain churning, unspoken question after unspoken question in her mind.

"Caterer tomorrow morning at nine," Emery said to Trip, before rising onto her toes to give him a soft peck on the lips. Only he was having no part of soft and held her to him, giving her the sort of kiss that Kate knew would embarrass Emery thoroughly. But instead of her friend reprimanding him as she pulled away, she smiled and said, "I love you."

He kissed her again. "And I you."

For a second, Kate couldn't decide if she wanted to grin at her best friend's antics or roll her eyes. It'd make it a lot easier if she had her own guy to kiss and smile at it, but instead all she had was memories.

The sounds of others arriving at the farm echoed all around them, reminding Kate just how out of place she was. Emery belonged here, not her. She focused on the small anthill in a patch of grass by the barn, refusing to look up, though she ached to see if Alex was watching her. If he remembered their time together fondly or if she'd been another notch on his belt, long since forgotten.

"Alex?" Emery called.

When he didn't answer, Kate looked up, only to find him focused inside the barn, already tuning everything else out.

"Earth to Alex?" Emery repeated.

He turned then, but Kate could tell his thoughts had long since

left the threesome and were focused on the mare in the barn scheduled to foal that day. "Yeah?"

"We wanted to have the wedding party over to Trip's tomorrow for
a barbeque. Will you come?"

His eyes drifted almost imperceptibly to Kate, but the impact on
her was immediate. How that man could lock her in place with one
gaze blew her mind. Trip might be the leader of the Hamilton family,
but he didn't have that thoughtful glint in his eyes like Alex. It was as
if his mind worked out complex puzzles the rest of them couldn't even
see. It fascinated Kate, and also scared her. A mind like that would
never feel content in one place. It was likely the reason he'd gone
from college to college, job to job, unable to sit still, unable to settle
down. Like a wild stallion, his heart would never beat easily unless it
was running.

"The wedding party?"

Trip took a step toward his brother then, but Kate didn't want
them to be hard on Alex on her behalf. She was fine. They should be
fine, too. This didn't have to get uncomfortable. So she and Alex
hung out a few times. They'd been friends more than anything else.

"Yes, come." She bit her lip, forcing herself to focus on him.

Alex grinned back at her. "Is that an order, Ms. Littleton?"

She smiled back, enjoying the easiness that slipped into his eyes.
"Bet your ass it is. Teacher's orders. Besides, Trip promised to have
one of Patty's Bundt cakes there. I know you can't resist cake."

Their gazes locked.

"No, I can't."

Instantly, Kate thought of the last slice of cake they had shared.
He'd asked for a bite, a wicked spark in his eyes, and she'd lifted her
fork to his lips. That perfect mouth of his wrapped around her fork,
his eyes on hers, and suddenly the plate clanged to the floor, and he
had her in his lap, their hands everywhere, lips connecting, tongues
intertwining. It had taken a surprisingly small amount of time to un-
dress each other, and even less time to shove the nagging voice in her
head to the corner, ordering her to shut her eyes if she didn't want to
watch. Because Kate needed that night. She needed it like she needed
to breathe. And though a part of her wanted more, she knew that
night would be the last night for them.

"So it's settled. Seven good for everyone? And maybe we should have two cakes," Emery said, her expression thoughtful. "That way we'll have plenty."

Alex turned back for the barn. "Nah, I'll just share some of Kate's." He winked at her, then started for the barn again, when Kate called out.

"Actually, I share my cake with someone else now." Ugh. Why did she say that?

Alex stopped and peered over his shoulder at her. "Is that right?"

No, not even close. But she refused to let him think he could just take a bite from her cake anytime he liked. She crossed her arms and held her head high. "Yes."

He pinned her with that look of his again. The one that made her feel as though she was the only person standing around, the only person in the world. The only person who mattered. And for a moment, she thought he might be jealous, when instead he said, "Happy to hear it. See you around, Ms. Littleton."

Kate stared after him, wishing she could think of something smart to say back, but all she managed was a slight nod before following Emery away from the barn.

When would she learn? If she tested Alex Hamilton, she was the one to get burned.

www.ingramcontent.com/pod-product-compliance
Lightning Source LLC
Chambersburg PA
CBHW031409250626
47155CB00004B/1467